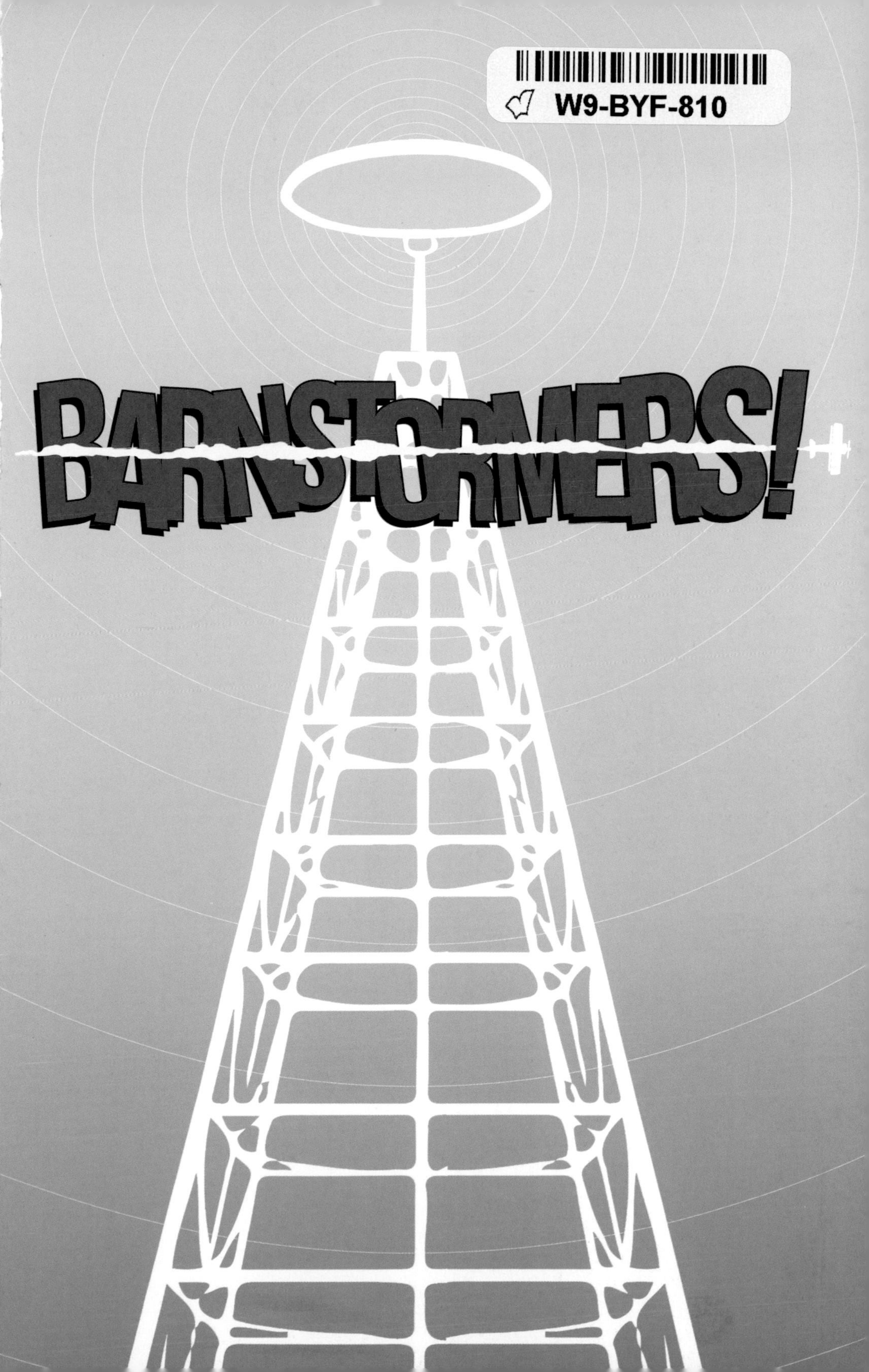
BARNSTORMERS!

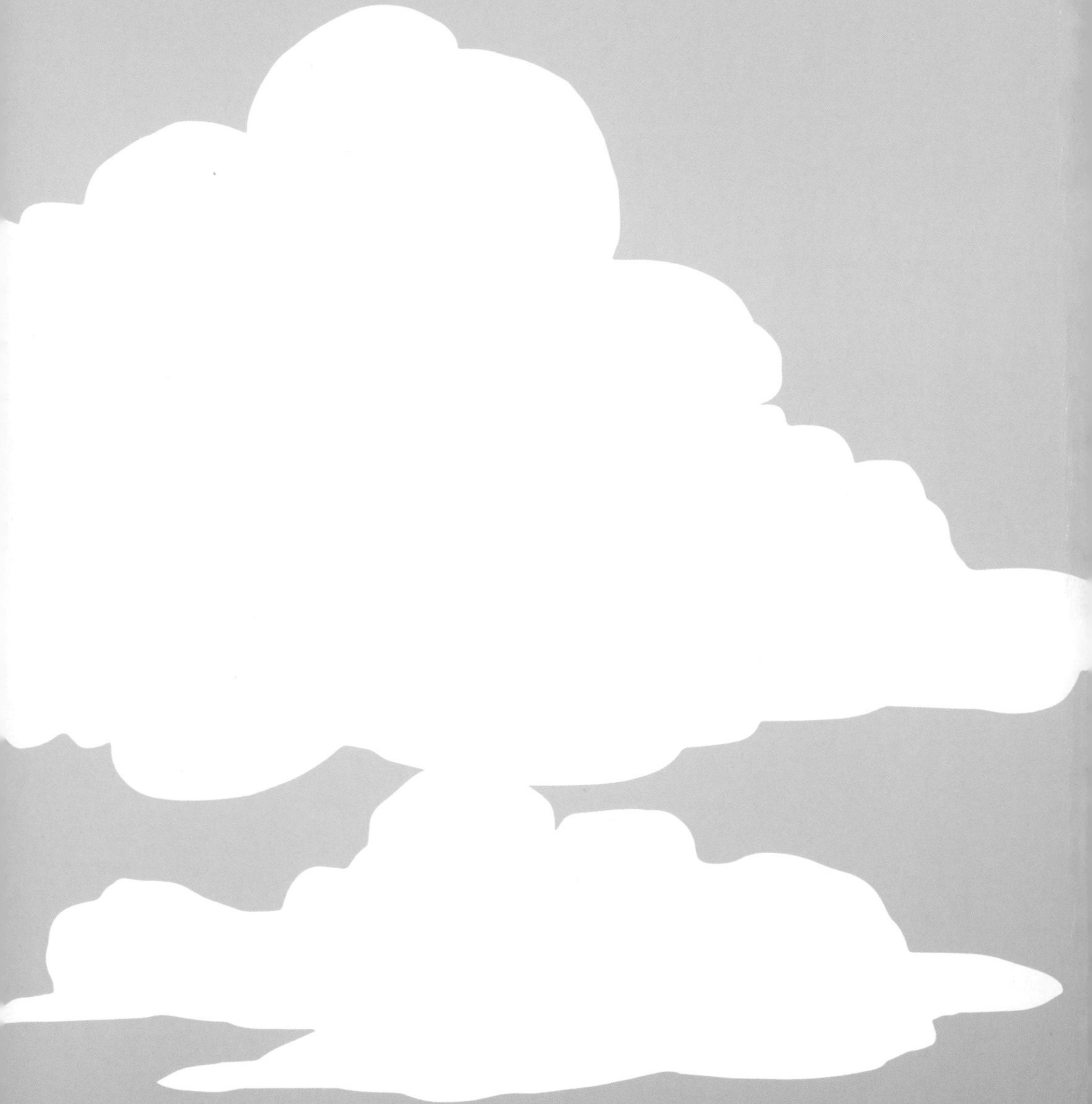

BARNSTORMERS!

WRITTEN BY KENNY PORTER
ILLUSTRATED BY RENNY CASTELLANI

INSIGHT
COMICS

SAN RAFAEL • LOS ANGELES • LONDON

FOREWORD

Kenny made an instant impression. I mean, I took my comic book writing class online, so I was no longer meeting my students face-to-face the way I had when I started up Comics Experience. But Kenny broke through the digital veil quickly. Most students I have really want to write comics—they work hard, have good ideas, and follow through on assignments and expectations. But Kenny was different. The work came through feeling natural already. It didn't require much massaging; it had an ease to it. And I noticed right away. As the course developed, Kenny continued to excel.

And when the course was over, Kenny joined our Creators Workshop and continued to turn out very good work. Then he won the Top Cow Talent contest that year, which didn't surprise me. Over the months and years that followed, I've gotten to know Kenny fairly well. And I know what makes him so good. It's not that he's some unnatural talent that the world has never seen before; it's that he puts the work in. He works his butt off, and the result is that his writing reads as though it's effortless. I love that contradiction. When Kenny first brought me *Barnstormers!*, it was in a different form. Still an idea. He wrote the five opening pages for my Introduction to Writing Comics course, but it was clear there was more to the idea. The five-page story was fun and exciting and had a good character arc, but the characters had more stories they wanted to tell. Kenny then developed *Barnstormers!*, and I'd chime in here and there and give some advice—not that he needed it.

The *Raiders of the Lost Ark* adventure style of the story has always been its main appeal to me. But that style of storytelling needs lovable and compelling characters, and there's no one more compelling than a man named Roscoe. The supporting cast works well together, and it's the characters that keep me engaged reading *Barnstormers!*, though monsters don't hurt.

As a teacher and a comic book editor, I find that the most rewarding thing is to see someone who was a student surpass that role and become a contemporary or colleague. That's where Kenny and I are in our relationship now. It's not that there's nothing more that Kenny can learn, but rather that we can learn from each other. He experiments, I experiment, and we both learn. I don't feel like he needs my help or anyone else's—he just needs the right project to hit at the right time, and his writing career in comics will start to unfold.

That's one thing that I hope you'll see in the pages beyond this introduction. You'll find a fun romp with engaging characters and exciting action—I have no doubt of that (it helps that I've read it). But I hope that you'll also recognize on some level the craft of Kenny and Renata's work. I've spoken more about Kenny as I know him personally, but the art fits so perfectly to this story that I hope you'll see the talent and drive to bring a project like this to work. And in turn, I hope that realization will give you ample reason to search out Kenny and Renny's future projects as well. I think you'll be glad you did.

Every graphic novel is a work of passion. But not all works of passion are demonstrably good. I believe *Barnstormers!* is demonstrably good, and I know why that is. Its creators are passionate about the project, but they are also workhorses, pushing themselves to make it seem easy. And it should. Reading *Barnstormers!* should be easy for you. You should be able to sit back and read it casually and have a great time. If it's easy for you to read, you can bet it was hard work to put together.

I hope your read of *Barnstormers!* is as much fun as my first reading of it. Oh, it's changed a lot since then, but I think it's only gotten better.

Andy Schmidt
Former Marvel Comics editor, Comics Experience

A BOLD NEW WORLD!

The year is 1928. Pilots from the Great War (World War I) find themselves thirsty for daredevil antics and adventure. With the cost of warplanes plummeting, pilots buy them at wholesale and launch into business for themselves. These "barnstormers" land at local farms, performing stunts and giving rides to make a living.

But giant occult monsters have escaped the conflicts of the Great War! Barnstormers find themselves enterprising as adventurers and monster hunters.

For barnstormers Roscoe Adams and his wingman, Clyde Turner, no job is too dangerous! No monster is too big! And they don't accept personal checks!

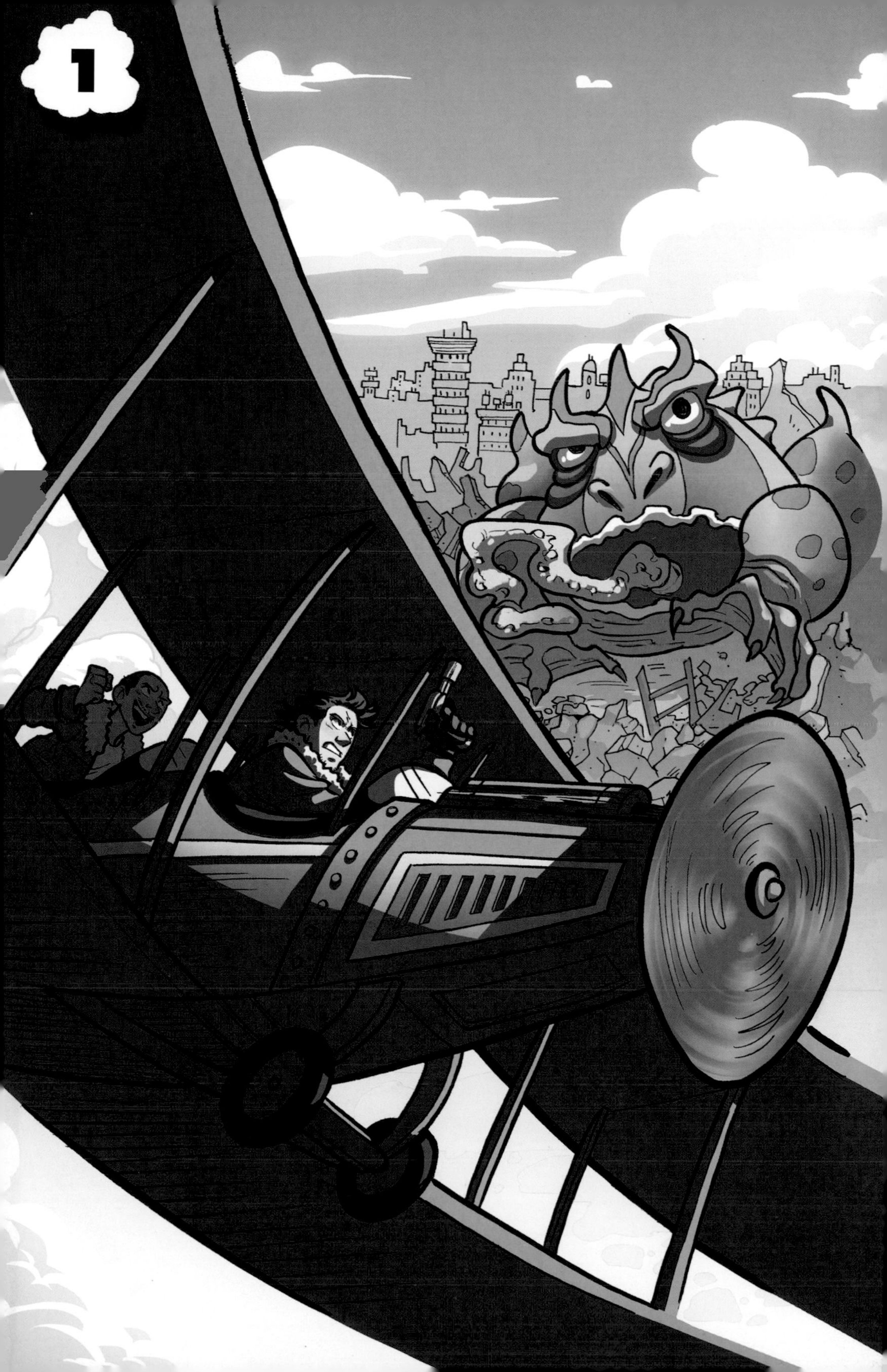
1

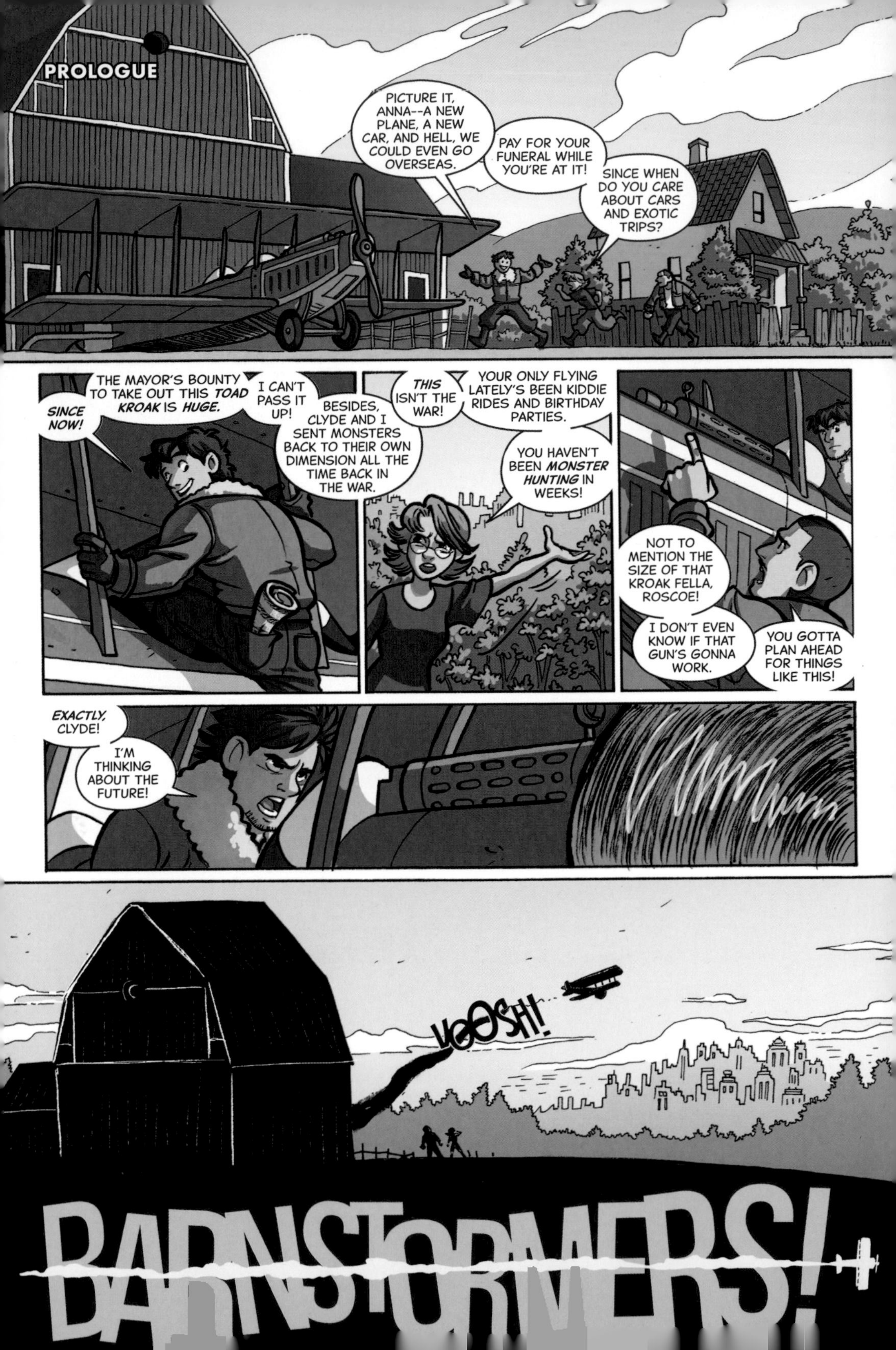
PROLOGUE
PICTURE IT, ANNA--A NEW PLANE, A NEW CAR, AND HELL, WE COULD EVEN GO OVERSEAS.
PAY FOR YOUR FUNERAL WHILE YOU'RE AT IT!
SINCE WHEN DO YOU CARE ABOUT CARS AND EXOTIC TRIPS?
SINCE NOW!
THE MAYOR'S BOUNTY TO TAKE OUT THIS TOAD KROAK IS HUGE.
I CAN'T PASS IT UP!
BESIDES, CLYDE AND I SENT MONSTERS BACK TO THEIR OWN DIMENSION ALL THE TIME BACK IN THE WAR.
THIS ISN'T THE WAR!
YOUR ONLY FLYING LATELY'S BEEN KIDDIE RIDES AND BIRTHDAY PARTIES.
YOU HAVEN'T BEEN MONSTER HUNTING IN WEEKS!
NOT TO MENTION THE SIZE OF THAT KROAK FELLA, ROSCOE!
I DON'T EVEN KNOW IF THAT GUN'S GONNA WORK.
YOU GOTTA PLAN AHEAD FOR THINGS LIKE THIS!
EXACTLY, CLYDE!
I'M THINKING ABOUT THE FUTURE!
VOOSH!
BARNSTORMERS!

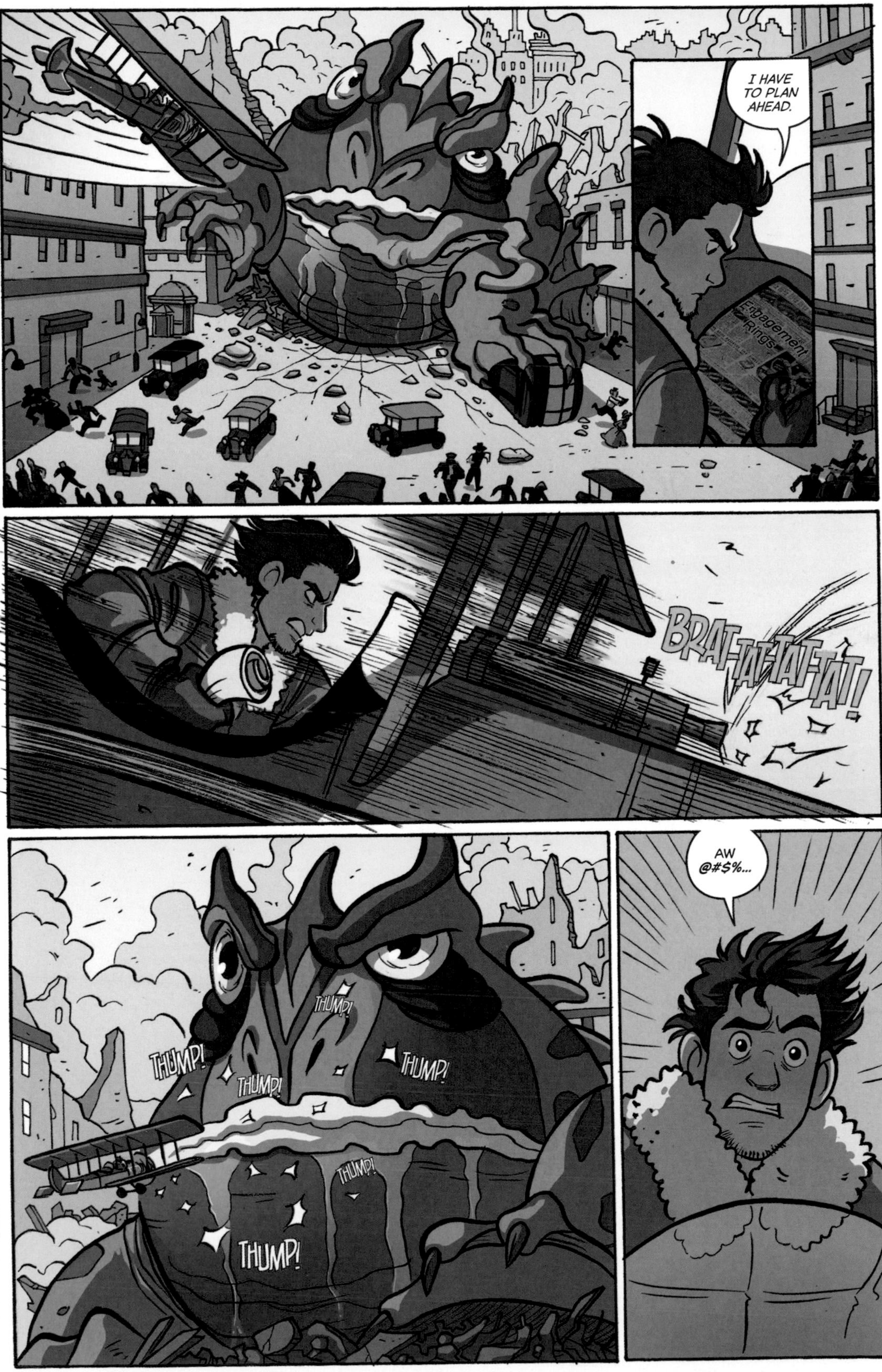
I HAVE TO PLAN AHEAD.
Engagement Rings
BRAT-TAT-TAT-TAT!
THUMP!
THUMP!
THUMP!
THUMP!
THUMP!
THUMP!
AW @#$%...

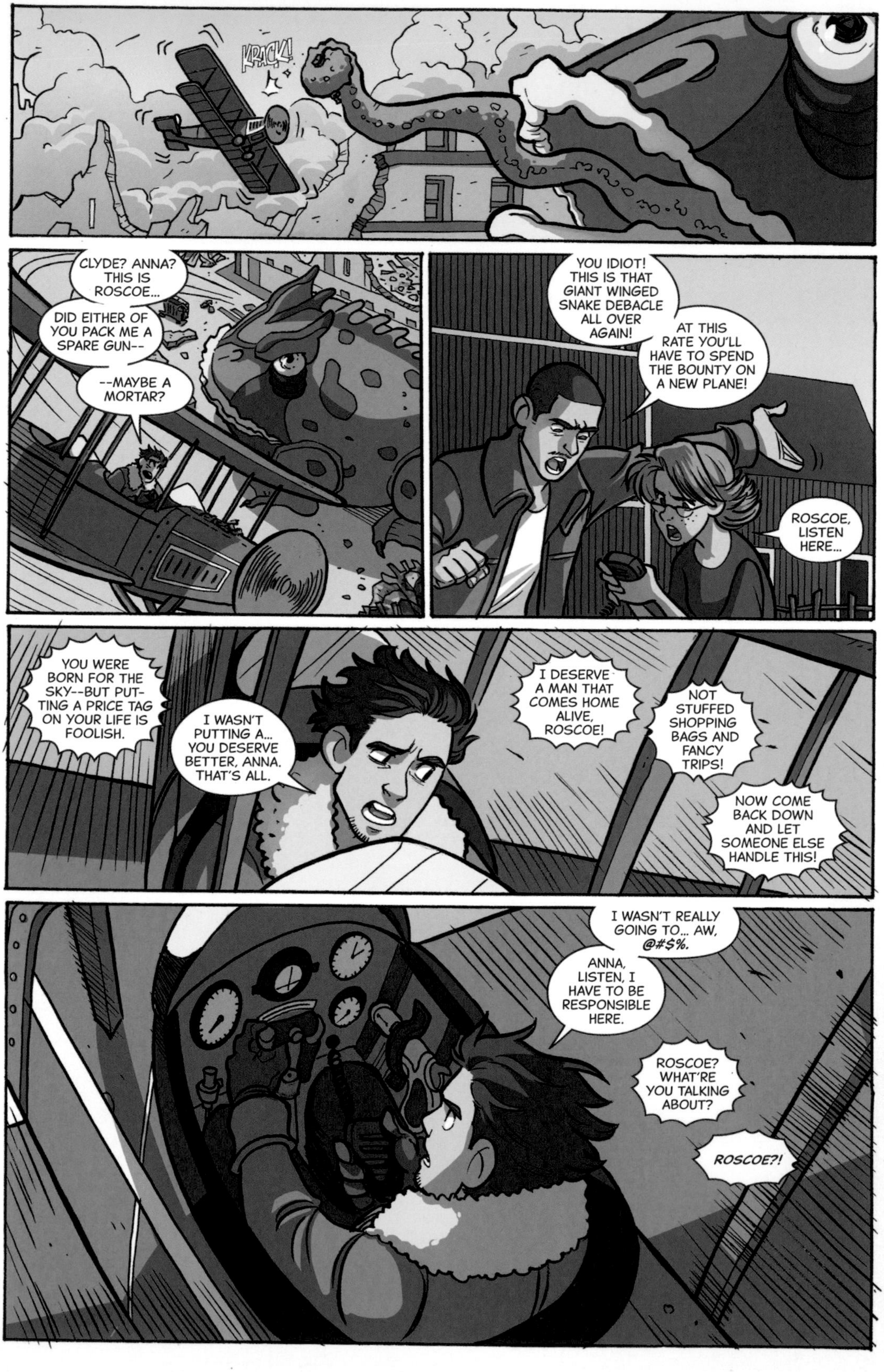
KRACK!
CLYDE? ANNA? THIS IS ROSCOE...
DID EITHER OF YOU PACK ME A SPARE GUN--
--MAYBE A MORTAR?
YOU IDIOT! THIS IS THAT GIANT WINGED SNAKE DEBACLE ALL OVER AGAIN!
AT THIS RATE YOU'LL HAVE TO SPEND THE BOUNTY ON A NEW PLANE!
ROSCOE, LISTEN HERE...
YOU WERE BORN FOR THE SKY--BUT PUTTING A PRICE TAG ON YOUR LIFE IS FOOLISH.
I WASN'T PUTTING A... YOU DESERVE BETTER, ANNA. THAT'S ALL.
I DESERVE A MAN THAT COMES HOME ALIVE, ROSCOE!
NOT STUFFED SHOPPING BAGS AND FANCY TRIPS!
NOW COME BACK DOWN AND LET SOMEONE ELSE HANDLE THIS!
I WASN'T REALLY GOING TO... AW, @#$%.
ANNA, LISTEN, I HAVE TO BE RESPONSIBLE HERE.
ROSCOE? WHAT'RE YOU TALKING ABOUT?
ROSCOE?!

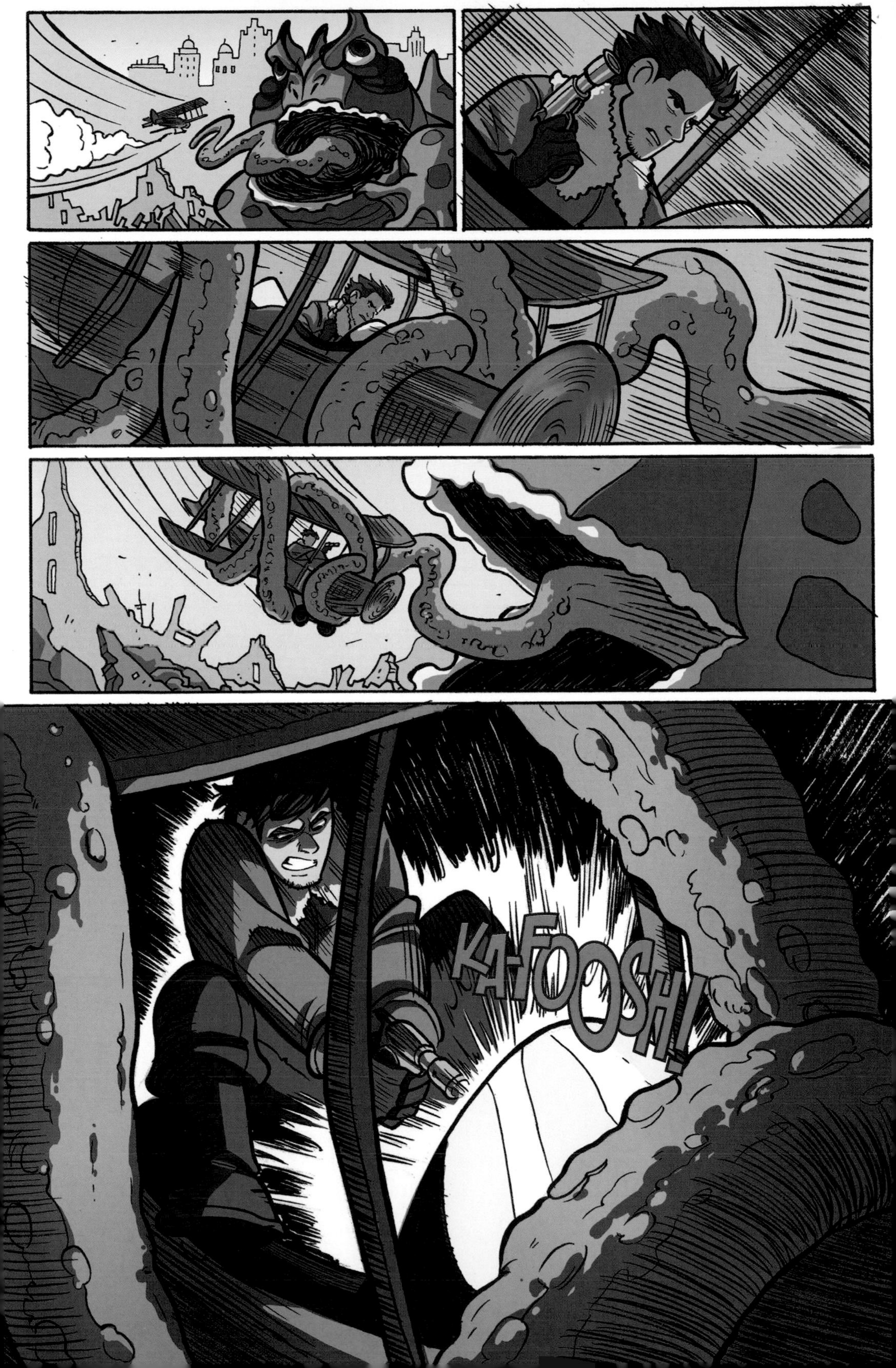
KA-FOOSH!

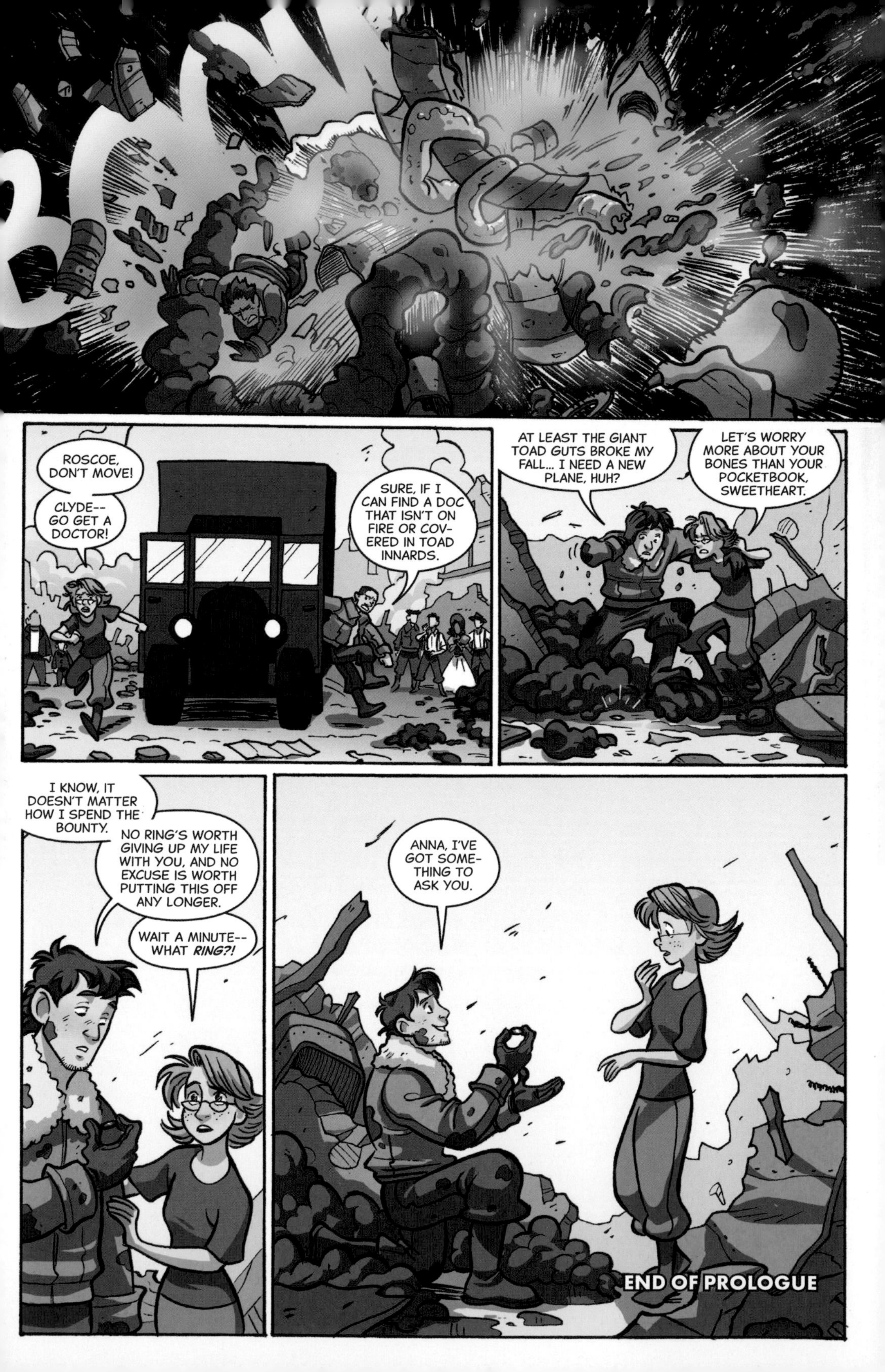
BOOM
ROSCOE, DON'T MOVE!
CLYDE-- GO GET A DOCTOR!
SURE, IF I CAN FIND A DOC THAT ISN'T ON FIRE OR COVERED IN TOAD INNARDS.
AT LEAST THE GIANT TOAD GUTS BROKE MY FALL... I NEED A NEW PLANE, HUH?
LET'S WORRY MORE ABOUT YOUR BONES THAN YOUR POCKETBOOK, SWEETHEART.
I KNOW, IT DOESN'T MATTER HOW I SPEND THE BOUNTY.
NO RING'S WORTH GIVING UP MY LIFE WITH YOU, AND NO EXCUSE IS WORTH PUTTING THIS OFF ANY LONGER.
WAIT A MINUTE-- WHAT *RING?!*
ANNA, I'VE GOT SOMETHING TO ASK YOU.
END OF PROLOGUE

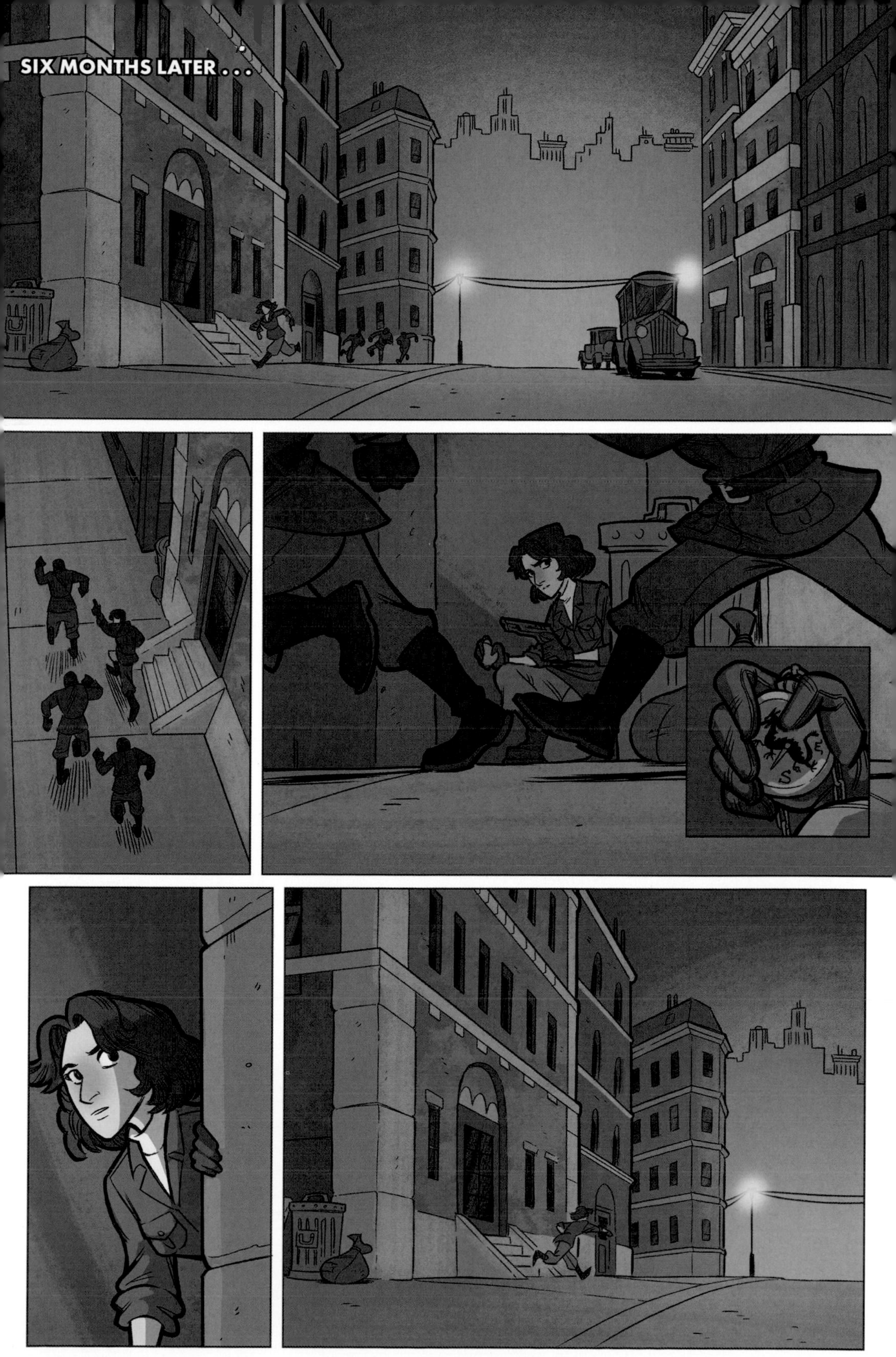
SIX MONTHS LATER . . .

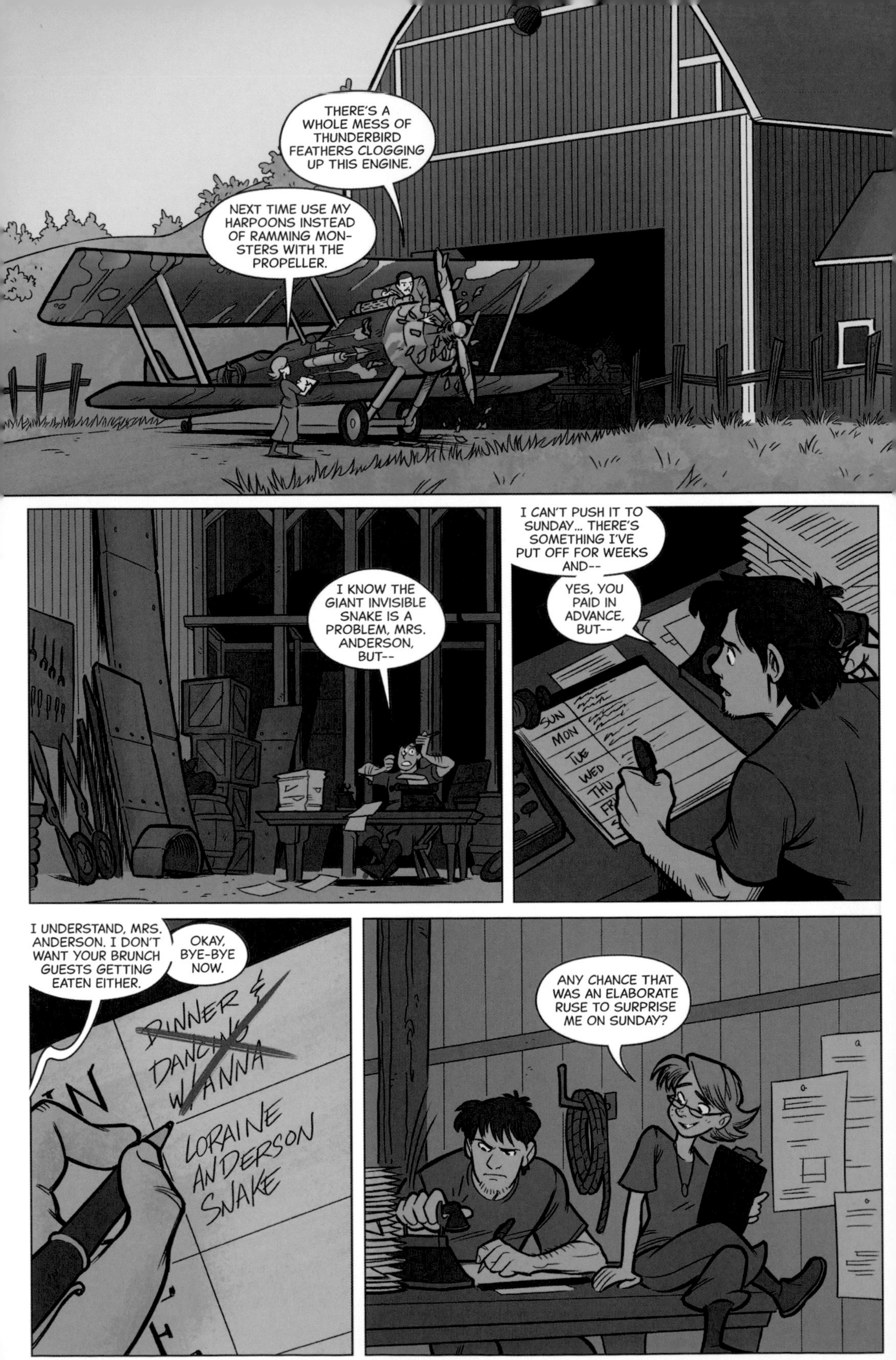
THERE'S A WHOLE MESS OF THUNDERBIRD FEATHERS CLOGGING UP THIS ENGINE.
NEXT TIME USE MY HARPOONS INSTEAD OF RAMMING MONSTERS WITH THE PROPELLER.
I KNOW THE GIANT INVISIBLE SNAKE IS A PROBLEM, MRS. ANDERSON, BUT--
I CAN'T PUSH IT TO SUNDAY... THERE'S SOMETHING I'VE PUT OFF FOR WEEKS AND--
YES, YOU PAID IN ADVANCE, BUT--
SUN
MON
TUE
WED
THU
I UNDERSTAND, MRS. ANDERSON. I DON'T WANT YOUR BRUNCH GUESTS GETTING EATEN EITHER.
OKAY, BYE-BYE NOW.
DINNER & DANCING W/ ANNA
LORAINE ANDERSON SNAKE
ANY CHANCE THAT WAS AN ELABORATE RUSE TO SURPRISE ME ON SUNDAY?

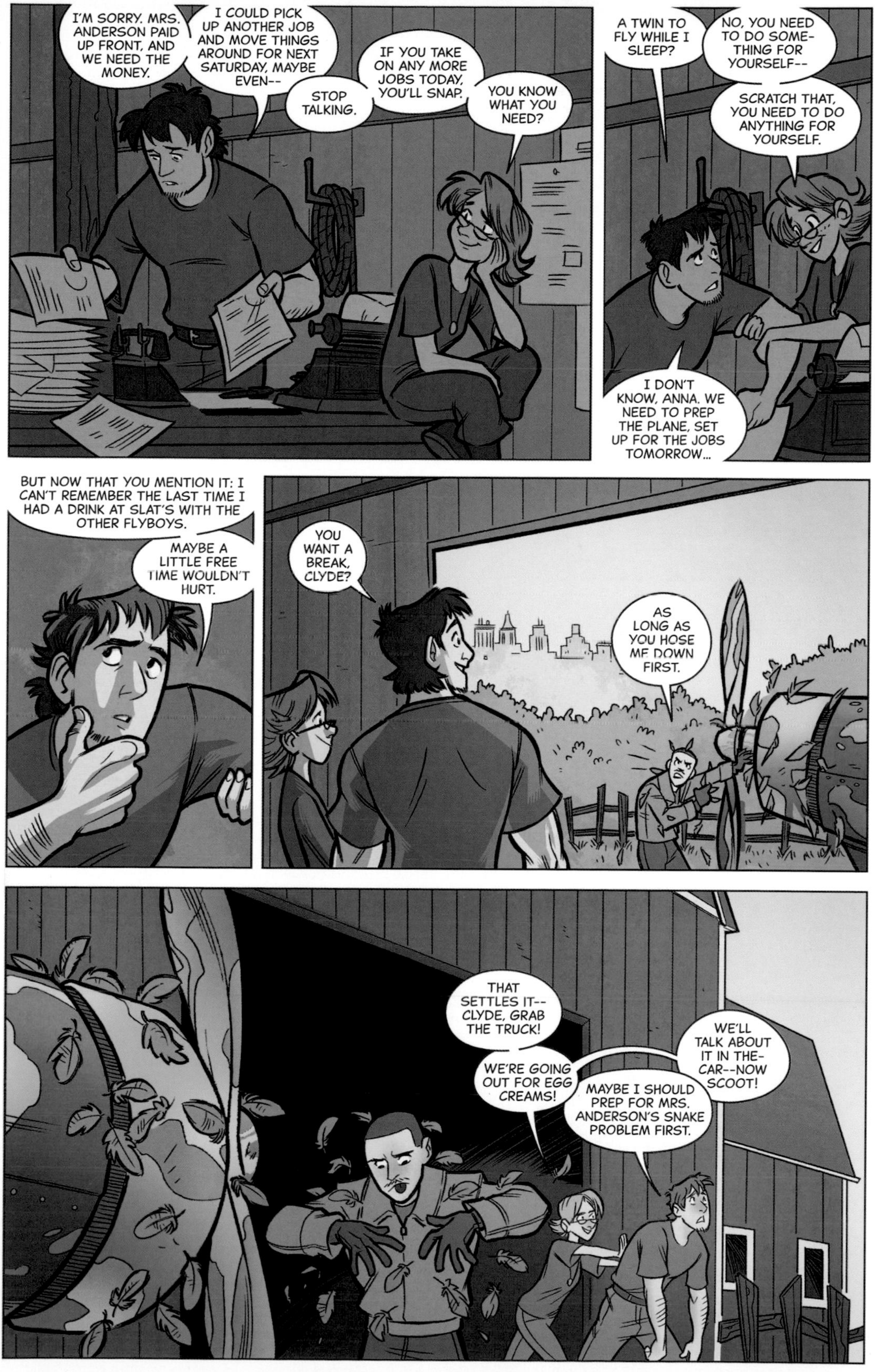

I'M SORRY. MRS. ANDERSON PAID UP FRONT, AND WE NEED THE MONEY.
I COULD PICK UP ANOTHER JOB AND MOVE THINGS AROUND FOR NEXT SATURDAY, MAYBE EVEN--
STOP TALKING.
IF YOU TAKE ON ANY MORE JOBS TODAY, YOU'LL SNAP.
YOU KNOW WHAT YOU NEED?
A TWIN TO FLY WHILE I SLEEP?
NO, YOU NEED TO DO SOME-THING FOR YOURSELF--
SCRATCH THAT, YOU NEED TO DO ANYTHING FOR YOURSELF.
I DON'T KNOW, ANNA. WE NEED TO PREP THE PLANE, SET UP FOR THE JOBS TOMORROW...
BUT NOW THAT YOU MENTION IT: I CAN'T REMEMBER THE LAST TIME I HAD A DRINK AT SLAT'S WITH THE OTHER FLYBOYS.
MAYBE A LITTLE FREE TIME WOULDN'T HURT.
YOU WANT A BREAK, CLYDE?
AS LONG AS YOU HOSE ME DOWN FIRST.
THAT SETTLES IT-- CLYDE, GRAB THE TRUCK!
WE'RE GOING OUT FOR EGG CREAMS!
MAYBE I SHOULD PREP FOR MRS. ANDERSON'S SNAKE PROBLEM FIRST.
WE'LL TALK ABOUT IT IN THE-CAR--NOW SCOOT!

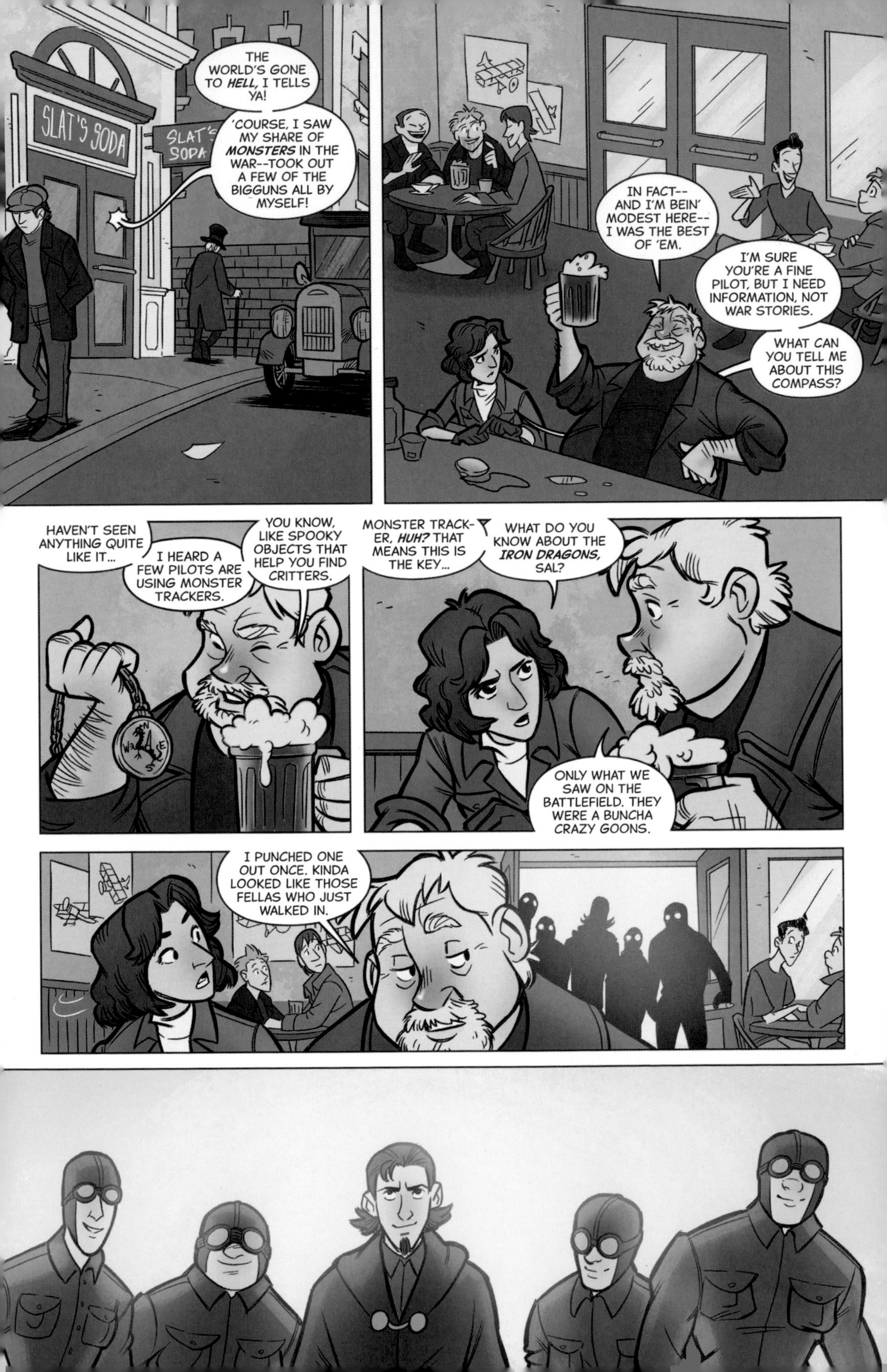
SLAT'S SODA
SLAT'S SODA
THE WORLD'S GONE TO HELL, I TELLS YA!
'COURSE, I SAW MY SHARE OF MONSTERS IN THE WAR--TOOK OUT A FEW OF THE BIGGUNS ALL BY MYSELF!
IN FACT--AND I'M BEIN' MODEST HERE--I WAS THE BEST OF 'EM.
I'M SURE YOU'RE A FINE PILOT, BUT I NEED INFORMATION, NOT WAR STORIES.
WHAT CAN YOU TELL ME ABOUT THIS COMPASS?
HAVEN'T SEEN ANYTHING QUITE LIKE IT...
I HEARD A FEW PILOTS ARE USING MONSTER TRACKERS.
YOU KNOW, LIKE SPOOKY OBJECTS THAT HELP YOU FIND CRITTERS.
MONSTER TRACKER, HUH? THAT MEANS THIS IS THE KEY...
WHAT DO YOU KNOW ABOUT THE IRON DRAGONS, SAL?
ONLY WHAT WE SAW ON THE BATTLEFIELD. THEY WERE A BUNCHA CRAZY GOONS.
I PUNCHED ONE OUT ONCE. KINDA LOOKED LIKE THOSE FELLAS WHO JUST WALKED IN.

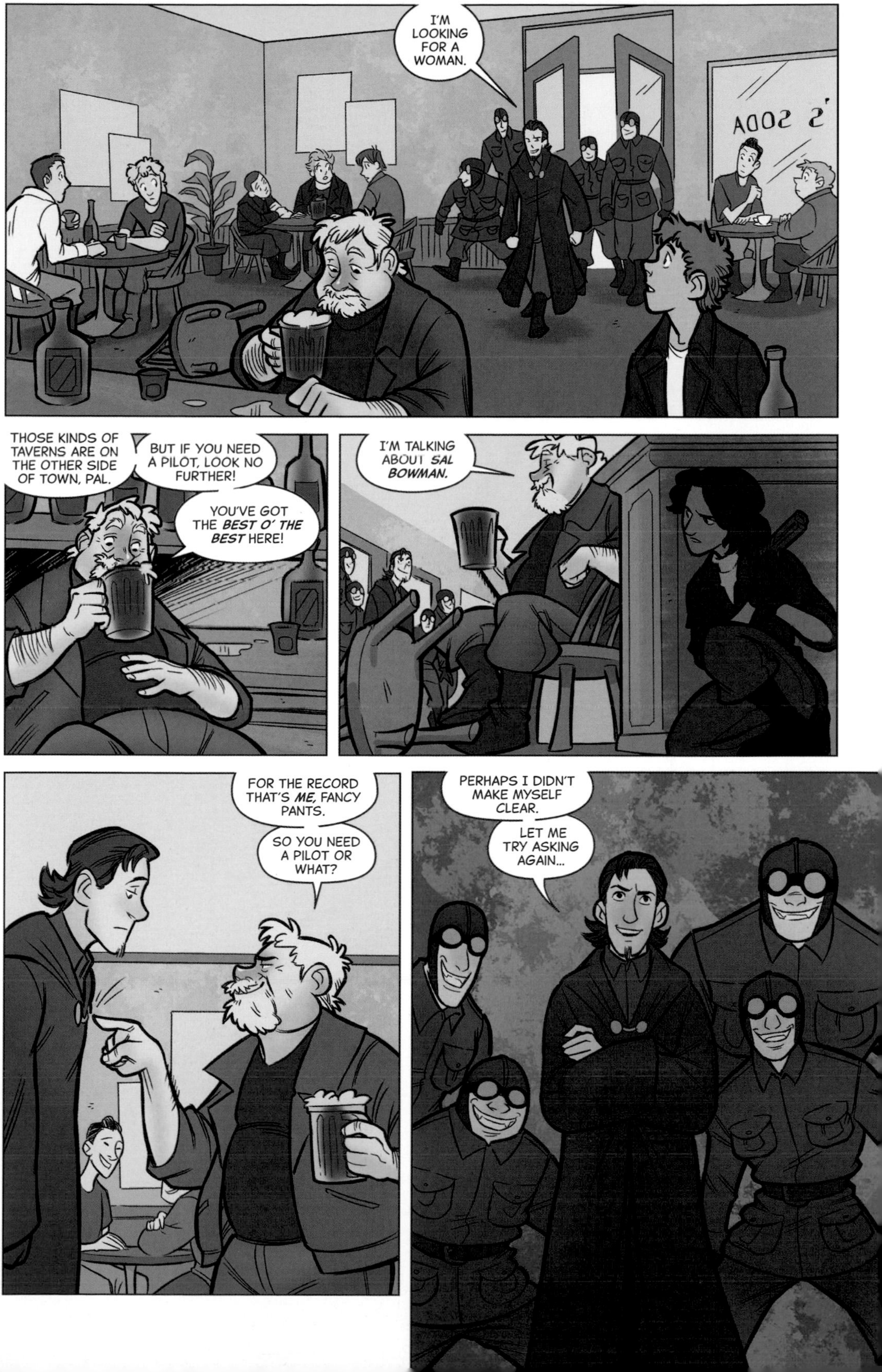
I'M LOOKING FOR A WOMAN.
'S SODA
THOSE KINDS OF TAVERNS ARE ON THE OTHER SIDE OF TOWN, PAL.
BUT IF YOU NEED A PILOT, LOOK NO FURTHER!
YOU'VE GOT THE BEST O' THE BEST HERE!
I'M TALKING ABOUT SAL BOWMAN.
FOR THE RECORD THAT'S ME, FANCY PANTS.
SO YOU NEED A PILOT OR WHAT?
PERHAPS I DIDN'T MAKE MYSELF CLEAR.
LET ME TRY ASKING AGAIN...

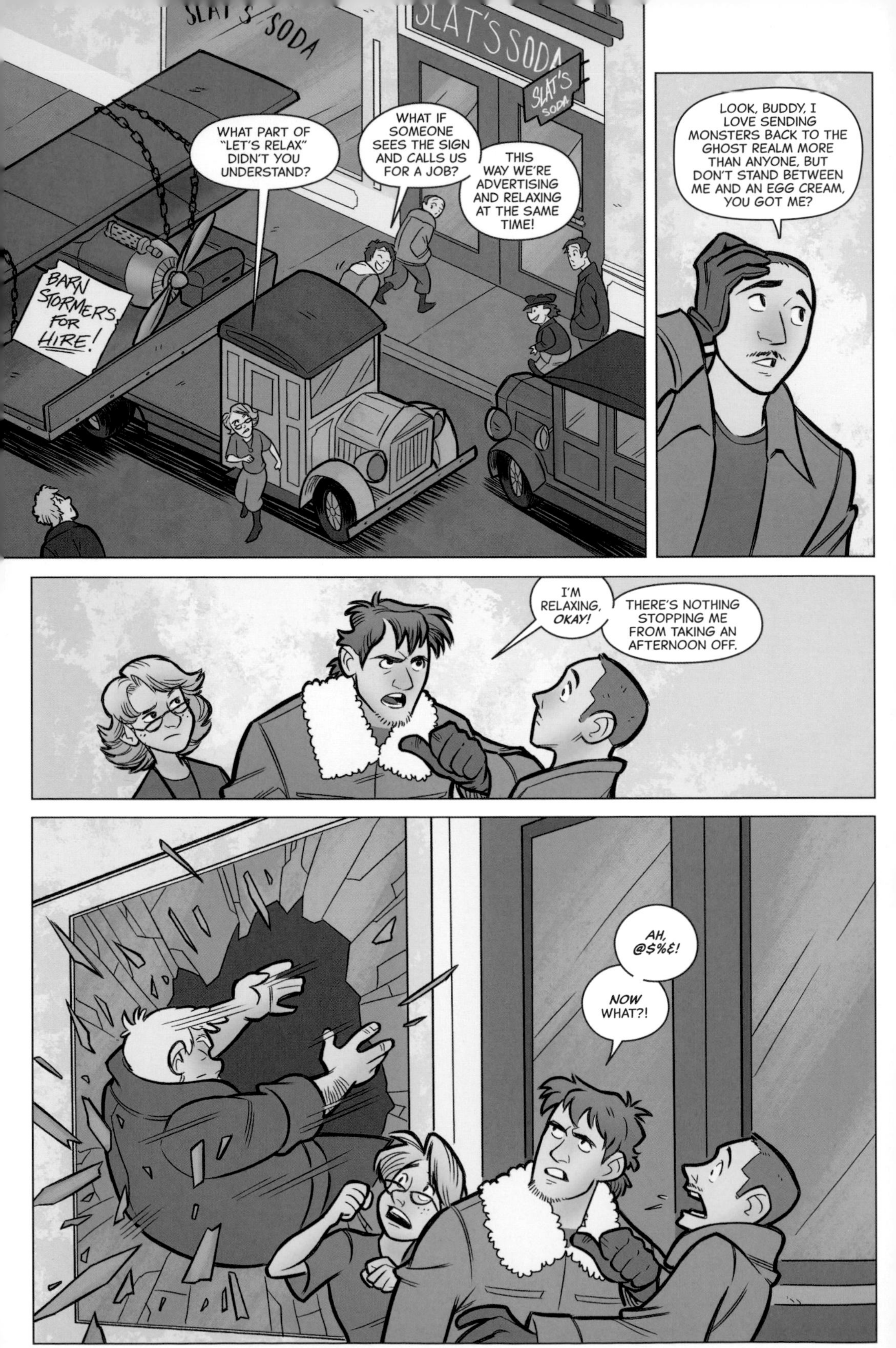
SLAT'S SODA
SLAT'S SODA
SLAT'S SODA
BARN STORMERS FOR HIRE!
WHAT PART OF "LET'S RELAX" DIDN'T YOU UNDERSTAND?
WHAT IF SOMEONE SEES THE SIGN AND CALLS US FOR A JOB?
THIS WAY WE'RE ADVERTISING AND RELAXING AT THE SAME TIME!
LOOK, BUDDY, I LOVE SENDING MONSTERS BACK TO THE GHOST REALM MORE THAN ANYONE, BUT DON'T STAND BETWEEN ME AND AN EGG CREAM, YOU GOT ME?
I'M RELAXING, OKAY!
THERE'S NOTHING STOPPING ME FROM TAKING AN AFTERNOON OFF.
AH, @$%£!
NOW WHAT?!

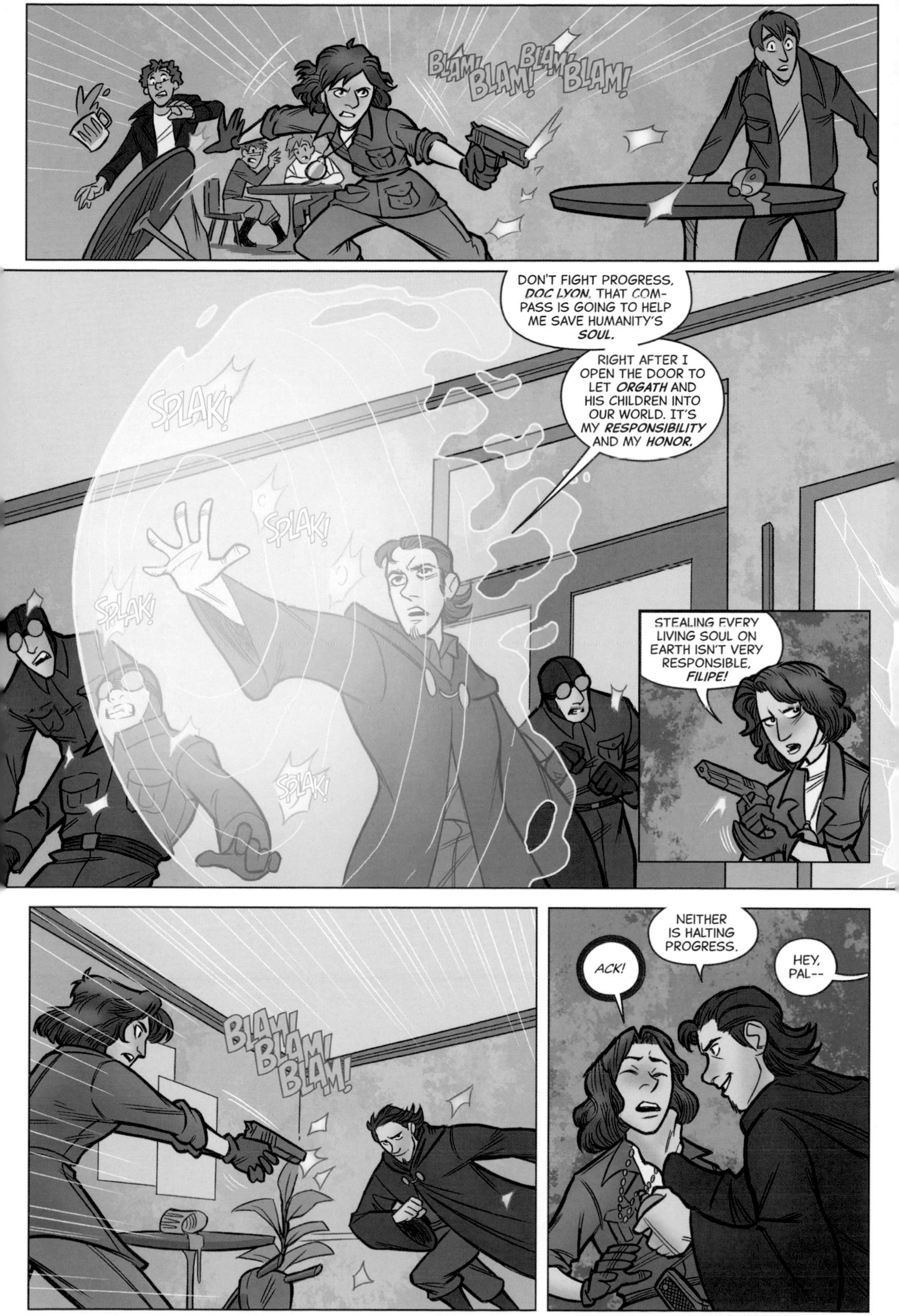
BLAM! BLAM! BLAM! BLAM!
DON'T FIGHT PROGRESS, DOC LYON. THAT COMPASS IS GOING TO HELP ME SAVE HUMANITY'S SOUL.
RIGHT AFTER I OPEN THE DOOR TO LET ORGATH AND HIS CHILDREN INTO OUR WORLD. IT'S MY RESPONSIBILITY AND MY HONOR.
SPLAK!
SPLAK!
SPLAK!
SPLAK!
STEALING EVERY LIVING SOUL ON EARTH ISN'T VERY RESPONSIBLE, FILIPE!
BLAM! BLAM! BLAM!
NEITHER IS HALTING PROGRESS.
ACK!
HEY, PAL--

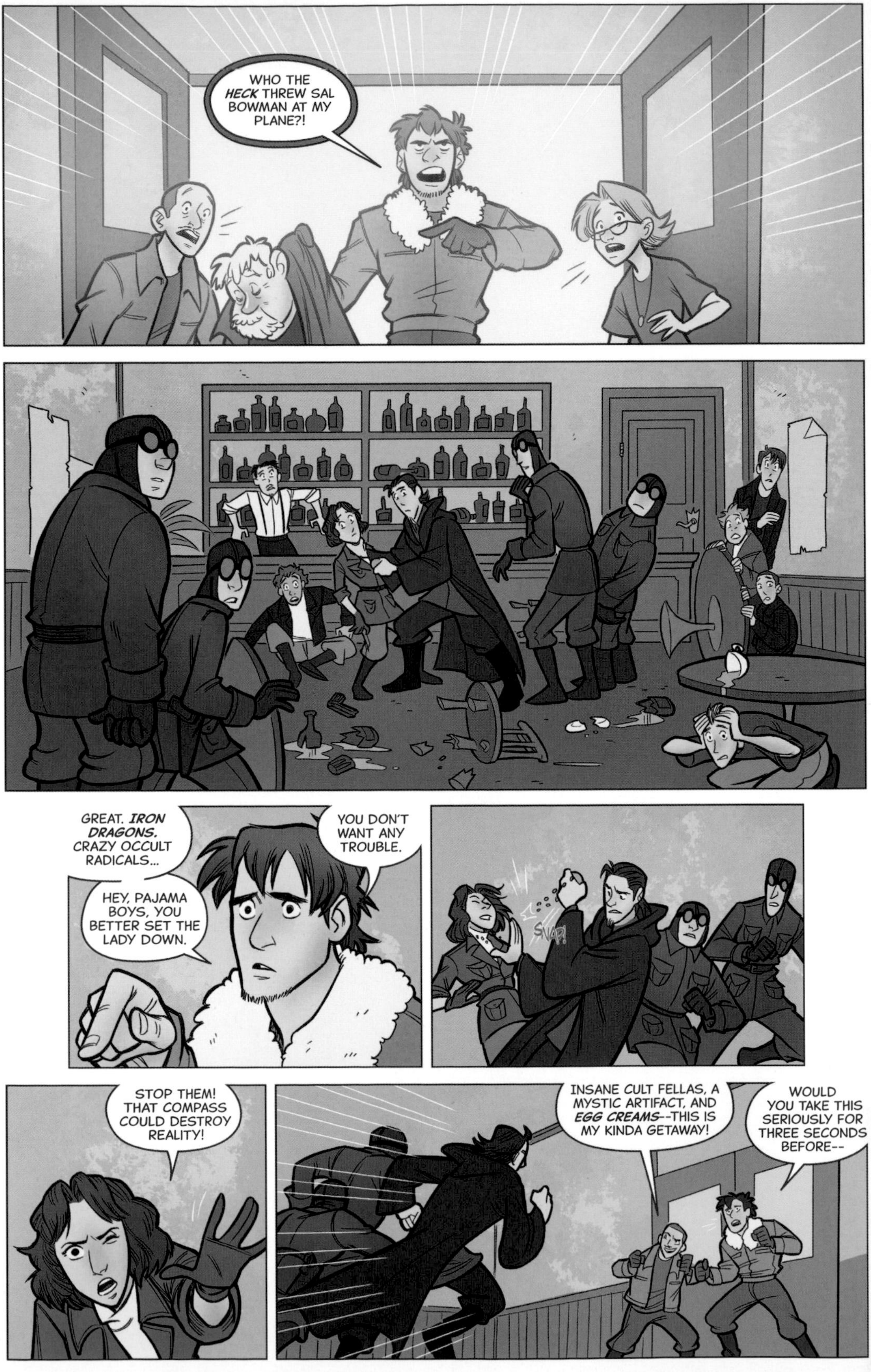
WHO THE *HECK* THREW SAL BOWMAN AT MY PLANE?!
GREAT. *IRON DRAGONS.* CRAZY OCCULT RADICALS...
YOU DON'T WANT ANY TROUBLE.
HEY, PAJAMA BOYS, YOU BETTER SET THE LADY DOWN.
SNAP!
STOP THEM! THAT COMPASS COULD DESTROY REALITY!
INSANE CULT FELLAS, A MYSTIC ARTIFACT, AND *EGG CREAMS*--THIS IS MY KINDA GETAWAY!
WOULD YOU TAKE THIS SERIOUSLY FOR THREE SECONDS BEFORE--

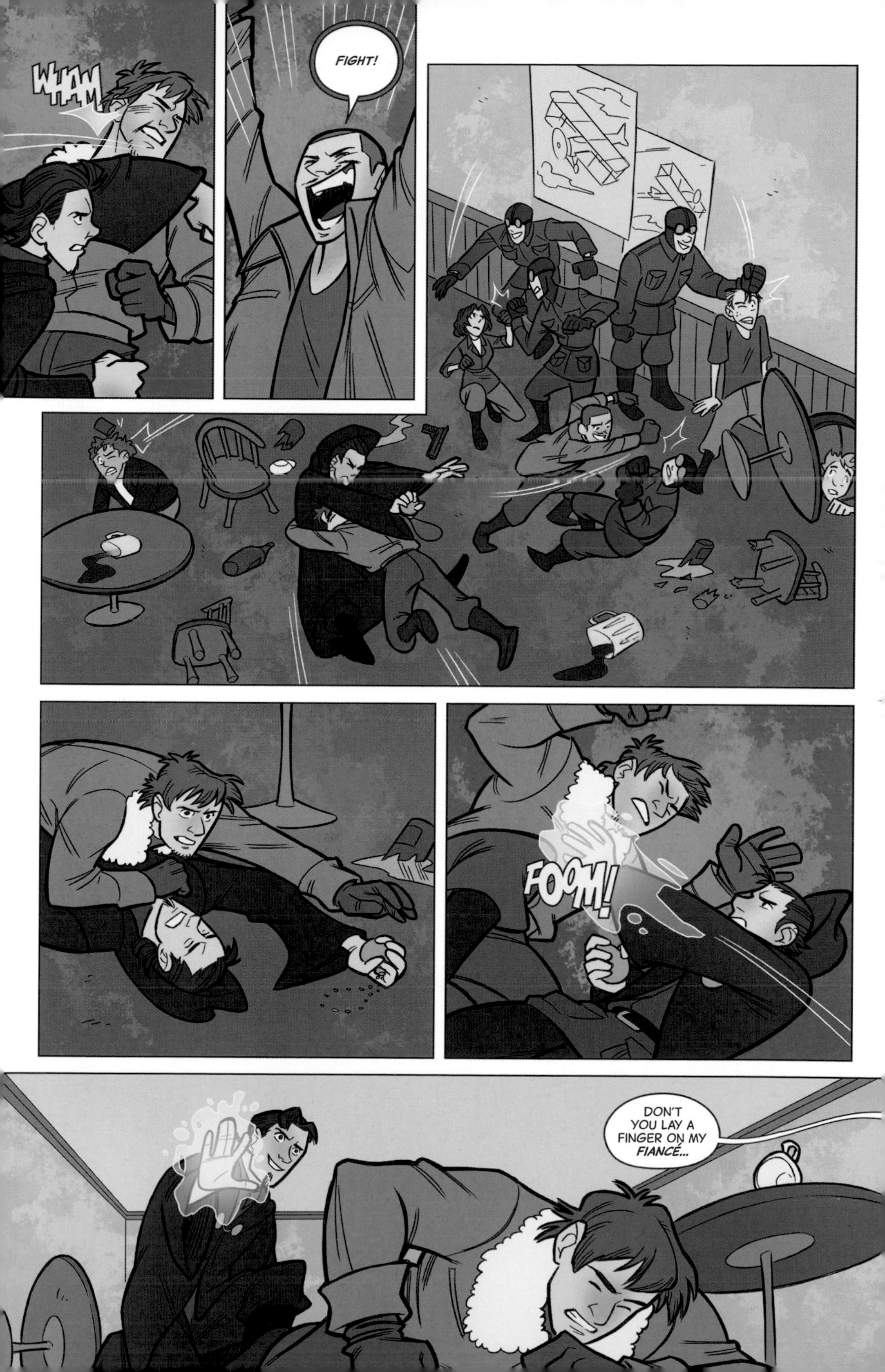
WHAM
FIGHT!
FOOM!
DON'T YOU LAY A FINGER ON MY FIANCÉ...

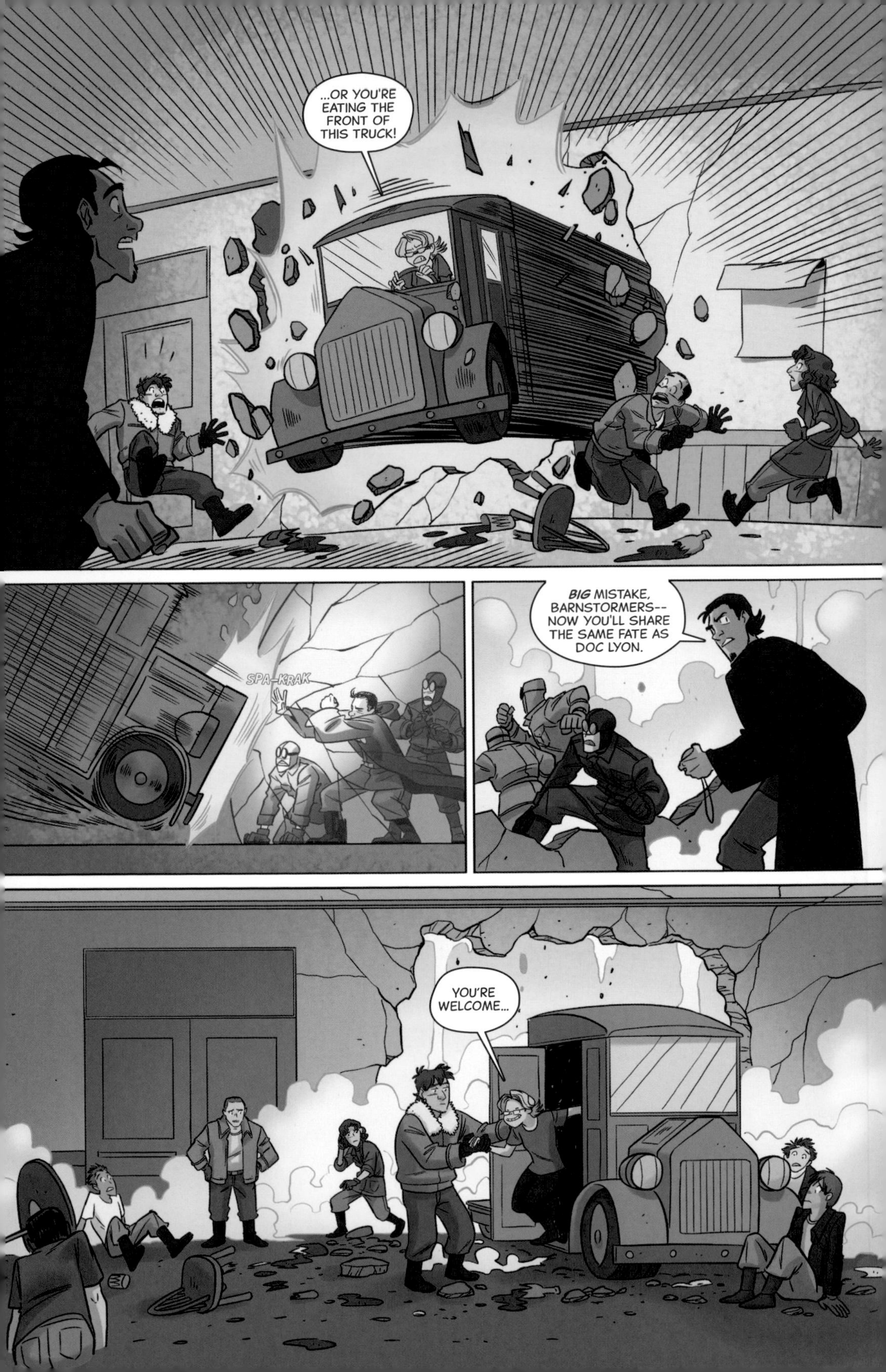
...OR YOU'RE EATING THE FRONT OF THIS TRUCK!
SPA-KRAK
BIG MISTAKE, BARNSTORMERS-- NOW YOU'LL SHARE THE SAME FATE AS DOC LYON.
YOU'RE WELCOME...

WITH *THIS,* THE PATH TO ORGATH WILL BE REVEALED.

THE WORLD CAN BE CLEANSED OF ITS SINS.

MASTER *FILIPE,* YOUR *PROTECTIVE MAGIC* IS RUNNING OUT AND THAT TRUCK PACKED A *WALLOP.*

WE NEED AN *ESCAPE* PLAN!

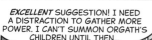

SLAT'S SODA

EXCELLENT SUGGESTION! I NEED A DISTRACTION TO GATHER MORE POWER. I CAN'T SUMMON ORGATH'S CHILDREN UNTIL THEN...

BUT WITH THIS MANY RAW MATERIALS...

!

GAHH!

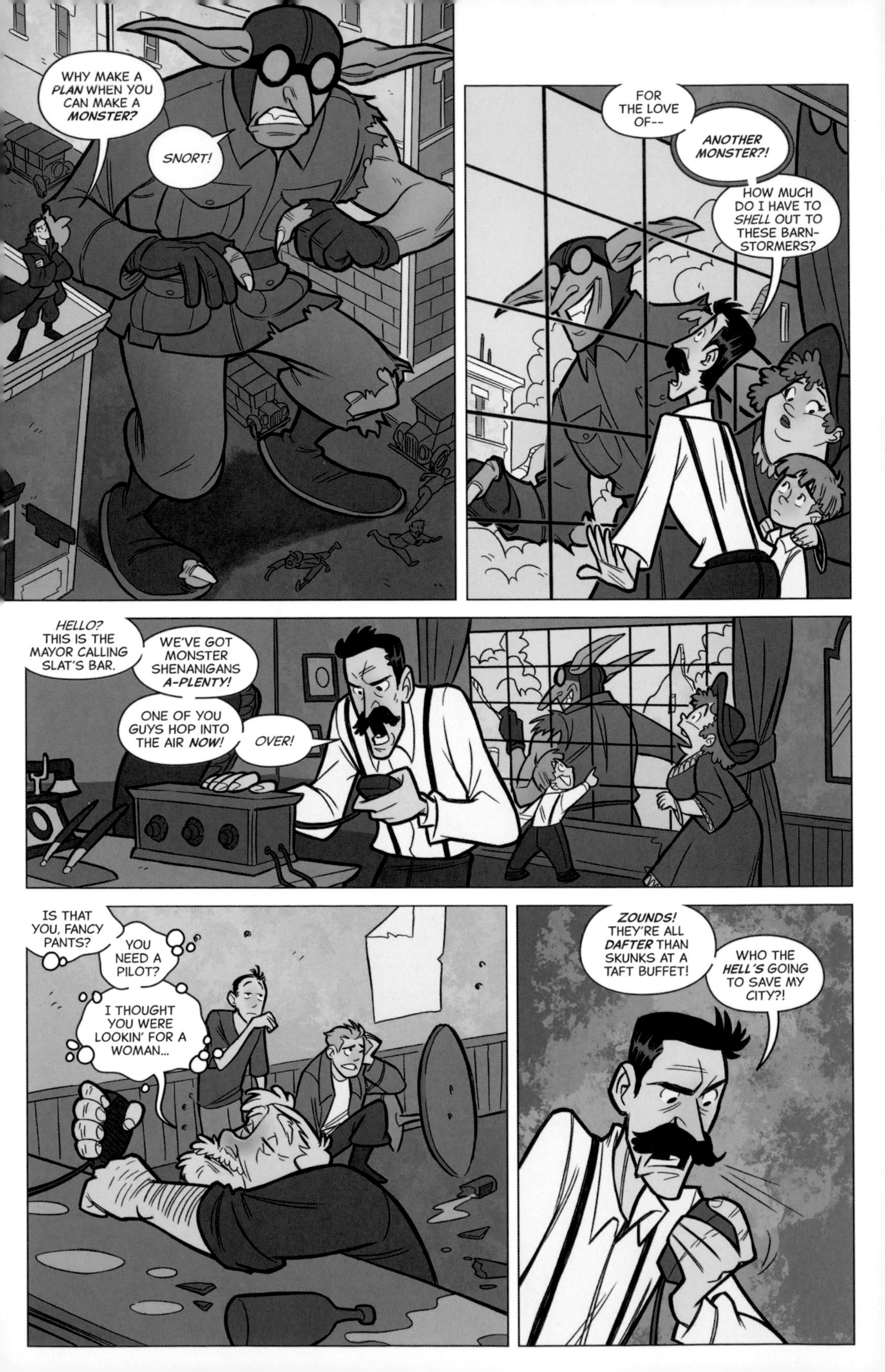
WHY MAKE A *PLAN* WHEN YOU CAN MAKE A *MONSTER?*
SNORT!
FOR THE LOVE OF--
ANOTHER MONSTER?!
HOW MUCH DO I HAVE TO *SHELL* OUT TO THESE BARN-STORMERS?
HELLO? THIS IS THE MAYOR CALLING SLAT'S BAR.
WE'VE GOT MONSTER SHENANIGANS *A-PLENTY!*
ONE OF YOU GUYS HOP INTO THE AIR *NOW!*
OVER!
IS THAT YOU, FANCY PANTS?
YOU NEED A PILOT?
I THOUGHT YOU WERE LOOKIN' FOR A WOMAN...
ZOUNDS! THEY'RE ALL *DAFTER* THAN SKUNKS AT A TAFT BUFFET!
WHO THE *HELL'S* GOING TO SAVE MY CITY?!

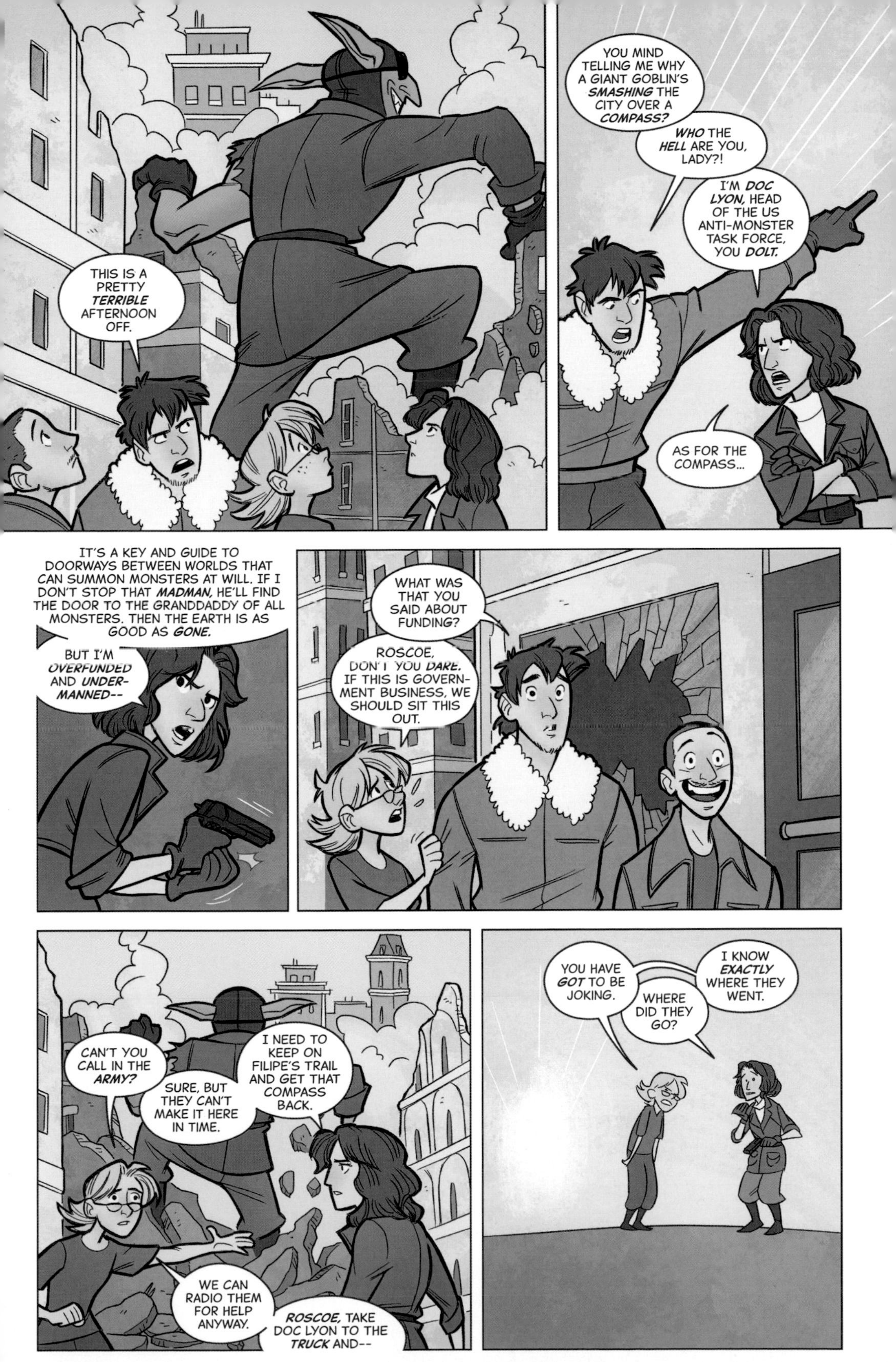
THIS IS A PRETTY TERRIBLE AFTERNOON OFF.
YOU MIND TELLING ME WHY A GIANT GOBLIN'S SMASHING THE CITY OVER A COMPASS?
WHO THE HELL ARE YOU, LADY?!
I'M DOC LYON, HEAD OF THE US ANTI-MONSTER TASK FORCE, YOU DOLT.
AS FOR THE COMPASS...
IT'S A KEY AND GUIDE TO DOORWAYS BETWEEN WORLDS THAT CAN SUMMON MONSTERS AT WILL. IF I DON'T STOP THAT MADMAN, HE'LL FIND THE DOOR TO THE GRANDDADDY OF ALL MONSTERS. THEN THE EARTH IS AS GOOD AS GONE.
BUT I'M OVERFUNDED AND UNDER-MANNED--
WHAT WAS THAT YOU SAID ABOUT FUNDING?
ROSCOE, DON'T YOU DARE. IF THIS IS GOVERN-MENT BUSINESS, WE SHOULD SIT THIS OUT.
CAN'T YOU CALL IN THE ARMY?
SURE, BUT THEY CAN'T MAKE IT HERE IN TIME.
I NEED TO KEEP ON FILIPE'S TRAIL AND GET THAT COMPASS BACK.
WE CAN RADIO THEM FOR HELP ANYWAY.
ROSCOE, TAKE DOC LYON TO THE TRUCK AND--
YOU HAVE GOT TO BE JOKING.
I KNOW EXACTLY WHERE THEY WENT.
WHERE DID THEY GO?

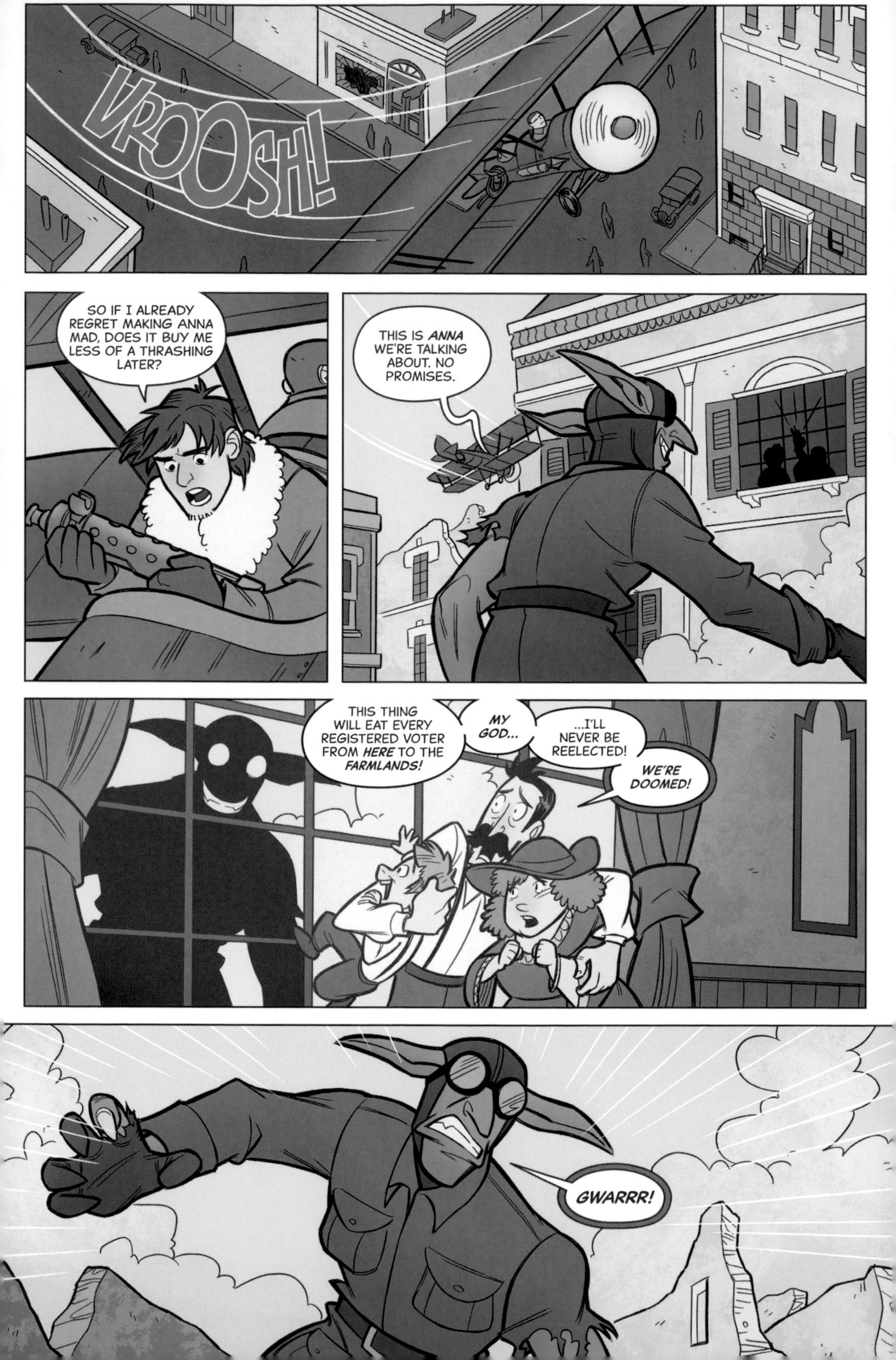
VROOSH!
SO IF I ALREADY REGRET MAKING ANNA MAD, DOES IT BUY ME LESS OF A THRASHING LATER?
THIS IS ANNA WE'RE TALKING ABOUT. NO PROMISES.
THIS THING WILL EAT EVERY REGISTERED VOTER FROM HERE TO THE FARMLANDS!
MY GOD...
...I'LL NEVER BE REELECTED!
WE'RE DOOMED!
GWARRR!

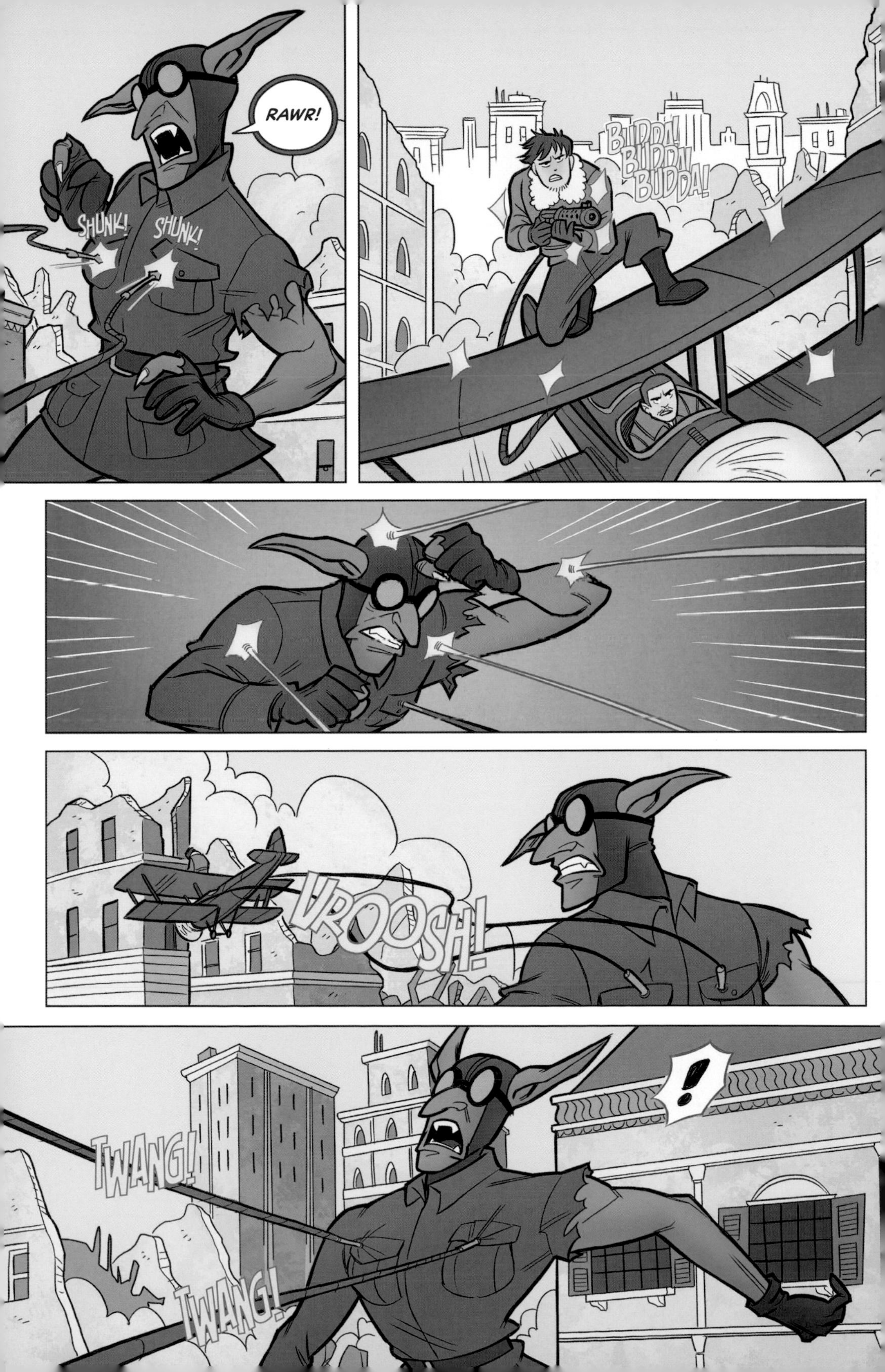
RAWR!
SHUNK!
SHUNK!
BUDDA!
BUDDA!
BUDDA!
VROOSH!
!
TWANG!
TWANG!

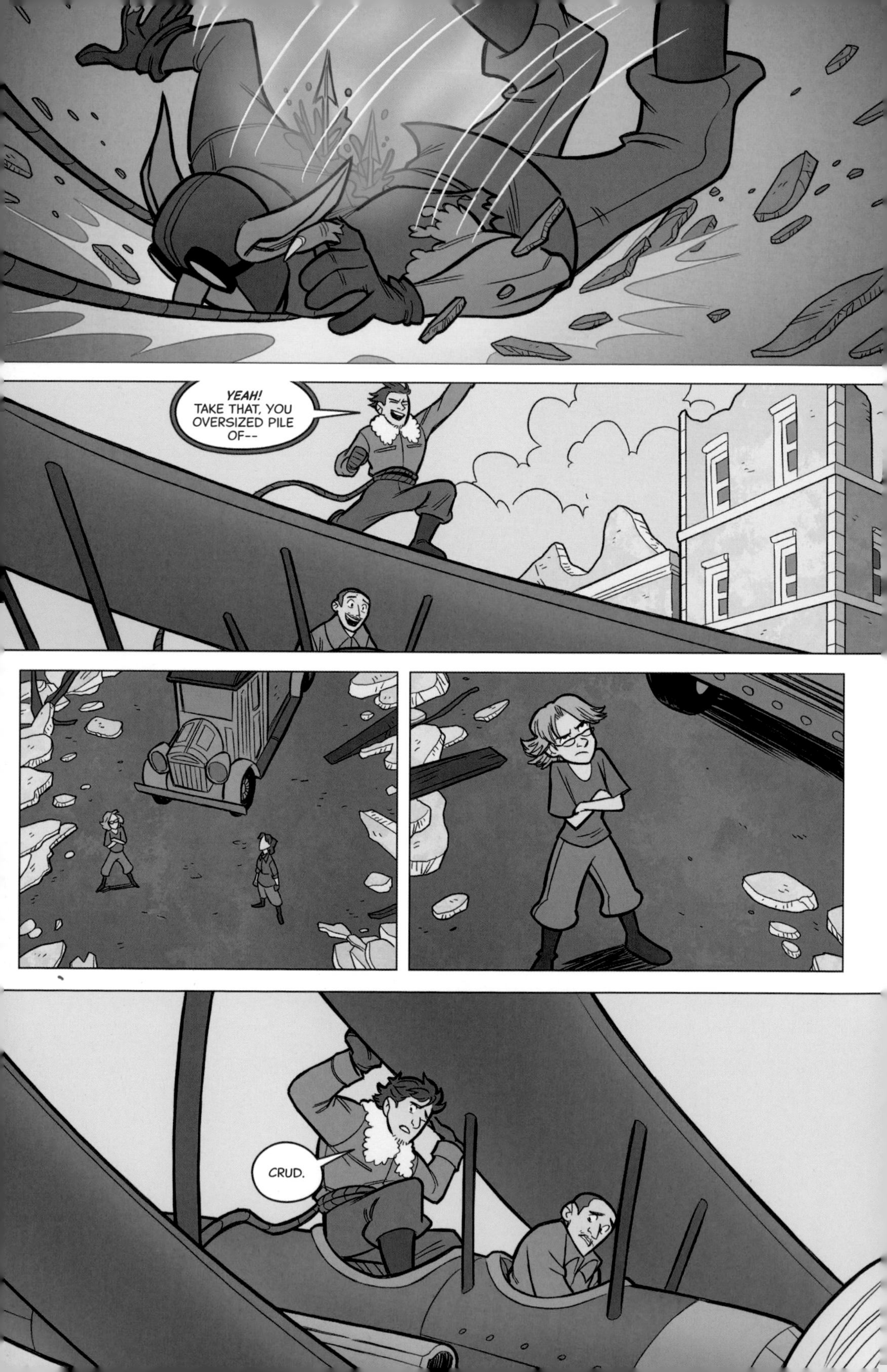
YEAH! TAKE THAT, YOU OVERSIZED PILE OF--
CRUD.

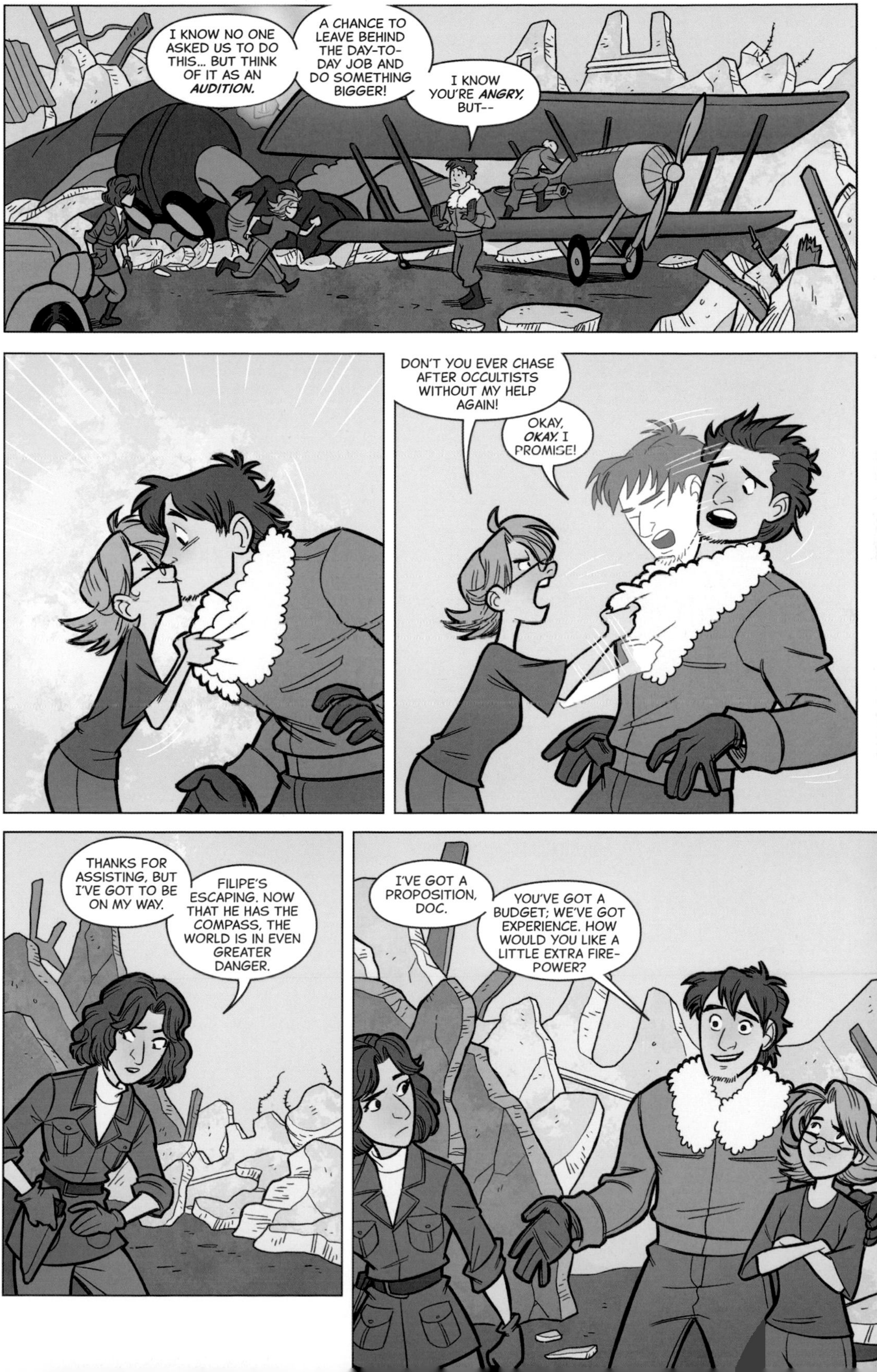
I KNOW NO ONE ASKED US TO DO THIS... BUT THINK OF IT AS AN *AUDITION.*
A CHANCE TO LEAVE BEHIND THE DAY-TO-DAY JOB AND DO SOMETHING BIGGER!
I KNOW YOU'RE *ANGRY,* BUT--
DON'T YOU EVER CHASE AFTER OCCULTISTS WITHOUT MY HELP AGAIN!
OKAY, *OKAY.* I PROMISE!
THANKS FOR ASSISTING, BUT I'VE GOT TO BE ON MY WAY.
FILIPE'S ESCAPING. NOW THAT HE HAS THE COMPASS, THE WORLD IS IN EVEN GREATER DANGER.
I'VE GOT A PROPOSITION, DOC.
YOU'VE GOT A BUDGET; WE'VE GOT EXPERIENCE. HOW WOULD YOU LIKE A LITTLE EXTRA FIRE-POWER?

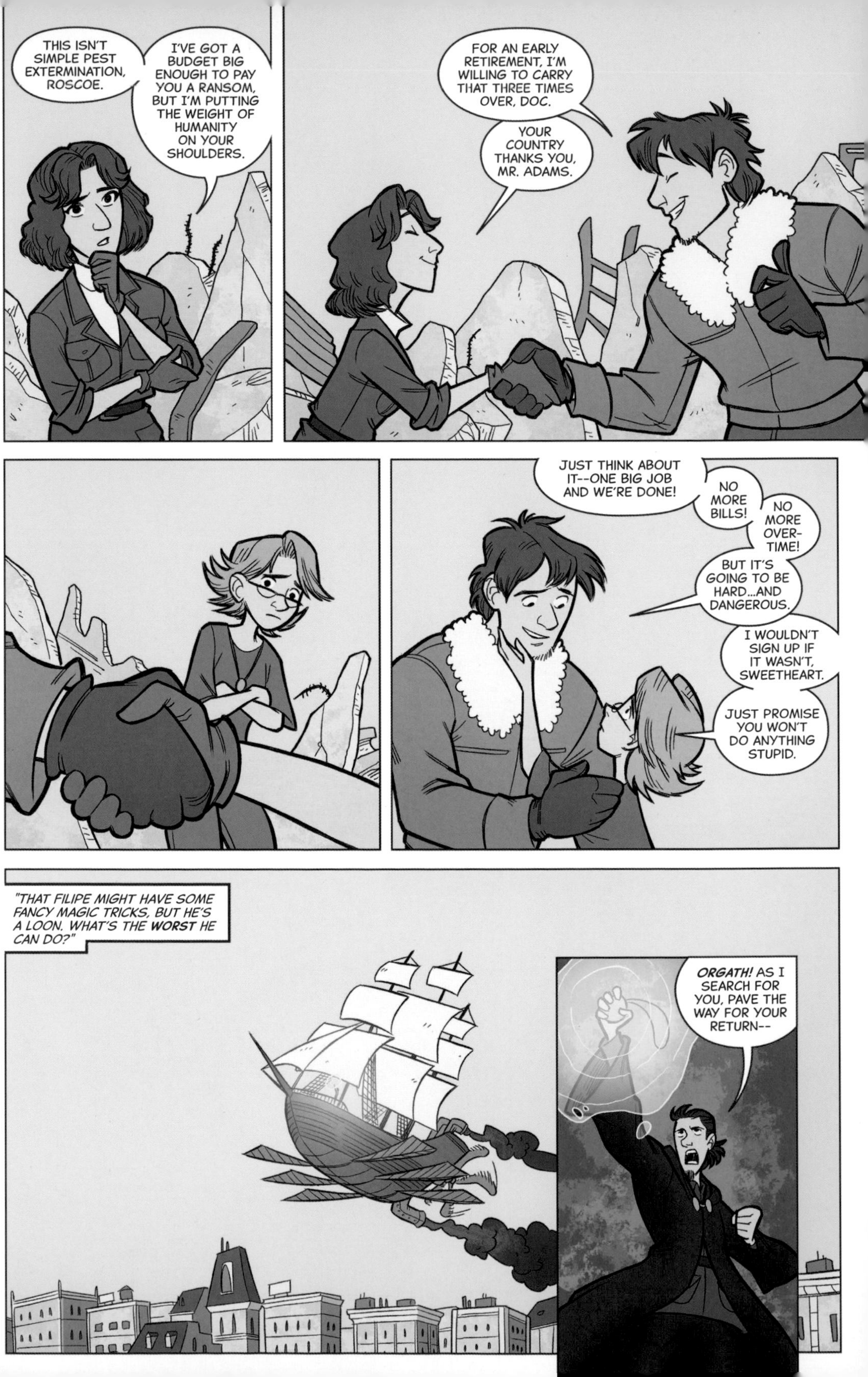
THIS ISN'T SIMPLE PEST EXTERMINATION, ROSCOE.
I'VE GOT A BUDGET BIG ENOUGH TO PAY YOU A RANSOM, BUT I'M PUTTING THE WEIGHT OF HUMANITY ON YOUR SHOULDERS.
FOR AN EARLY RETIREMENT, I'M WILLING TO CARRY THAT THREE TIMES OVER, DOC.
YOUR COUNTRY THANKS YOU, MR. ADAMS.
JUST THINK ABOUT IT--ONE BIG JOB AND WE'RE DONE!
NO MORE BILLS!
NO MORE OVER-TIME!
BUT IT'S GOING TO BE HARD...AND DANGEROUS.
I WOULDN'T SIGN UP IF IT WASN'T, SWEETHEART.
JUST PROMISE YOU WON'T DO ANYTHING STUPID.
"THAT FILIPE MIGHT HAVE SOME FANCY MAGIC TRICKS, BUT HE'S A LOON. WHAT'S THE **WORST** HE CAN DO?"
ORGATH! AS I SEARCH FOR YOU, PAVE THE WAY FOR YOUR RETURN--

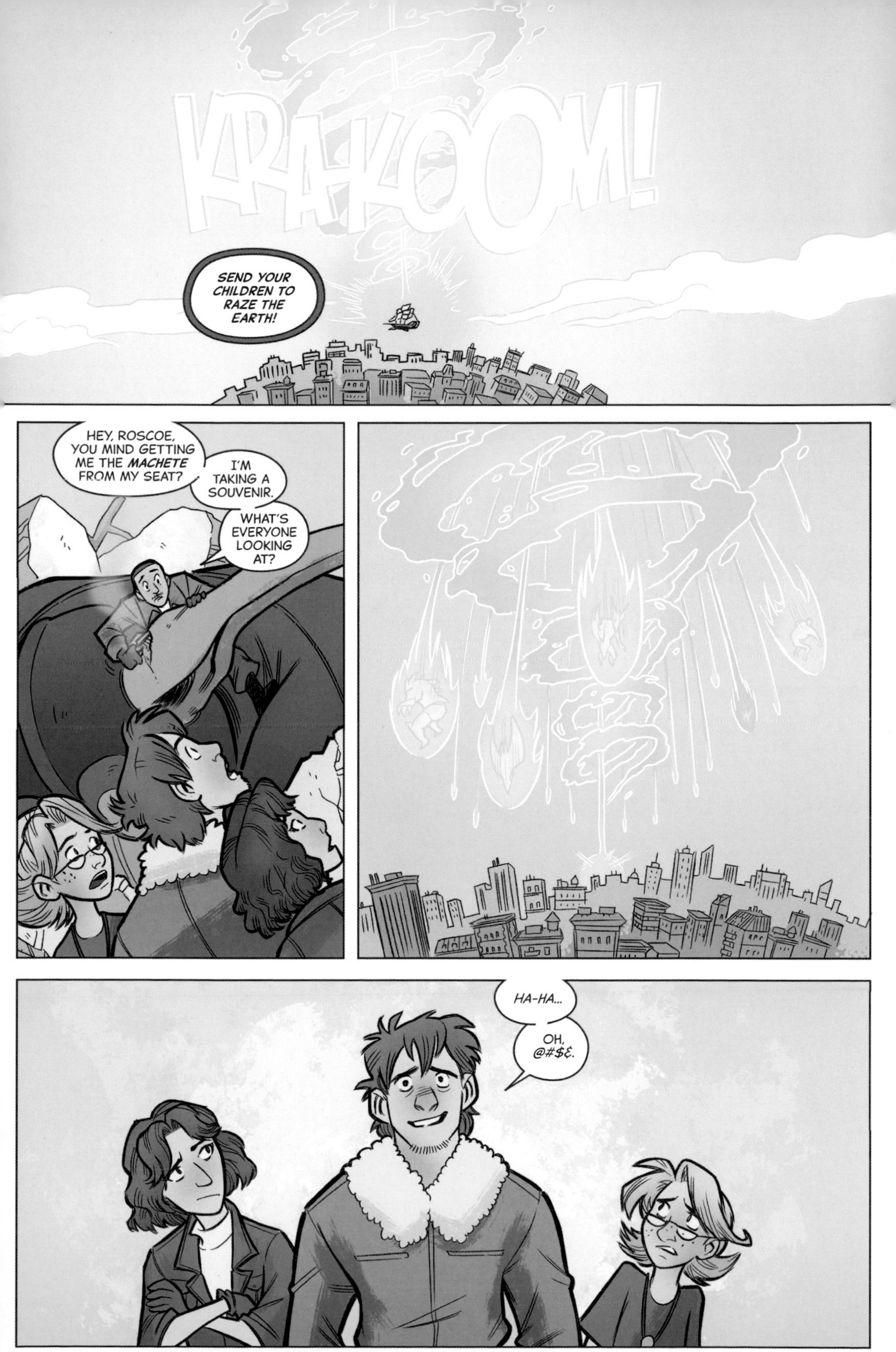
KRAKOOM!
SEND YOUR CHILDREN TO RAZE THE EARTH!
HEY, ROSCOE, YOU MIND GETTING ME THE MACHETE FROM MY SEAT?
I'M TAKING A SOUVENIR.
WHAT'S EVERYONE LOOKING AT?
HA-HA...
OH, @#$£.

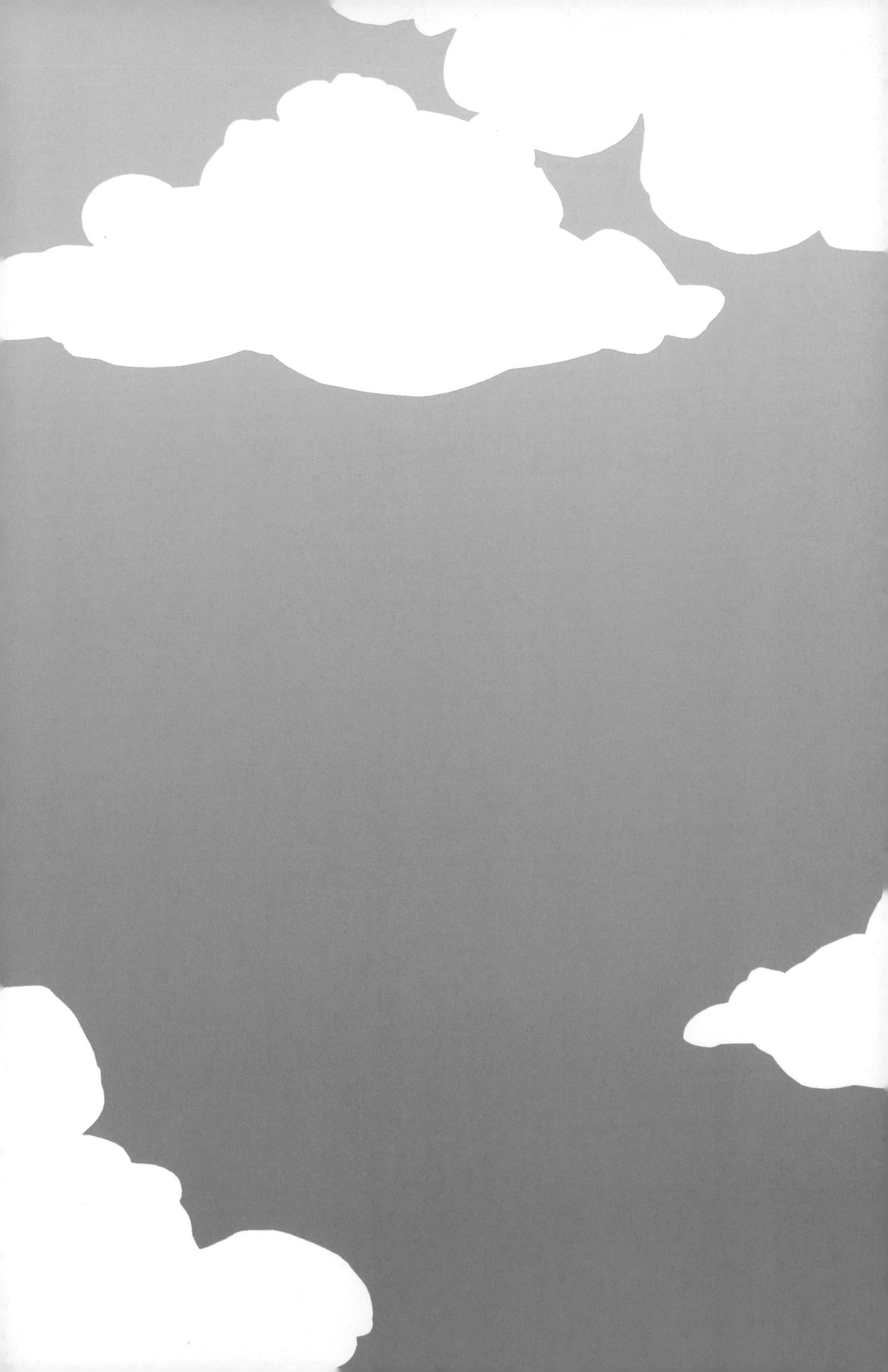

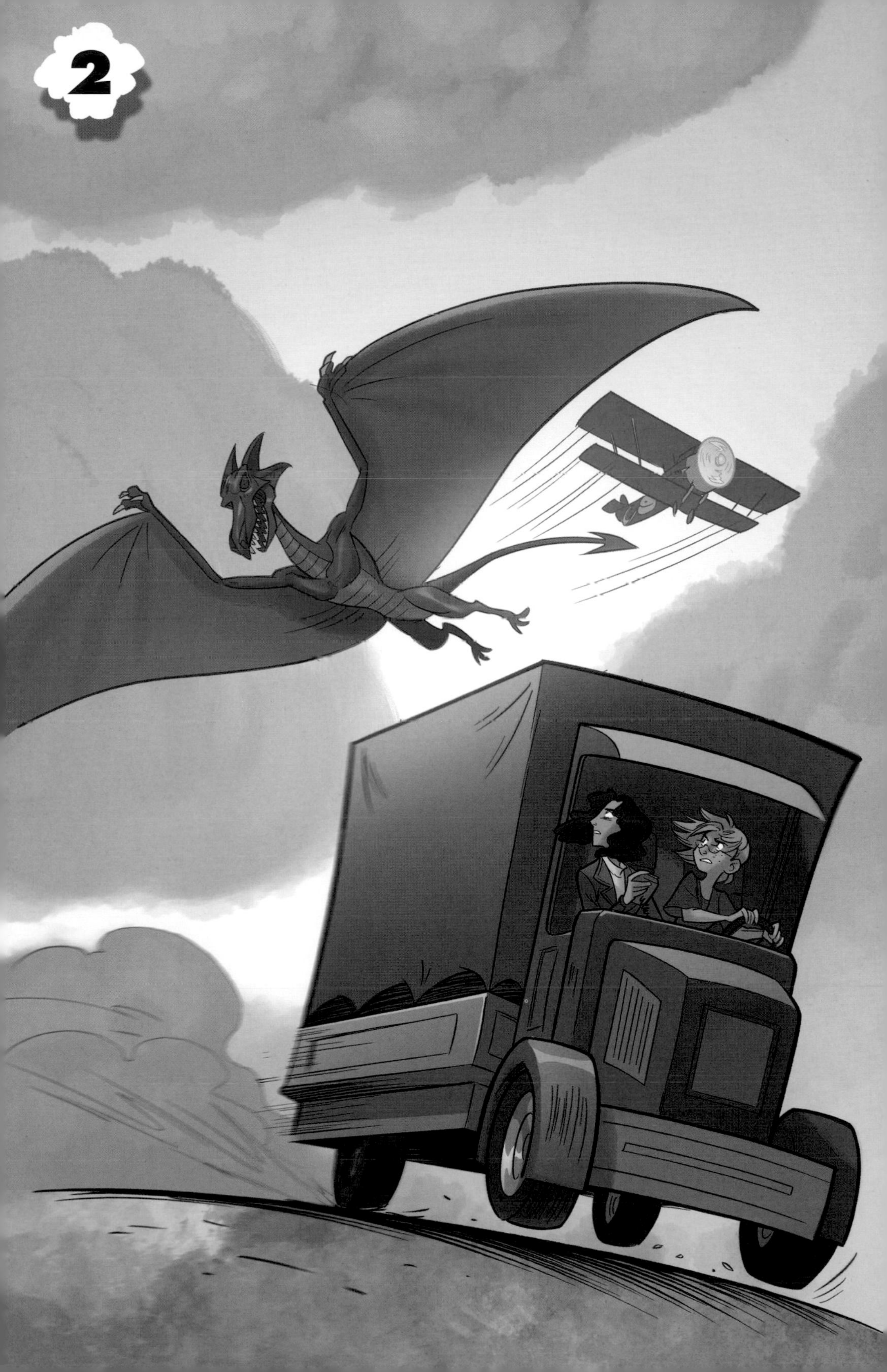
2

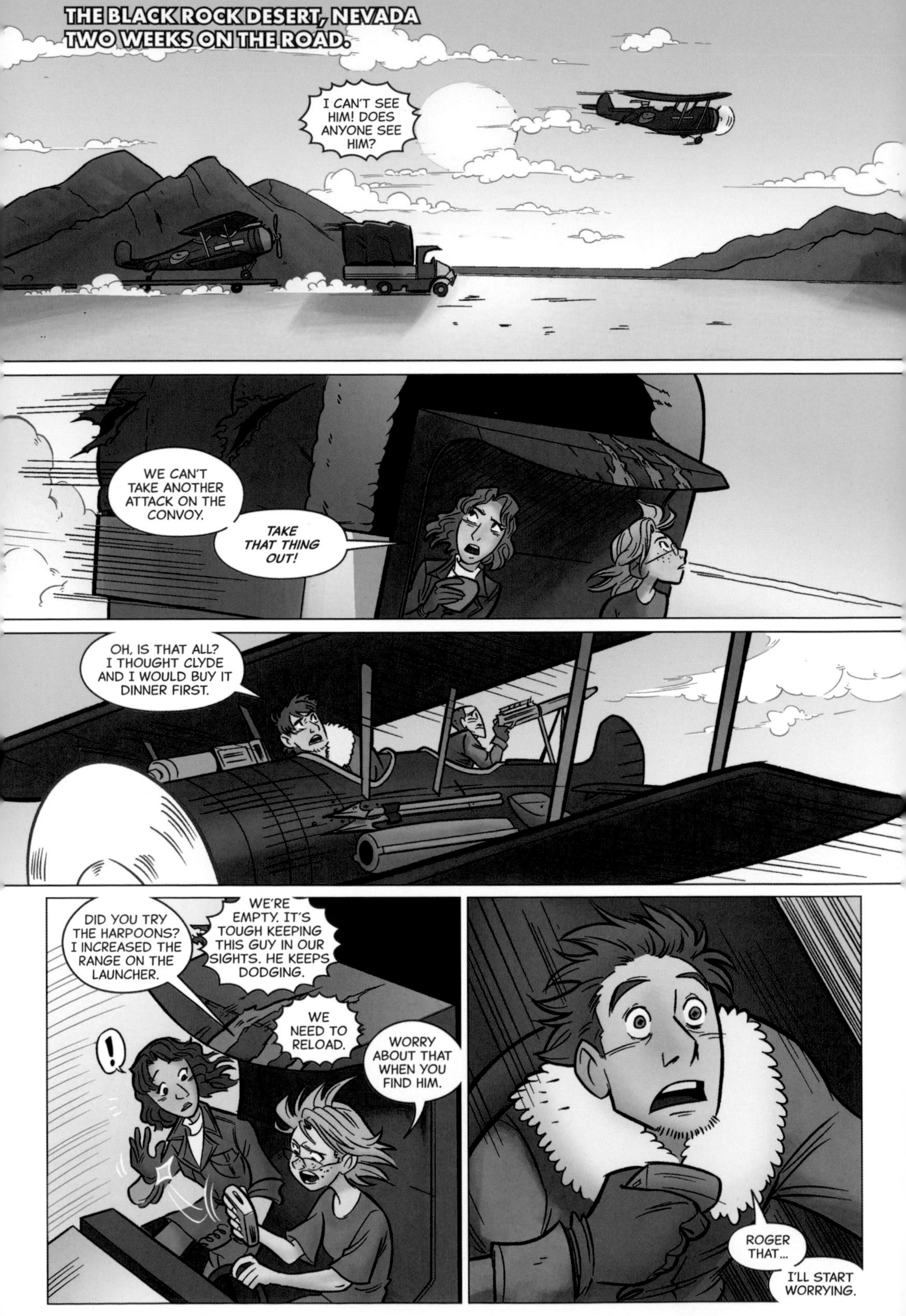
THE BLACK ROCK DESERT, NEVADA
TWO WEEKS ON THE ROAD.
I CAN'T SEE HIM! DOES ANYONE SEE HIM?
WE CAN'T TAKE ANOTHER ATTACK ON THE CONVOY.
TAKE THAT THING OUT!
OH, IS THAT ALL? I THOUGHT CLYDE AND I WOULD BUY IT DINNER FIRST.
DID YOU TRY THE HARPOONS? I INCREASED THE RANGE ON THE LAUNCHER.
WE'RE EMPTY. IT'S TOUGH KEEPING THIS GUY IN OUR SIGHTS. HE KEEPS DODGING.
WE NEED TO RELOAD.
!
WORRY ABOUT THAT WHEN YOU FIND HIM.
ROGER THAT...
I'LL START WORRYING.

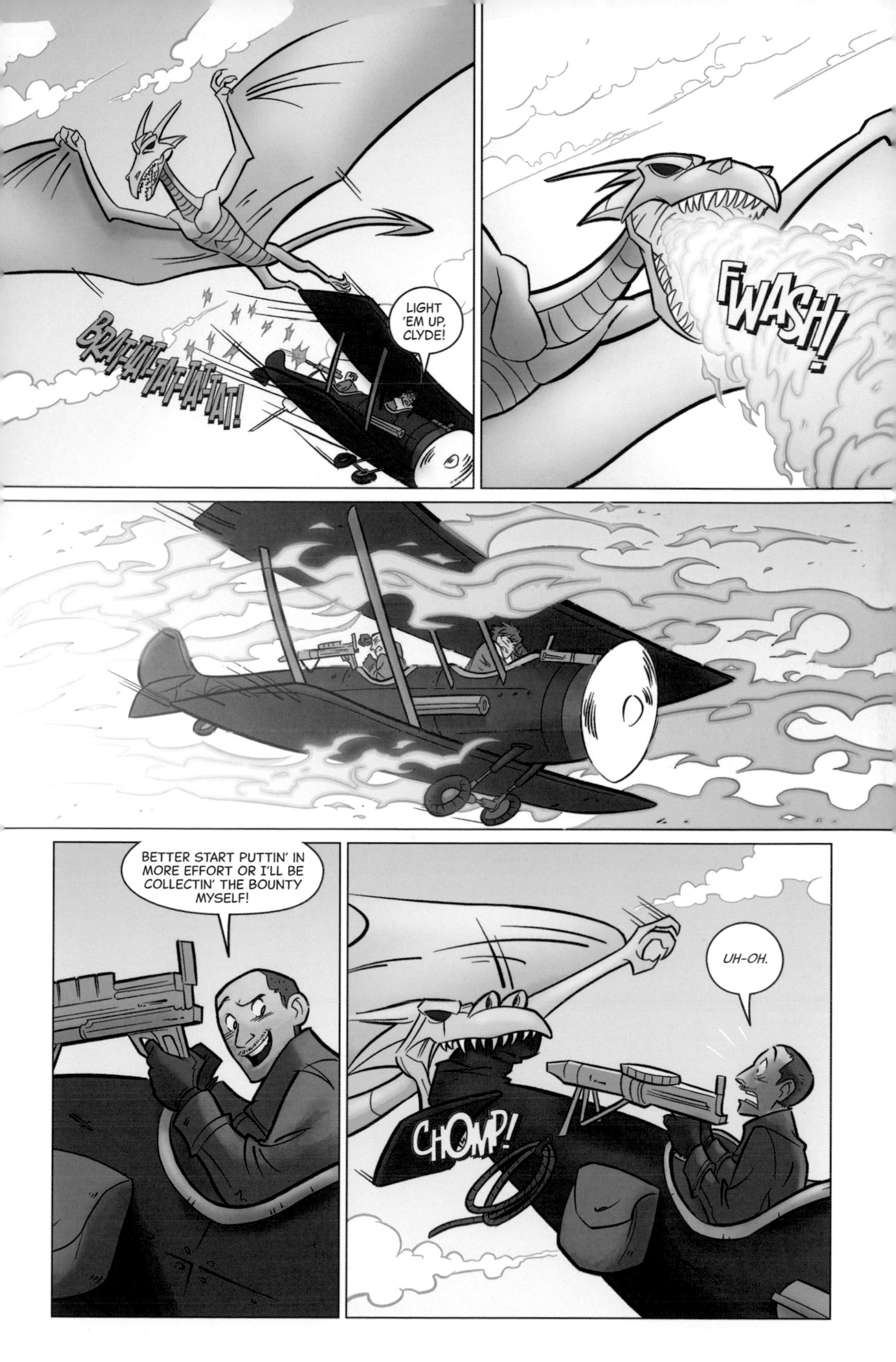
LIGHT 'EM UP, CLYDE!
BRAT-TAT-TAT-TAT-TAT!
FWASH!
BETTER START PUTTIN' IN MORE EFFORT OR I'LL BE COLLECTIN' THE BOUNTY MYSELF!
UH-OH.
CHOMP!

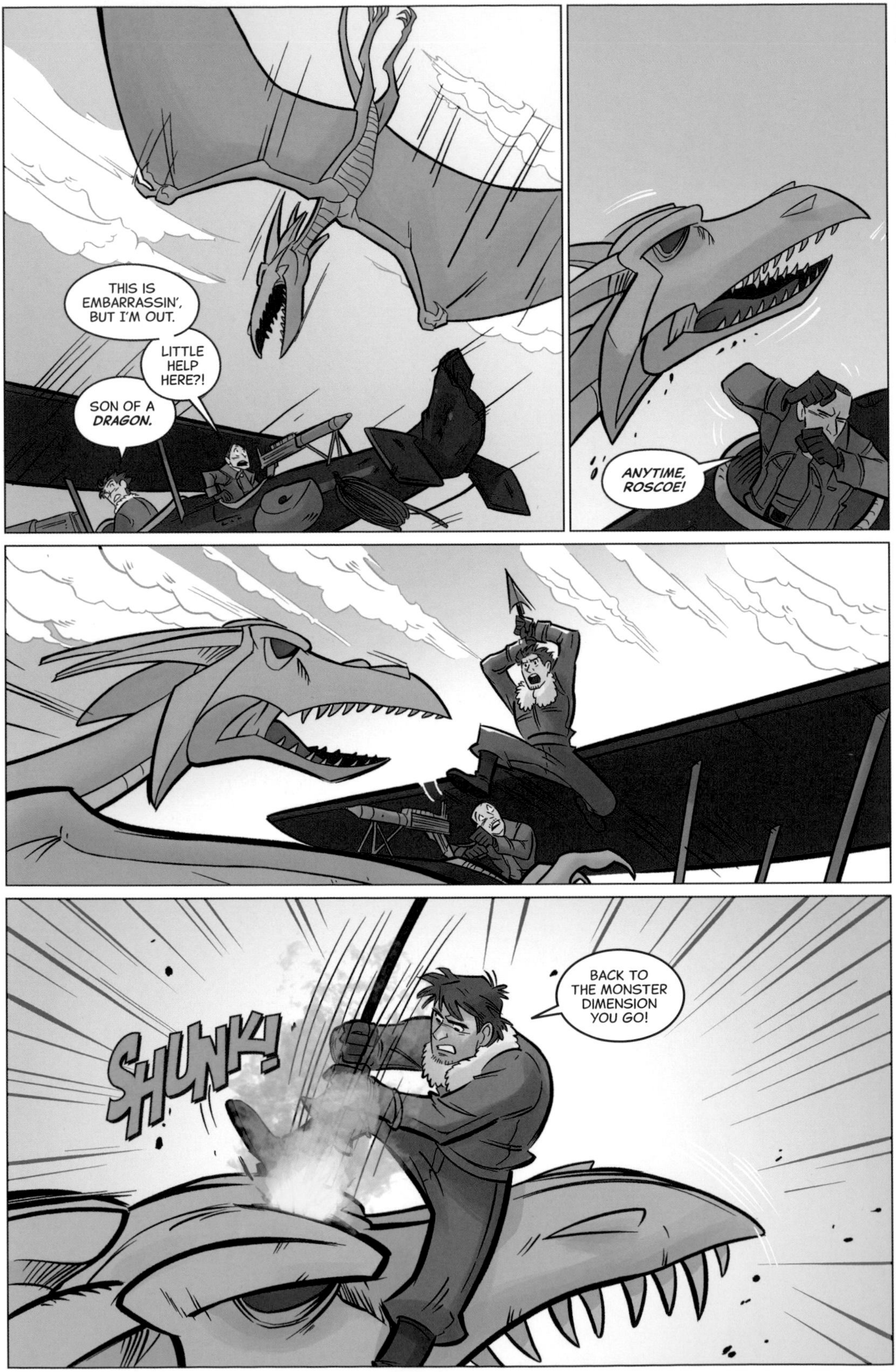
THIS IS EMBARRASSIN', BUT I'M OUT.
LITTLE HELP HERE?!
SON OF A *DRAGON.*
ANYTIME, ROSCOE!
SHUNK!
BACK TO THE MONSTER DIMENSION YOU GO!

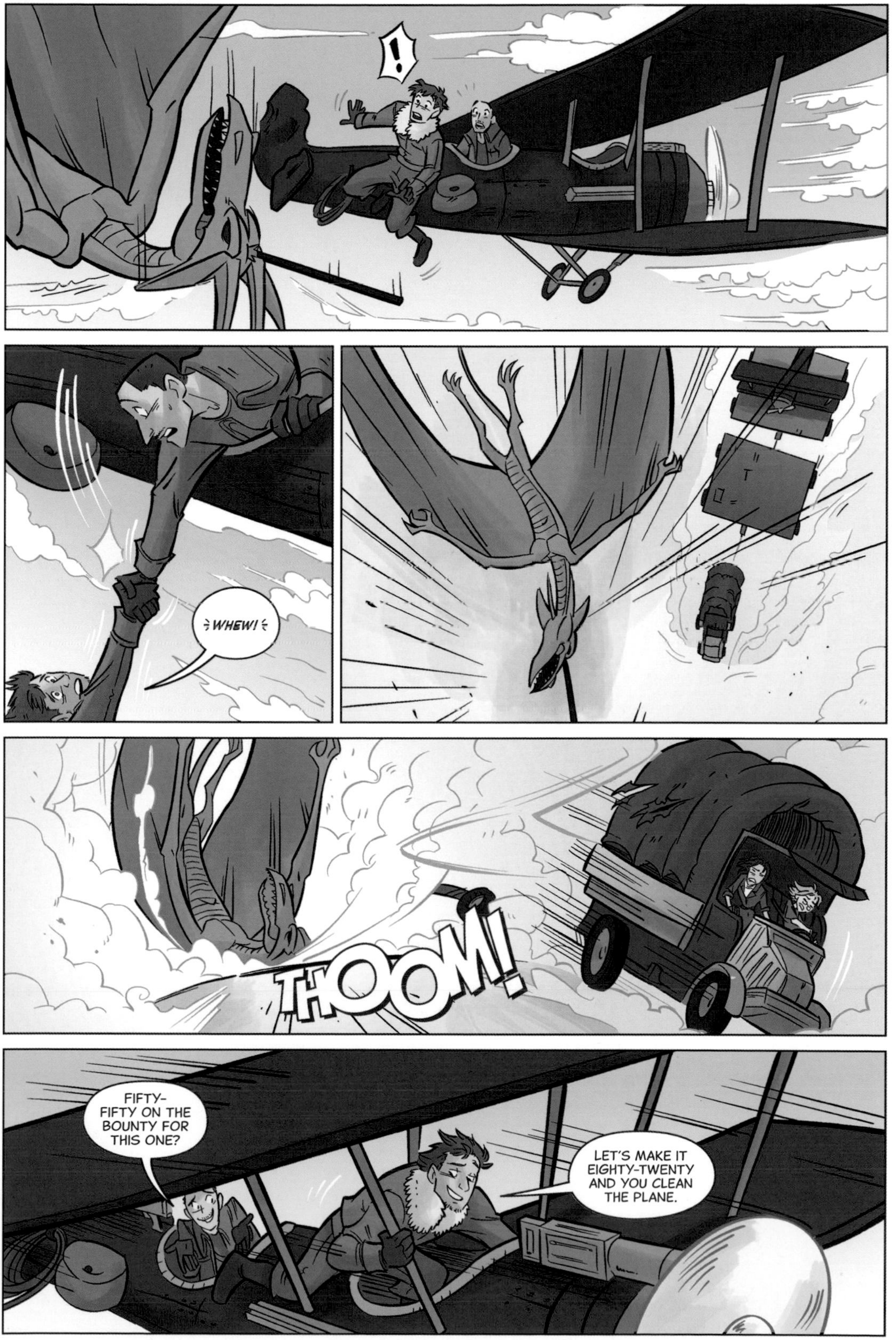
!
WHEW!
THOOM!
FIFTY-FIFTY ON THE BOUNTY FOR THIS ONE?
LET'S MAKE IT EIGHTY-TWENTY AND YOU CLEAN THE PLANE.

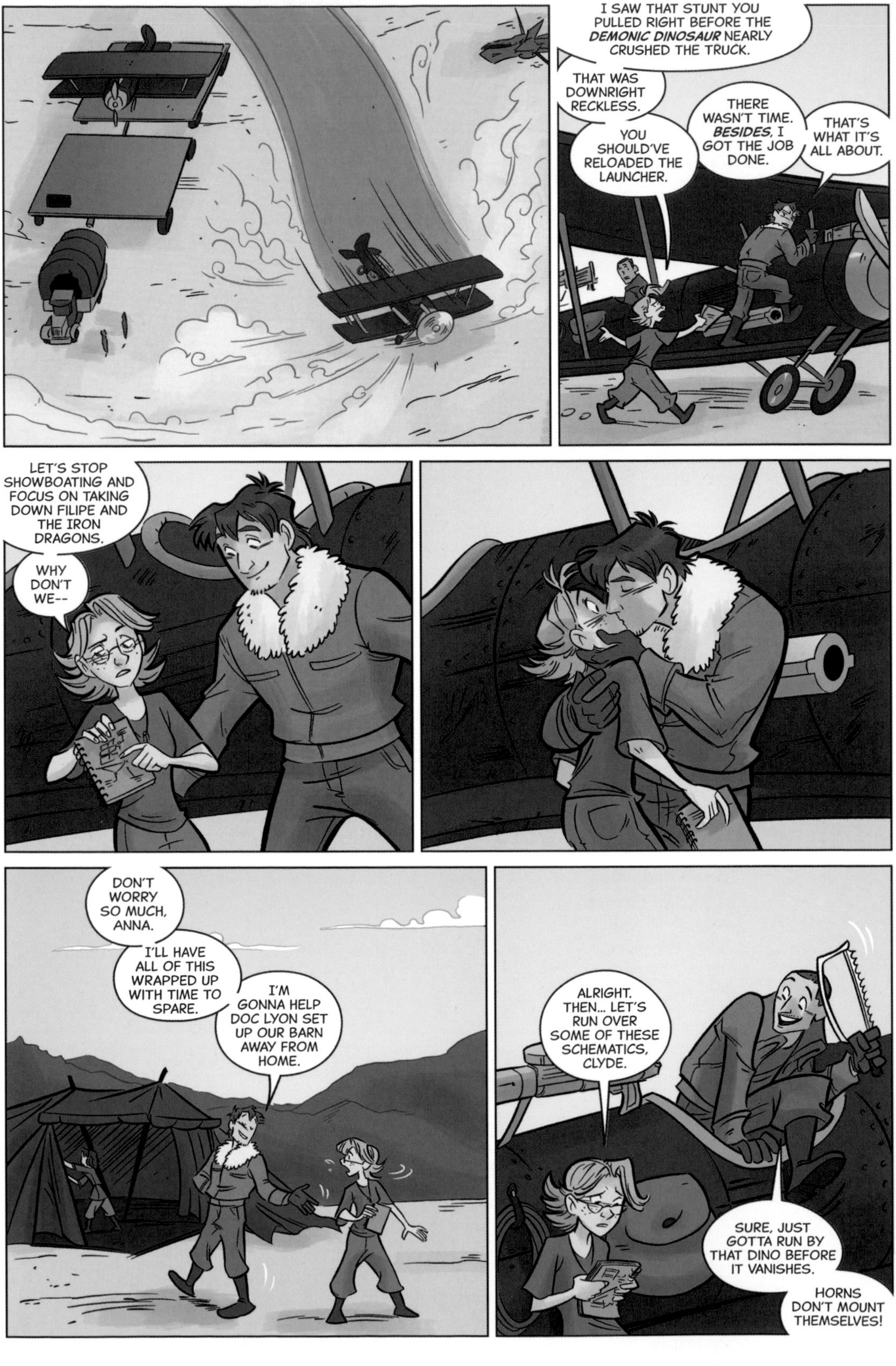
I SAW THAT STUNT YOU PULLED RIGHT BEFORE THE *DEMONIC DINOSAUR* NEARLY CRUSHED THE TRUCK.
THAT WAS DOWNRIGHT RECKLESS.
YOU SHOULD'VE RELOADED THE LAUNCHER.
THERE WASN'T TIME. *BESIDES*, I GOT THE JOB DONE.
THAT'S WHAT IT'S ALL ABOUT.
LET'S STOP SHOWBOATING AND FOCUS ON TAKING DOWN FILIPE AND THE IRON DRAGONS.
WHY DON'T WE--
DON'T WORRY SO MUCH, ANNA.
I'LL HAVE ALL OF THIS WRAPPED UP WITH TIME TO SPARE.
I'M GONNA HELP DOC LYON SET UP OUR BARN AWAY FROM HOME.
ALRIGHT. THEN... LET'S RUN OVER SOME OF THESE SCHEMATICS, CLYDE.
SURE, JUST GOTTA RUN BY THAT DINO BEFORE IT VANISHES.
HORNS DON'T MOUNT THEMSELVES!

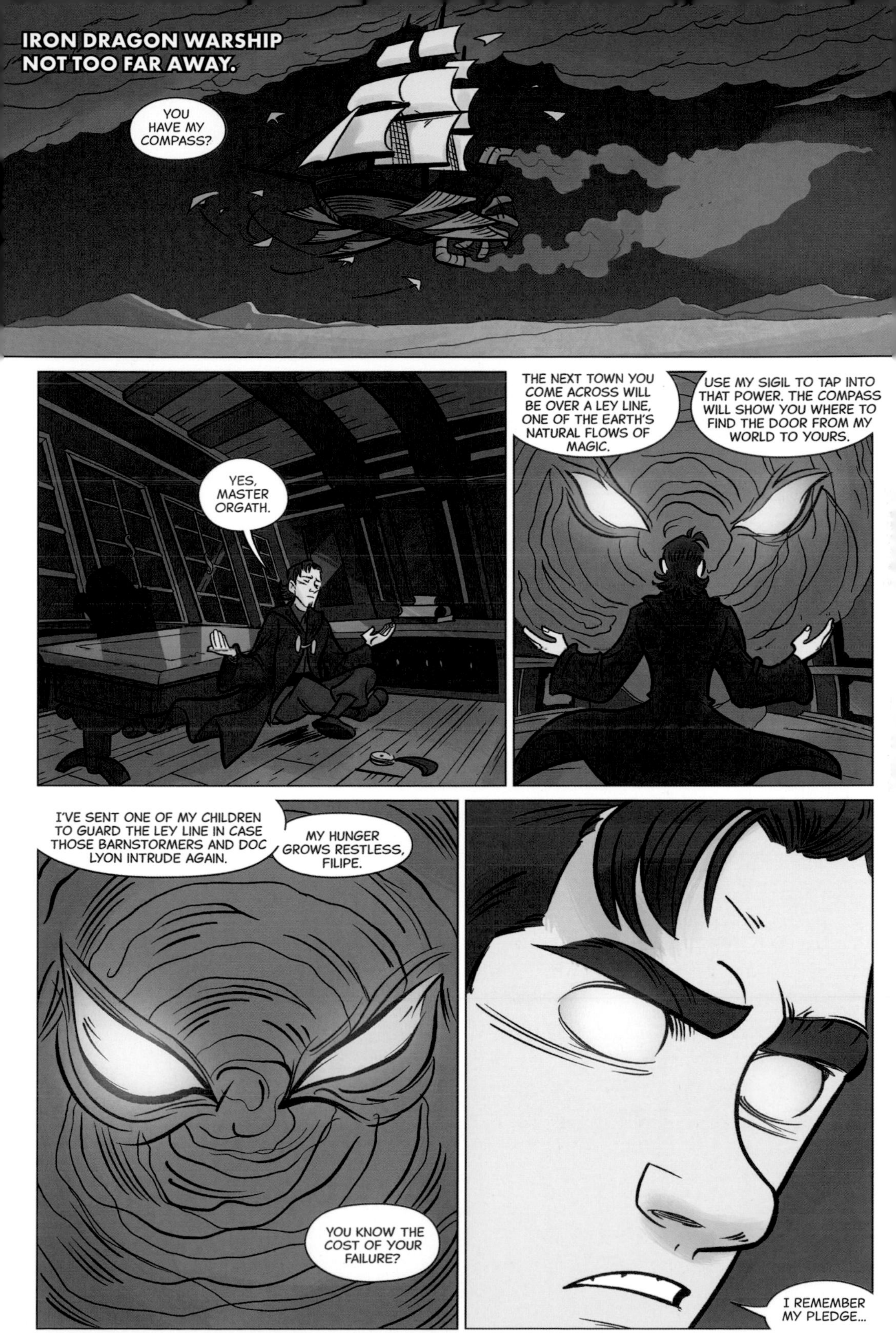
IRON DRAGON WARSHIP NOT TOO FAR AWAY.
YOU HAVE MY COMPASS?
YES, MASTER ORGATH.
THE NEXT TOWN YOU COME ACROSS WILL BE OVER A LEY LINE, ONE OF THE EARTH'S NATURAL FLOWS OF MAGIC.
USE MY SIGIL TO TAP INTO THAT POWER. THE COMPASS WILL SHOW YOU WHERE TO FIND THE DOOR FROM MY WORLD TO YOURS.
I'VE SENT ONE OF MY CHILDREN TO GUARD THE LEY LINE IN CASE THOSE BARNSTORMERS AND DOC LYON INTRUDE AGAIN.
MY HUNGER GROWS RESTLESS, FILIPE.
YOU KNOW THE COST OF YOUR FAILURE?
I REMEMBER MY PLEDGE...

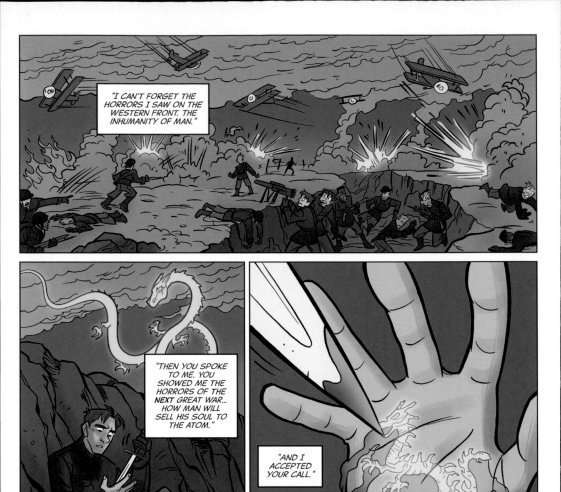

"I CAN'T FORGET THE HORRORS I SAW ON THE WESTERN FRONT. THE INHUMANITY OF MAN."

"THEN YOU SPOKE TO ME. YOU SHOWED ME THE HORRORS OF THE **NEXT** GREAT WAR... HOW MAN WILL SELL HIS SOUL TO THE ATOM."

"AND I ACCEPTED YOUR CALL."

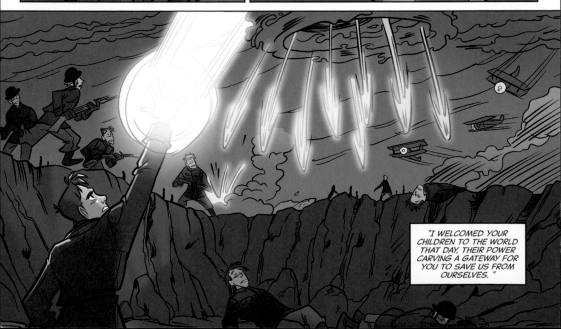

"I WELCOMED YOUR CHILDREN TO THE WORLD THAT DAY, THEIR POWER CARVING A GATEWAY FOR YOU TO SAVE US FROM OURSELVES. "

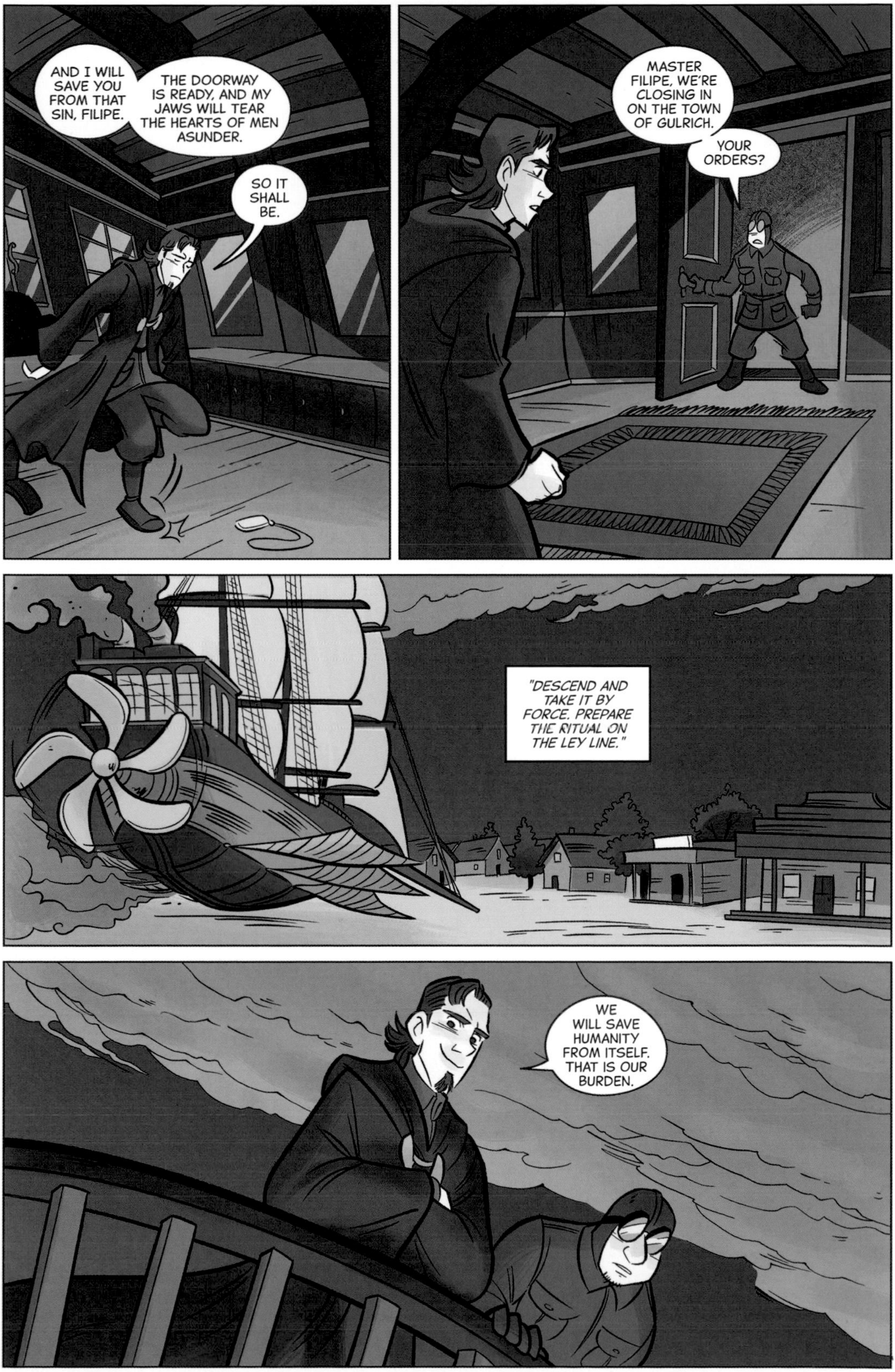
AND I WILL SAVE YOU FROM THAT SIN, FILIPE.
THE DOORWAY IS READY, AND MY JAWS WILL TEAR THE HEARTS OF MEN ASUNDER.
SO IT SHALL BE.
MASTER FILIPE, WE'RE CLOSING IN ON THE TOWN OF GULRICH.
YOUR ORDERS?
"DESCEND AND TAKE IT BY FORCE. PREPARE THE RITUAL ON THE LEY LINE."
WE WILL SAVE HUMANITY FROM ITSELF. THAT IS OUR BURDEN.

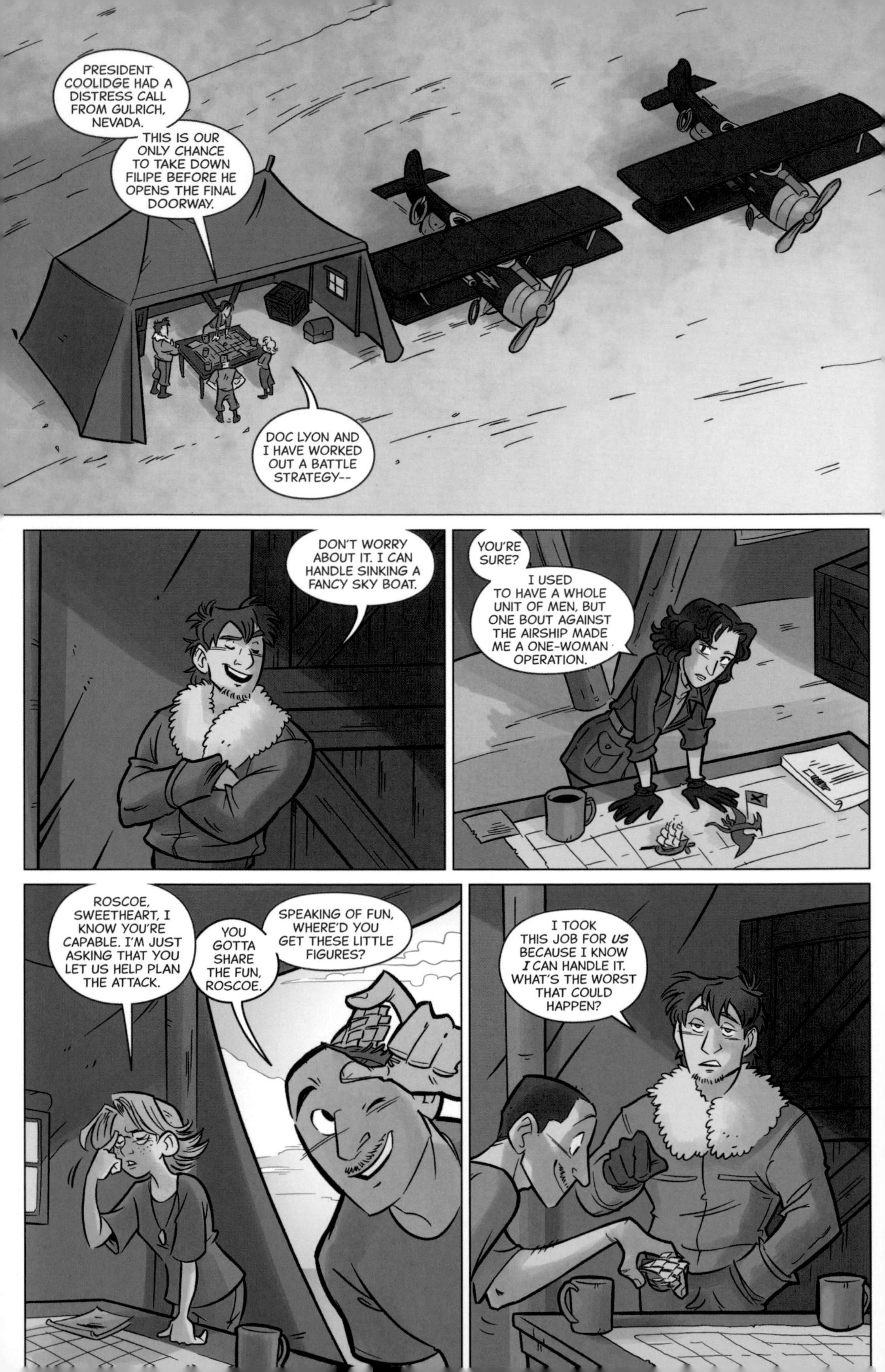
PRESIDENT COOLIDGE HAD A DISTRESS CALL FROM GULRICH, NEVADA.
THIS IS OUR ONLY CHANCE TO TAKE DOWN FILIPE BEFORE HE OPENS THE FINAL DOORWAY.
DOC LYON AND I HAVE WORKED OUT A BATTLE STRATEGY--
DON'T WORRY ABOUT IT. I CAN HANDLE SINKING A FANCY SKY BOAT.
YOU'RE SURE?
I USED TO HAVE A WHOLE UNIT OF MEN, BUT ONE BOUT AGAINST THE AIRSHIP MADE ME A ONE-WOMAN OPERATION.
ROSCOE, SWEETHEART, I KNOW YOU'RE CAPABLE. I'M JUST ASKING THAT YOU LET US HELP PLAN THE ATTACK.
YOU GOTTA SHARE THE FUN, ROSCOE.
SPEAKING OF FUN, WHERE'D YOU GET THESE LITTLE FIGURES?
I TOOK THIS JOB FOR *US* BECAUSE I KNOW *I* CAN HANDLE IT. WHAT'S THE WORST THAT COULD HAPPEN?

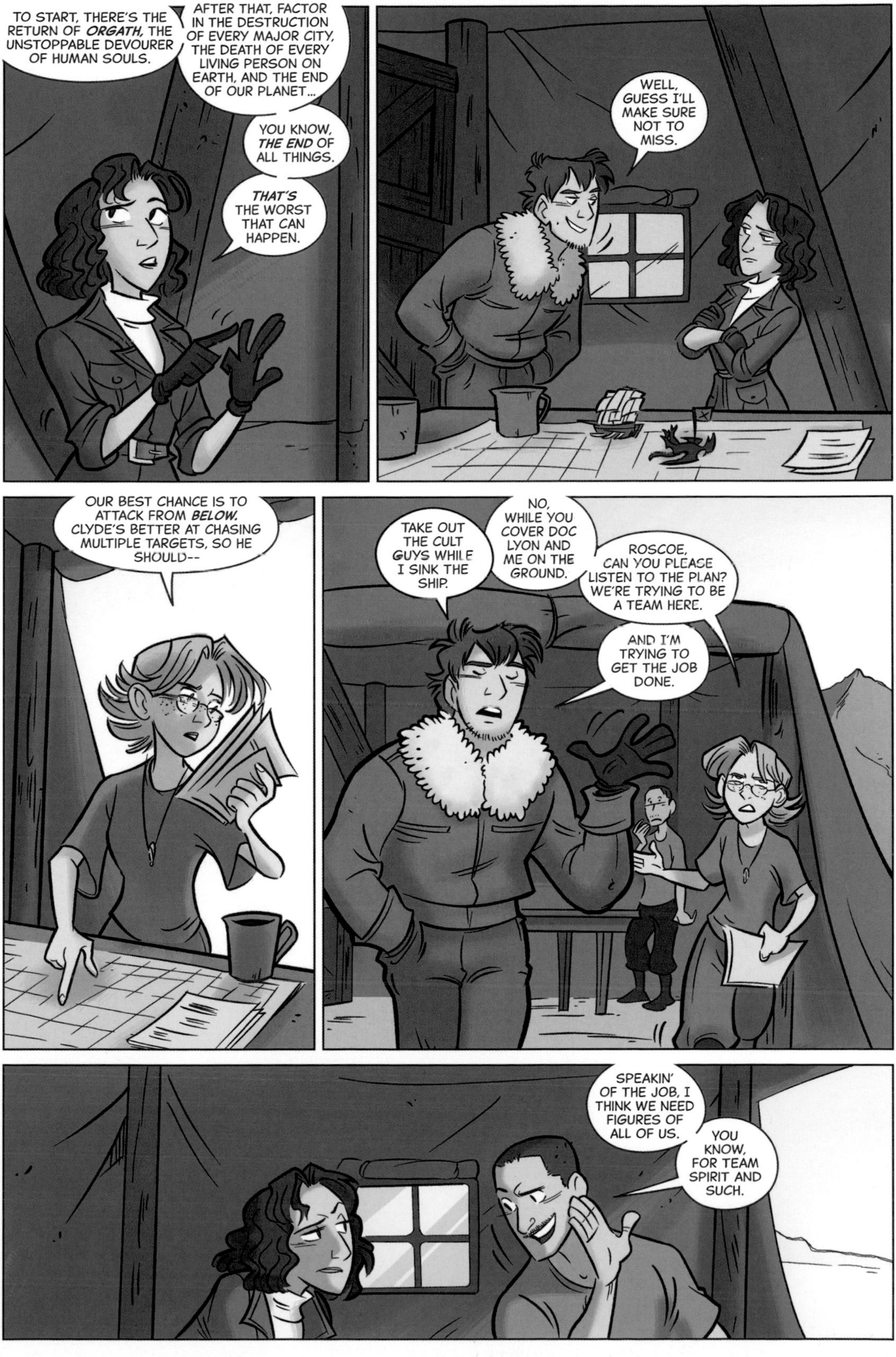
TO START, THERE'S THE RETURN OF *ORGATH,* THE UNSTOPPABLE DEVOURER OF HUMAN SOULS.
AFTER THAT, FACTOR IN THE DESTRUCTION OF EVERY MAJOR CITY, THE DEATH OF EVERY LIVING PERSON ON EARTH, AND THE END OF OUR PLANET...
YOU KNOW, *THE END* OF ALL THINGS.
THAT'S THE WORST THAT CAN HAPPEN.
WELL, GUESS I'LL MAKE SURE NOT TO MISS.
OUR BEST CHANCE IS TO ATTACK FROM *BELOW.* CLYDE'S BETTER AT CHASING MULTIPLE TARGETS, SO HE SHOULD--
TAKE OUT THE CULT GUYS WHILE I SINK THE SHIP.
NO, WHILE YOU COVER DOC LYON AND ME ON THE GROUND.
ROSCOE, CAN YOU PLEASE LISTEN TO THE PLAN? WE'RE TRYING TO BE A TEAM HERE.
AND I'M TRYING TO GET THE JOB DONE.
SPEAKIN' OF THE JOB, I THINK WE NEED FIGURES OF ALL OF US.
YOU KNOW, FOR TEAM SPIRIT AND SUCH.

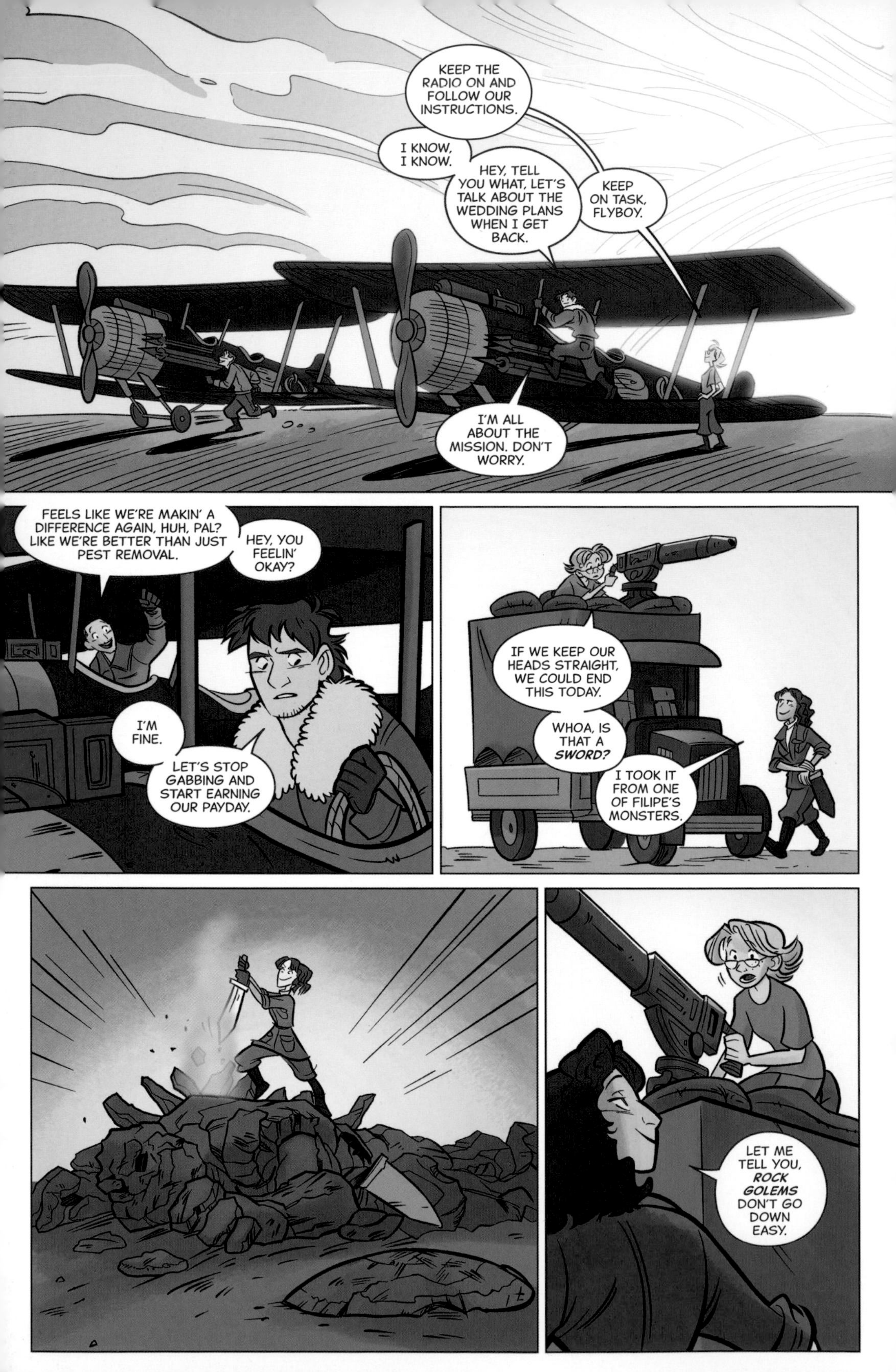
KEEP THE RADIO ON AND FOLLOW OUR INSTRUCTIONS.
I KNOW, I KNOW.
HEY, TELL YOU WHAT, LET'S TALK ABOUT THE WEDDING PLANS WHEN I GET BACK.
KEEP ON TASK, FLYBOY.
I'M ALL ABOUT THE MISSION. DON'T WORRY.
FEELS LIKE WE'RE MAKIN' A DIFFERENCE AGAIN, HUH, PAL? LIKE WE'RE BETTER THAN JUST PEST REMOVAL.
HEY, YOU FEELIN' OKAY?
I'M FINE.
LET'S STOP GABBING AND START EARNING OUR PAYDAY.
IF WE KEEP OUR HEADS STRAIGHT, WE COULD END THIS TODAY.
WHOA, IS THAT A *SWORD?*
I TOOK IT FROM ONE OF FILIPE'S MONSTERS.
LET ME TELL YOU, ***ROCK GOLEMS*** DON'T GO DOWN EASY.

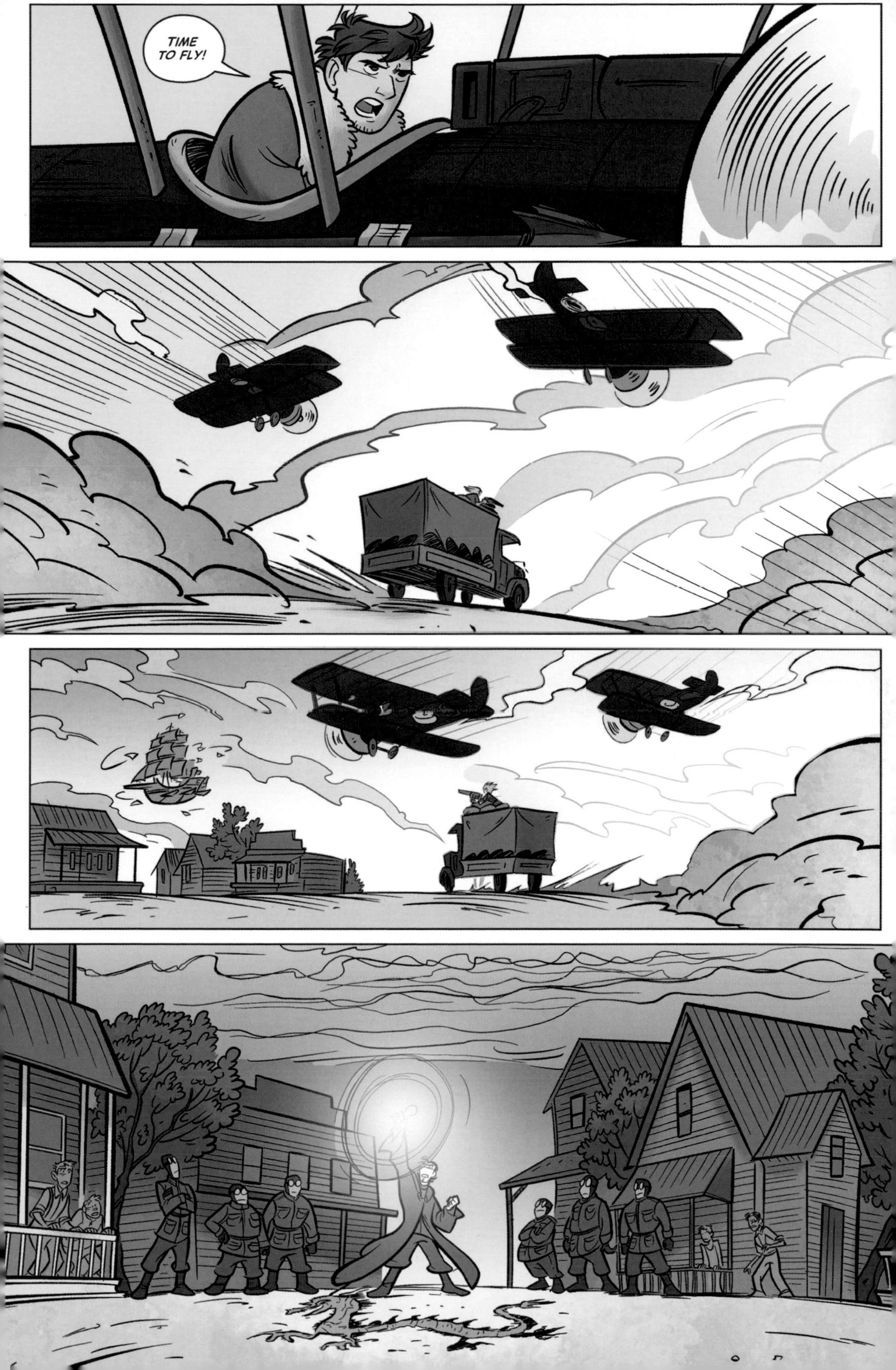
TIME TO FLY!

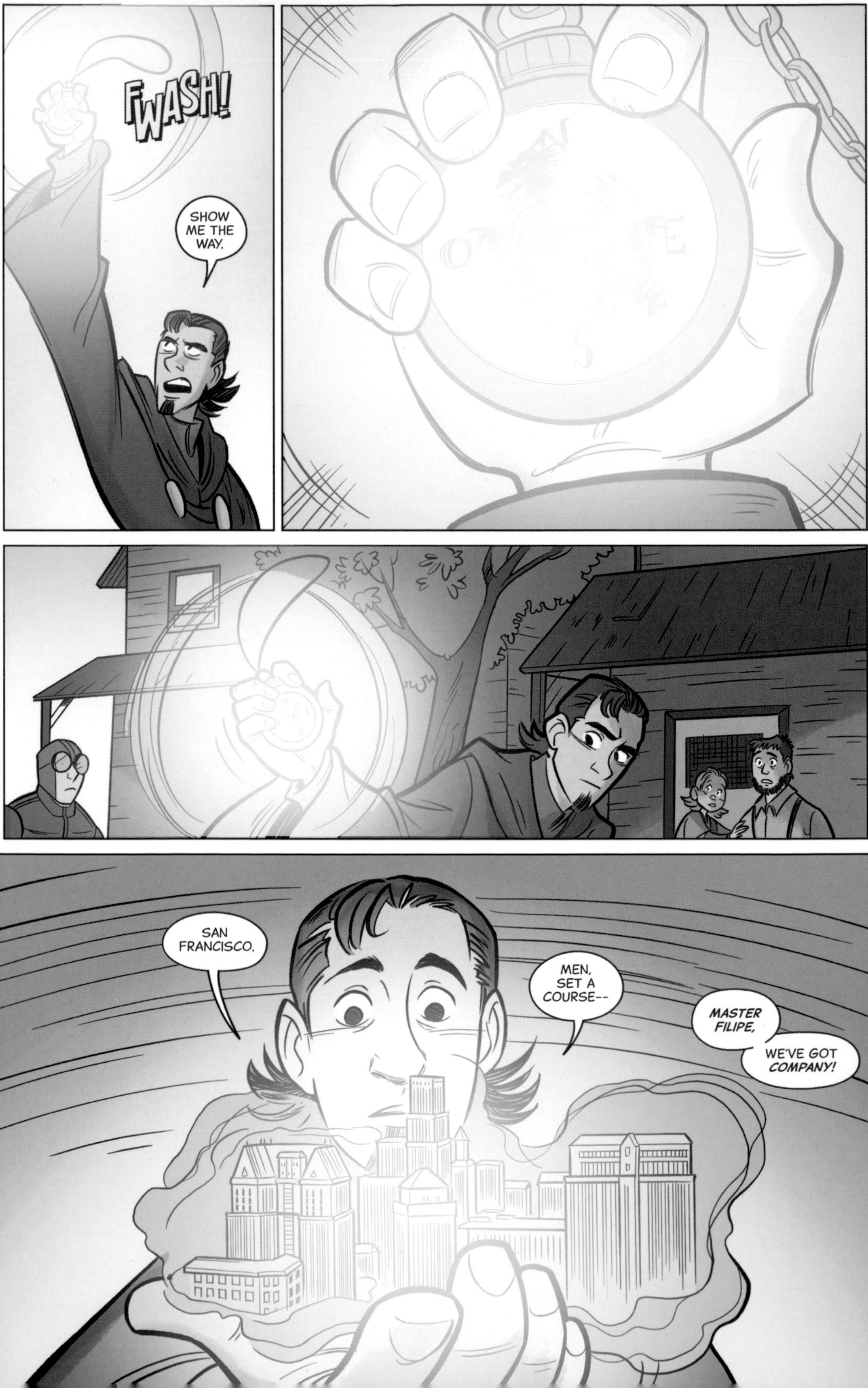

FWASH!
SHOW ME THE WAY.
SAN FRANCISCO.
MEN, SET A COURSE--
MASTER FILIPE,
WE'VE GOT COMPANY!

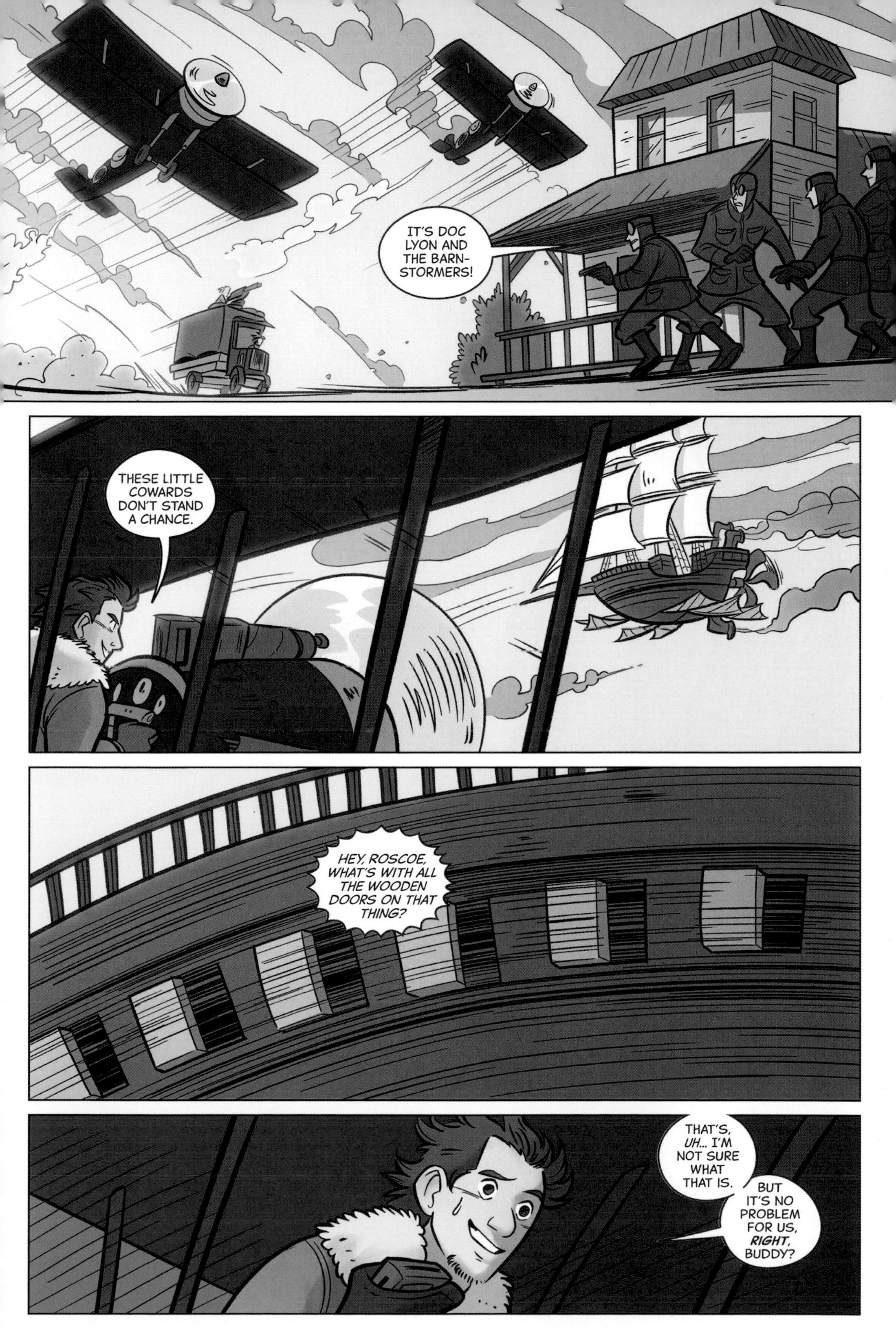

IT'S DOC LYON AND THE BARN-STORMERS!
THESE LITTLE COWARDS DON'T STAND A CHANCE.
HEY, ROSCOE, WHAT'S WITH ALL THE WOODEN DOORS ON THAT THING?
THAT'S, *UH...* I'M NOT SURE WHAT THAT IS.
BUT IT'S NO PROBLEM FOR US, ***RIGHT***, BUDDY?

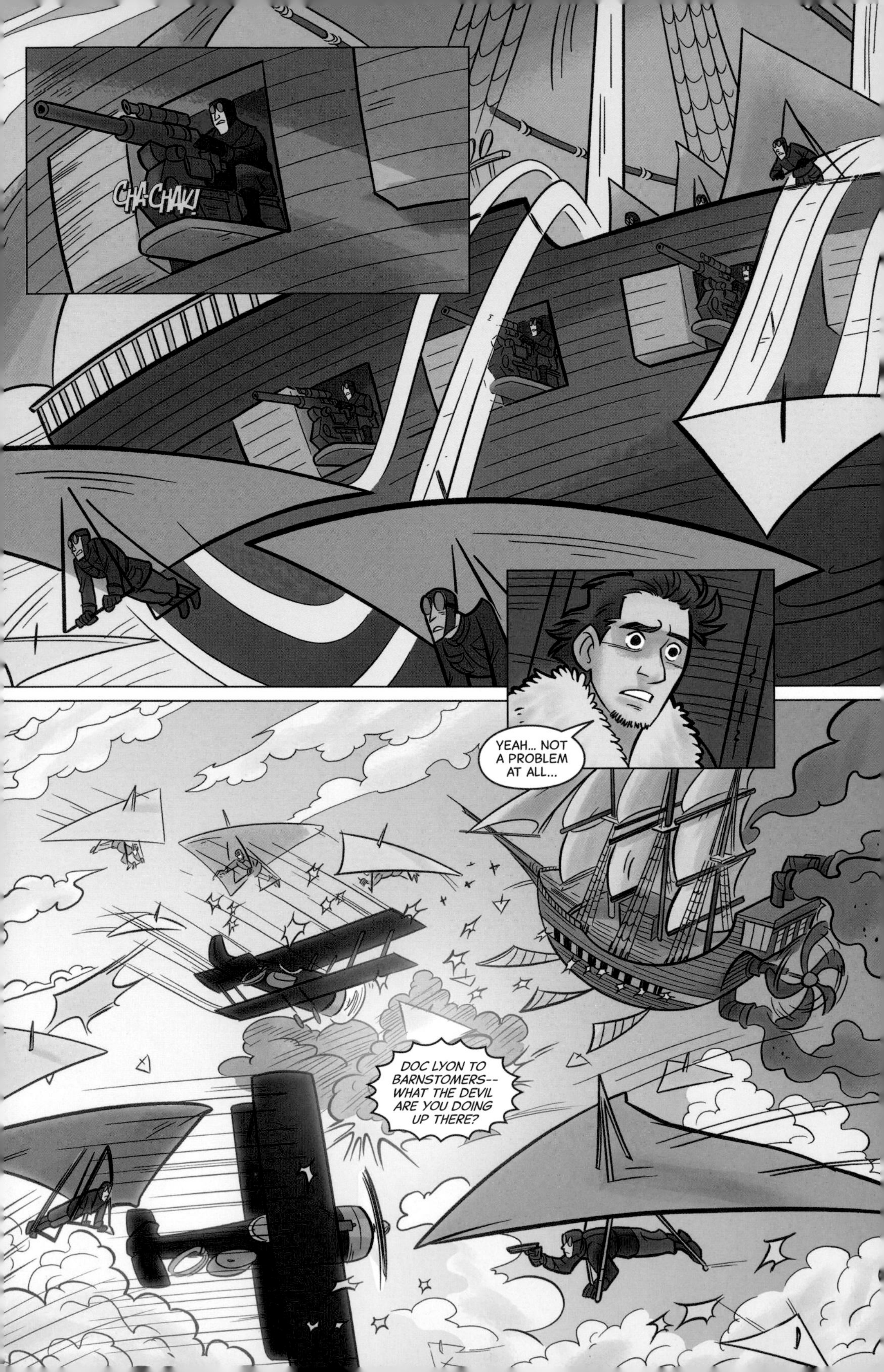
CHA-CHAK!
YEAH... NOT A PROBLEM AT ALL...
DOC LYON TO BARNSTOMERS-- WHAT THE DEVIL ARE YOU DOING UP THERE?

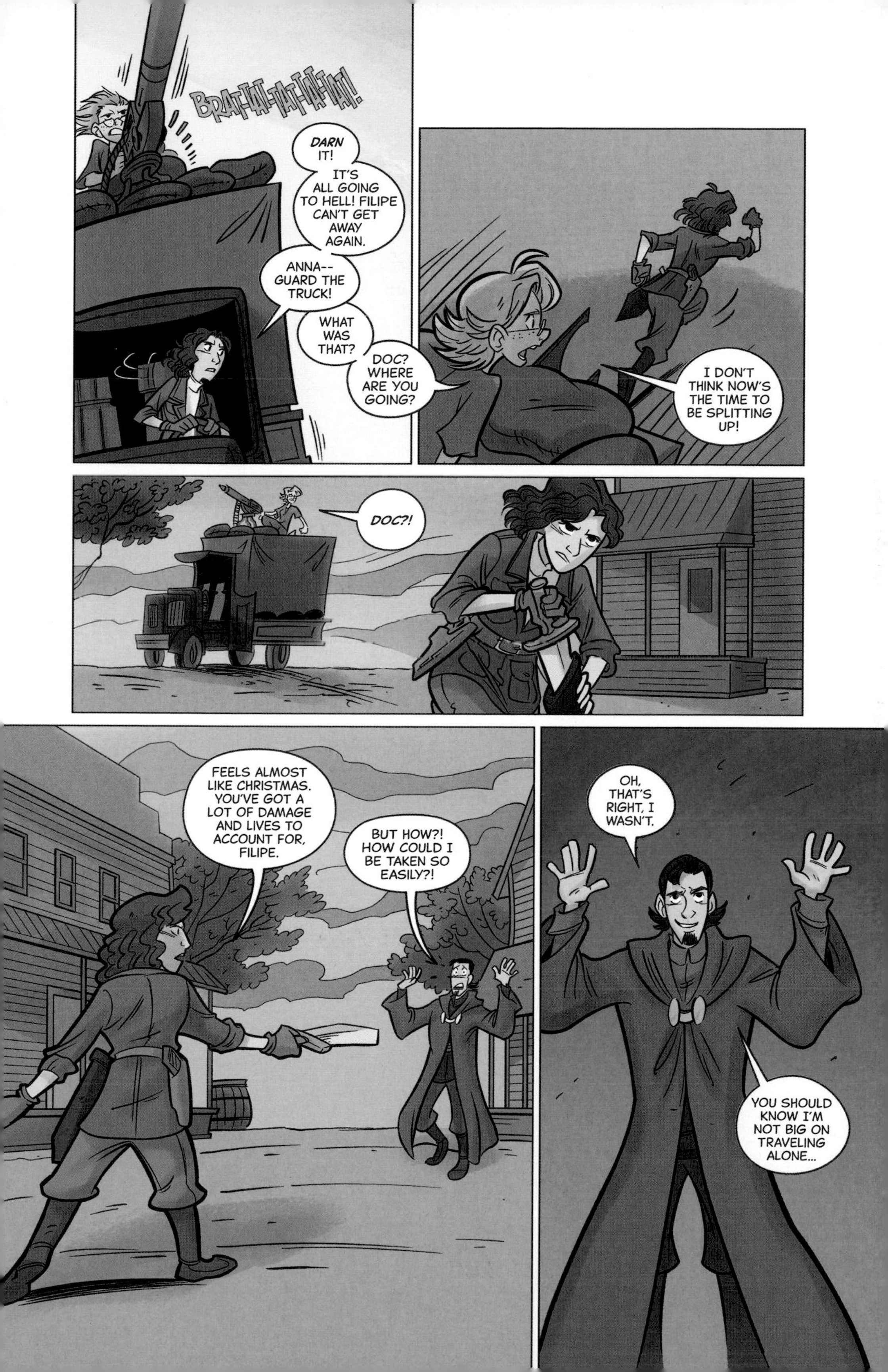
BRATTATATATATAT!
DARN IT!
IT'S ALL GOING TO HELL! FILIPE CAN'T GET AWAY AGAIN.
ANNA-- GUARD THE TRUCK!
WHAT WAS THAT?
DOC? WHERE ARE YOU GOING?
I DON'T THINK NOW'S THE TIME TO BE SPLITTING UP!
DOC?!
FEELS ALMOST LIKE CHRISTMAS. YOU'VE GOT A LOT OF DAMAGE AND LIVES TO ACCOUNT FOR, FILIPE.
BUT HOW?! HOW COULD I BE TAKEN SO EASILY?!
OH, THAT'S RIGHT, I WASN'T.
YOU SHOULD KNOW I'M NOT BIG ON TRAVELING ALONE...

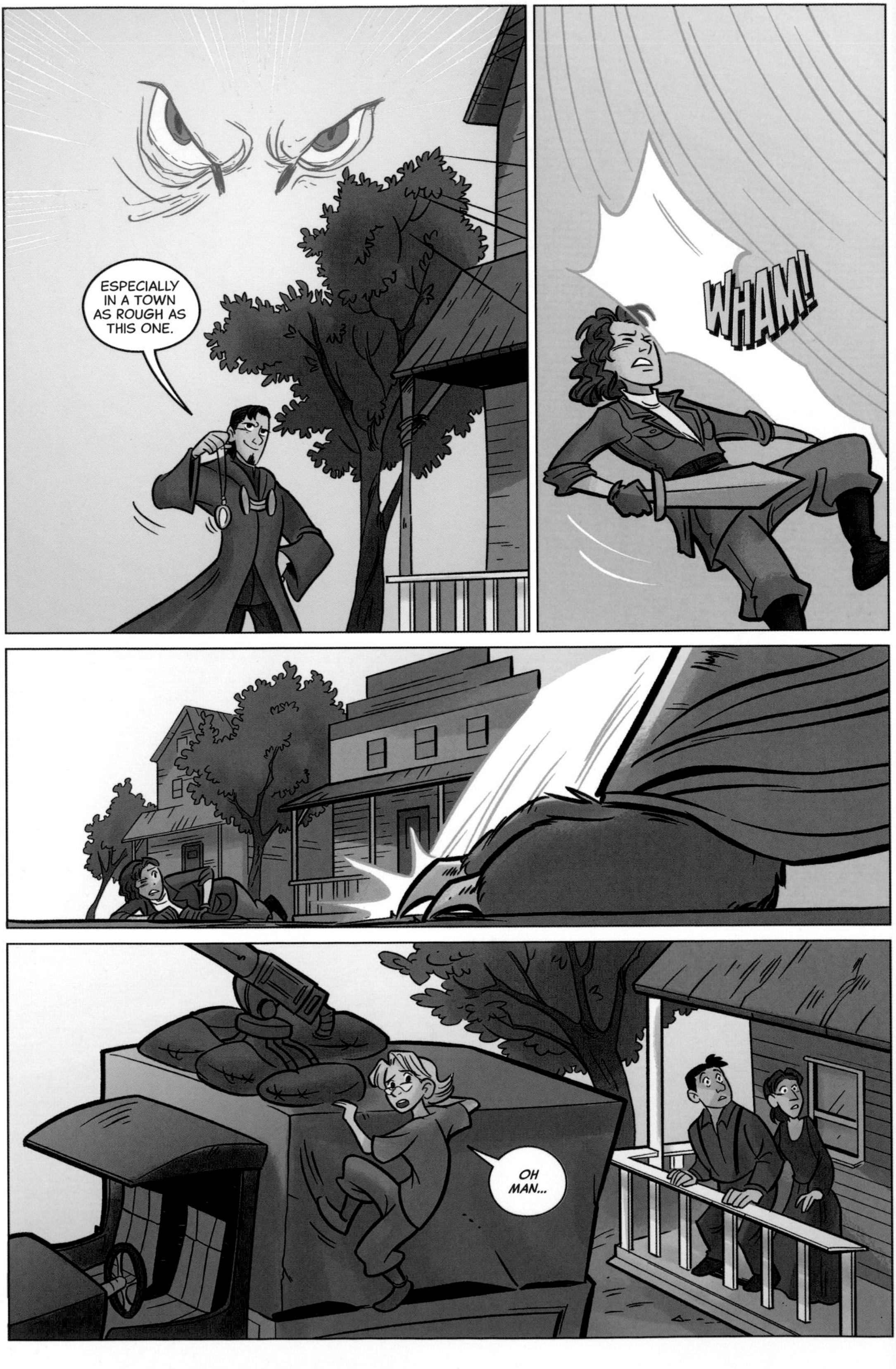
ESPECIALLY IN A TOWN AS ROUGH AS THIS ONE.
WHAM!
OH MAN...

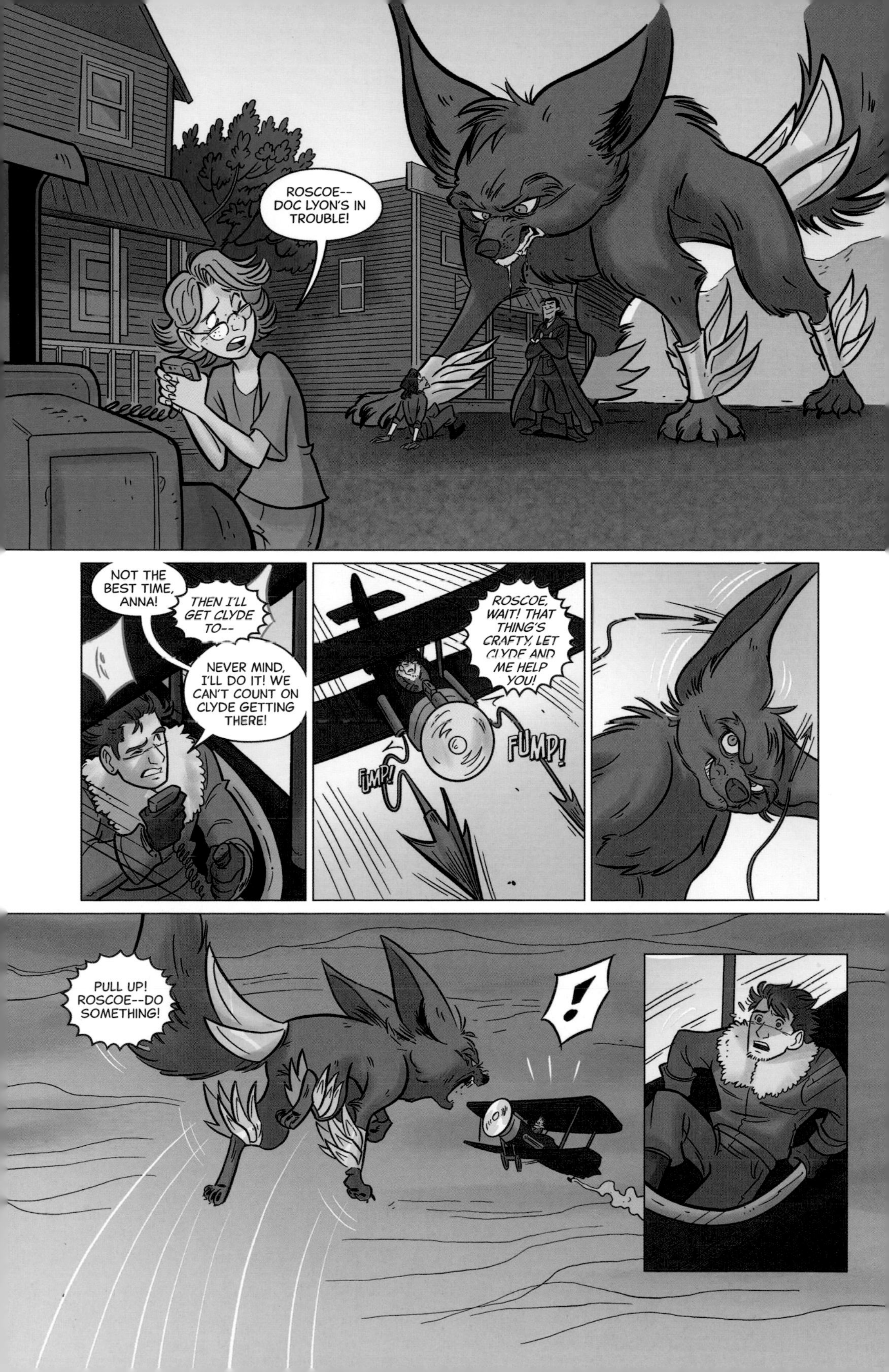
ROSCOE--DOC LYON'S IN TROUBLE!
NOT THE BEST TIME, ANNA!
THEN I'LL GET CLYDE TO--
NEVER MIND, I'LL DO IT! WE CAN'T COUNT ON CLYDE GETTING THERE!
ROSCOE, WAIT! THAT THING'S CRAFTY, LET CLYDE AND ME HELP YOU!
FUMP!
FUMP!
PULL UP! ROSCOE--DO SOMETHING!
!

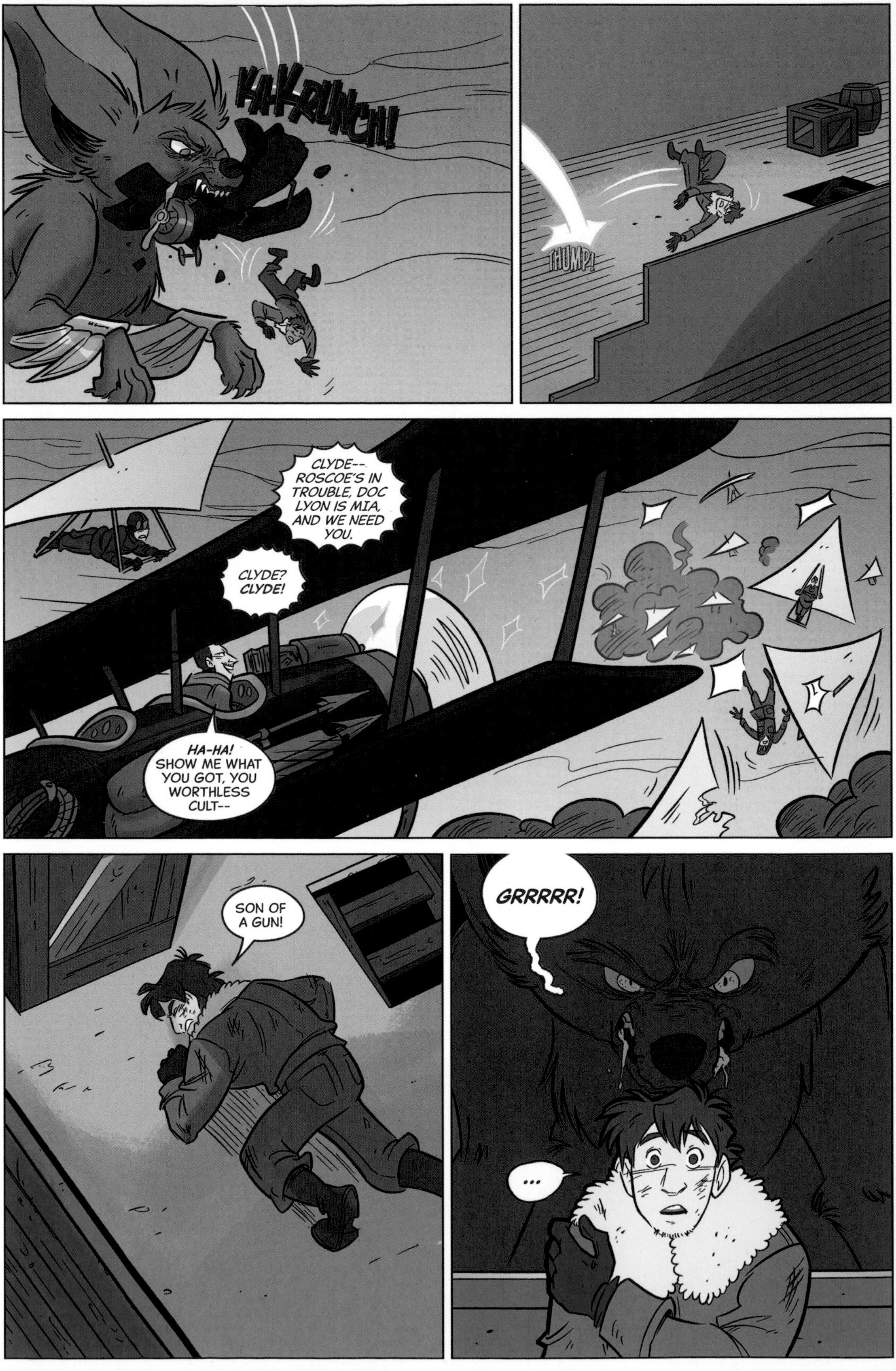
KA-KRUNCH!
THUMP!
CLYDE-- ROSCOE'S IN TROUBLE, DOC LYON IS MIA, AND WE NEED YOU.
CLYDE? CLYDE!
HA-HA! SHOW ME WHAT YOU GOT, YOU WORTHLESS CULT--
SON OF A GUN!
GRRRRR!
...

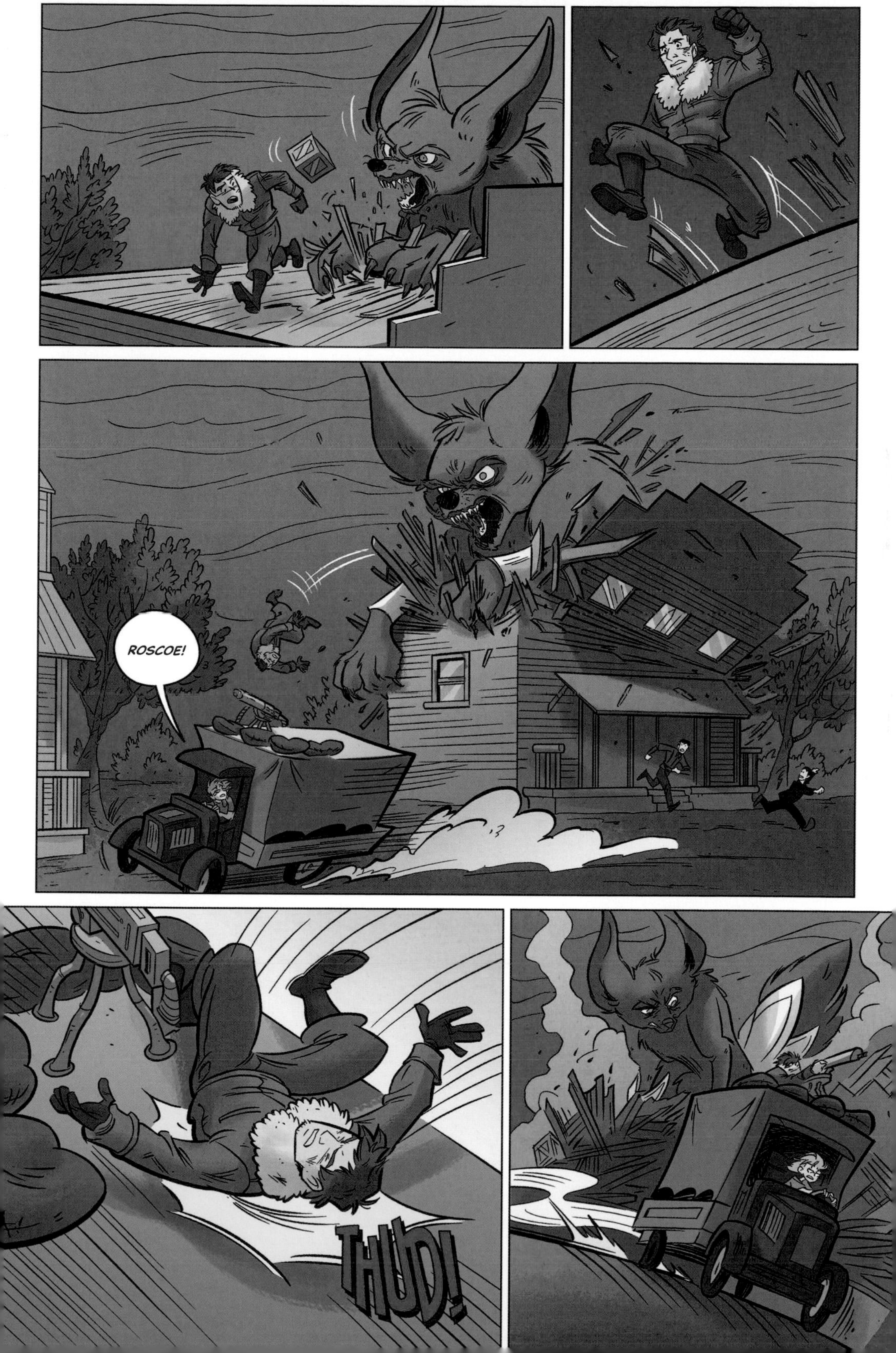
ROSCOE!
THUD!

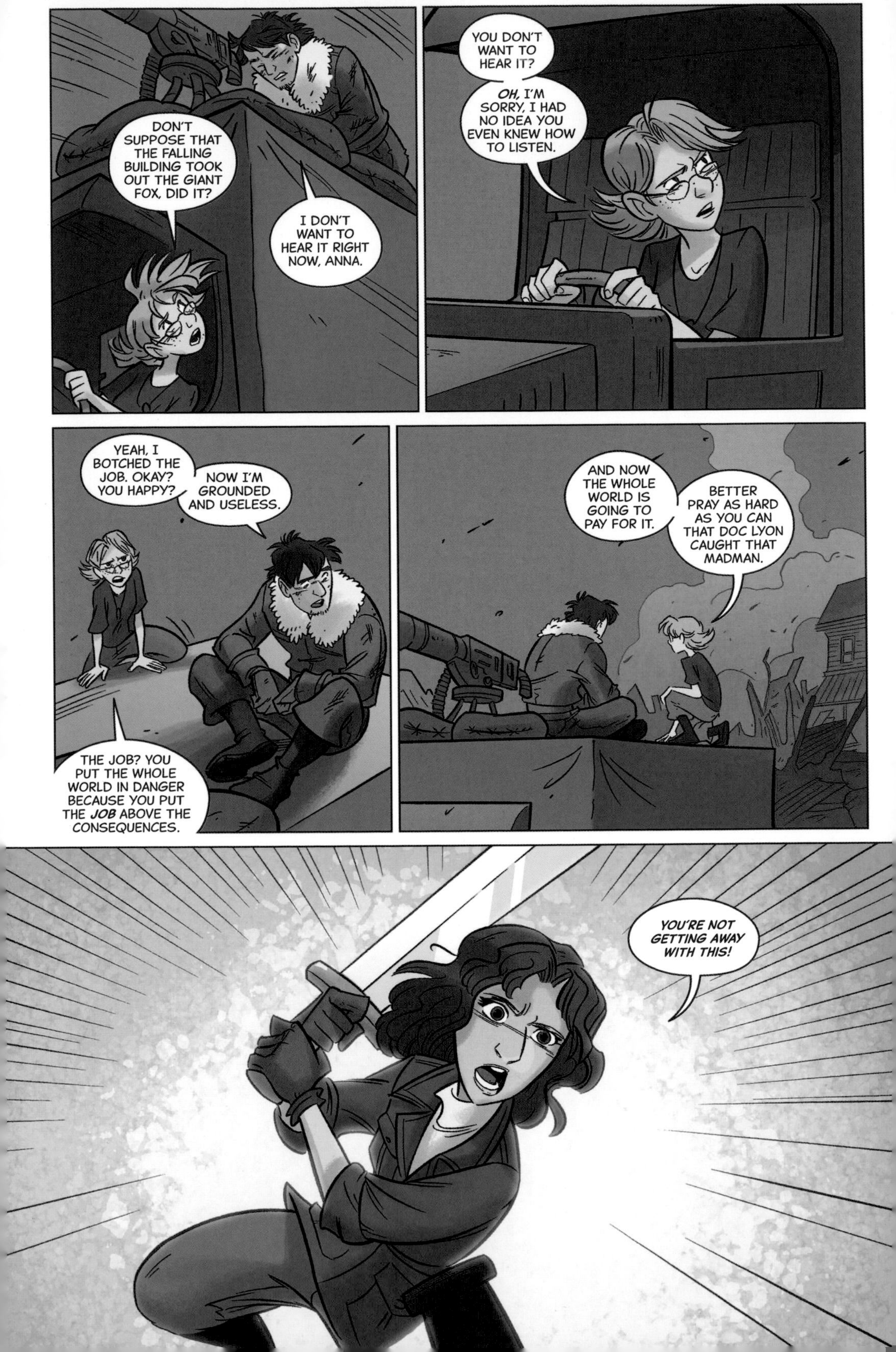
DON'T SUPPOSE THAT THE FALLING BUILDING TOOK OUT THE GIANT FOX, DID IT?
I DON'T WANT TO HEAR IT RIGHT NOW, ANNA.
YOU DON'T WANT TO HEAR IT?
OH, I'M SORRY, I HAD NO IDEA YOU EVEN KNEW HOW TO LISTEN.
YEAH, I BOTCHED THE JOB. OKAY? YOU HAPPY?
NOW I'M GROUNDED AND USELESS.
THE JOB? YOU PUT THE WHOLE WORLD IN DANGER BECAUSE YOU PUT THE JOB ABOVE THE CONSEQUENCES.
AND NOW THE WHOLE WORLD IS GOING TO PAY FOR IT.
BETTER PRAY AS HARD AS YOU CAN THAT DOC LYON CAUGHT THAT MADMAN.
YOU'RE NOT GETTING AWAY WITH THIS!

SWOOSH!

YOU'RE DETERMINED, I'LL GIVE YOU THAT. ABOUT AS DETERMINED AS YOUR FOOLISH FRIENDS.

WHACK!

AND JUST AS SLOW, I'M AFRAID.

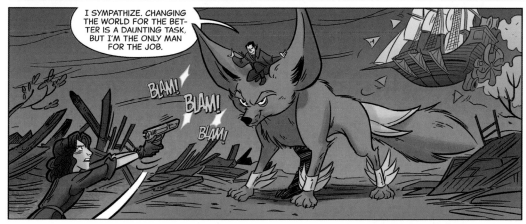

I SYMPATHIZE. CHANGING THE WORLD FOR THE BETTER IS A DAUNTING TASK, BUT I'M THE ONLY MAN FOR THE JOB.

BLAM! BLAM! BLAM!

SAY GOODBYE TO THE OLD WORLD, DOC LYON!

CLACK!

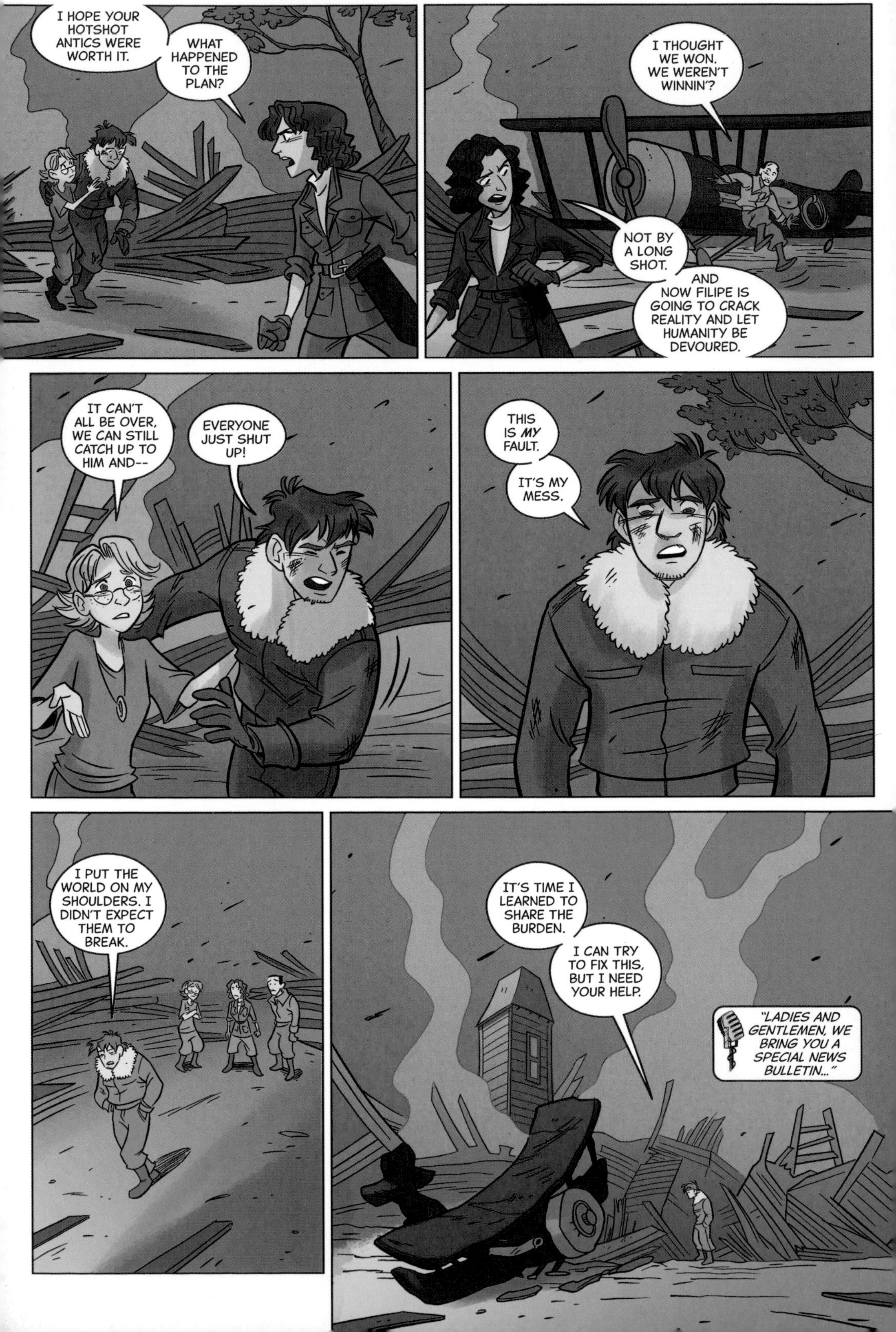
I HOPE YOUR HOTSHOT ANTICS WERE WORTH IT.
WHAT HAPPENED TO THE PLAN?
I THOUGHT WE WON. WE WEREN'T WINNIN'?
NOT BY A LONG SHOT.
AND NOW FILIPE IS GOING TO CRACK REALITY AND LET HUMANITY BE DEVOURED.
IT CAN'T ALL BE OVER, WE CAN STILL CATCH UP TO HIM AND--
EVERYONE JUST SHUT UP!
THIS IS *MY* FAULT.
IT'S MY MESS.
I PUT THE WORLD ON MY SHOULDERS. I DIDN'T EXPECT THEM TO BREAK.
IT'S TIME I LEARNED TO SHARE THE BURDEN.
I CAN TRY TO FIX THIS, BUT I NEED YOUR HELP.
"LADIES AND GENTLEMEN, WE BRING YOU A SPECIAL NEWS BULLETIN..."

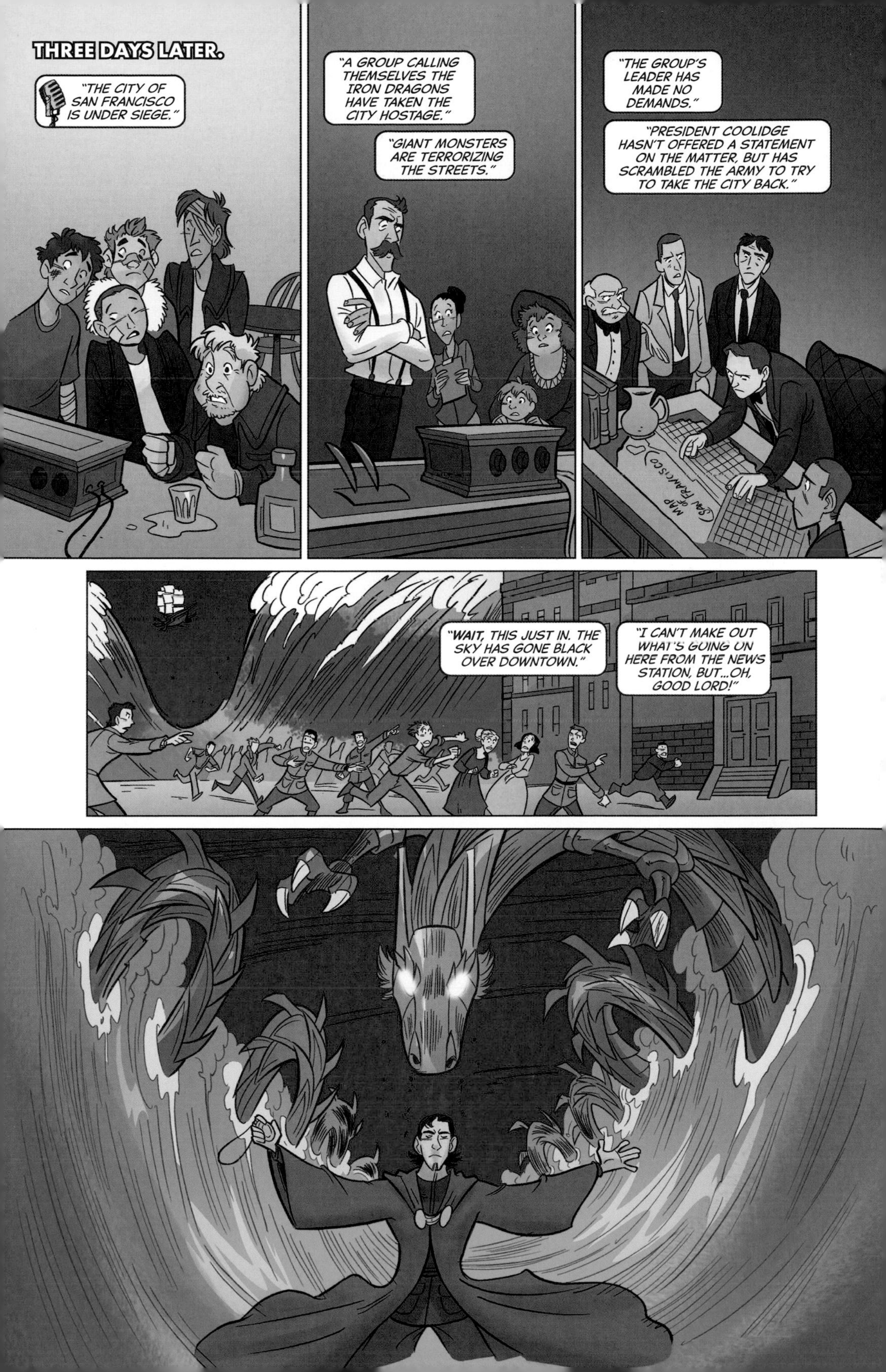
THREE DAYS LATER.
"THE CITY OF SAN FRANCISCO IS UNDER SIEGE."
"A GROUP CALLING THEMSELVES THE IRON DRAGONS HAVE TAKEN THE CITY HOSTAGE."
"GIANT MONSTERS ARE TERRORIZING THE STREETS."
"THE GROUP'S LEADER HAS MADE NO DEMANDS."
"PRESIDENT COOLIDGE HASN'T OFFERED A STATEMENT ON THE MATTER, BUT HAS SCRAMBLED THE ARMY TO TRY TO TAKE THE CITY BACK."
"WAIT, THIS JUST IN. THE SKY HAS GONE BLACK OVER DOWNTOWN."
"I CAN'T MAKE OUT WHAT'S GOING ON HERE FROM THE NEWS STATION, BUT...OH, GOOD LORD!"

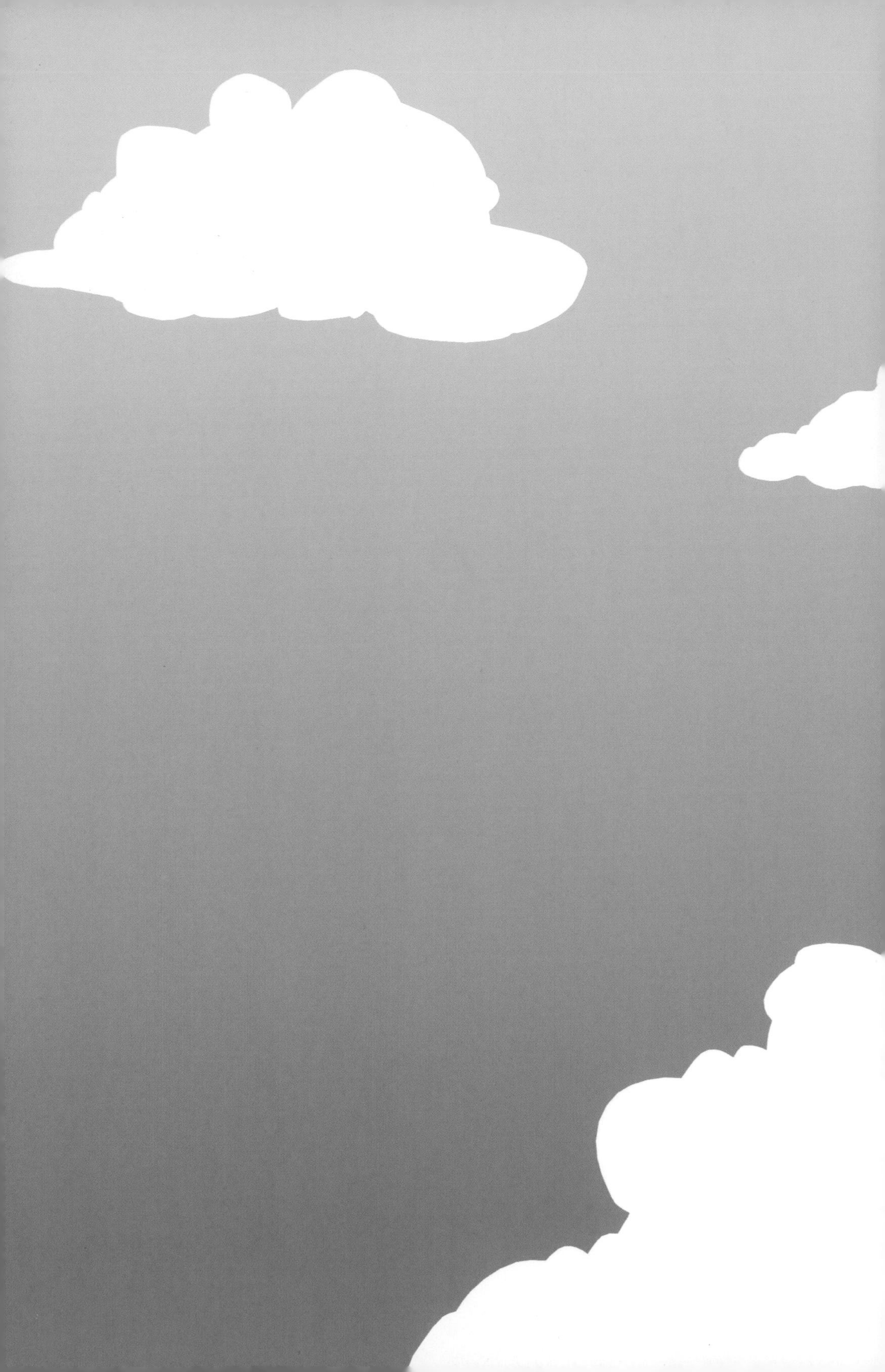

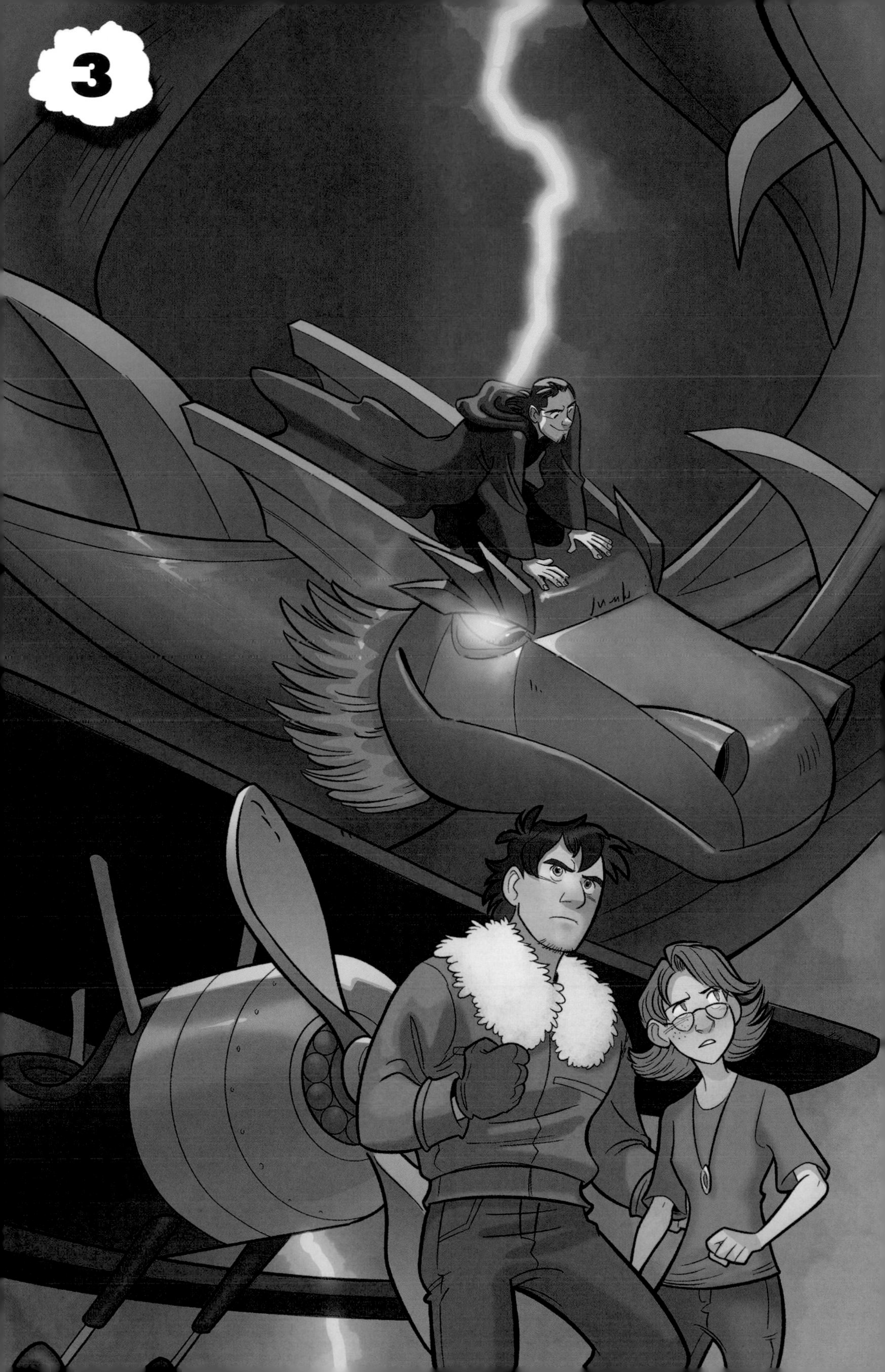
3

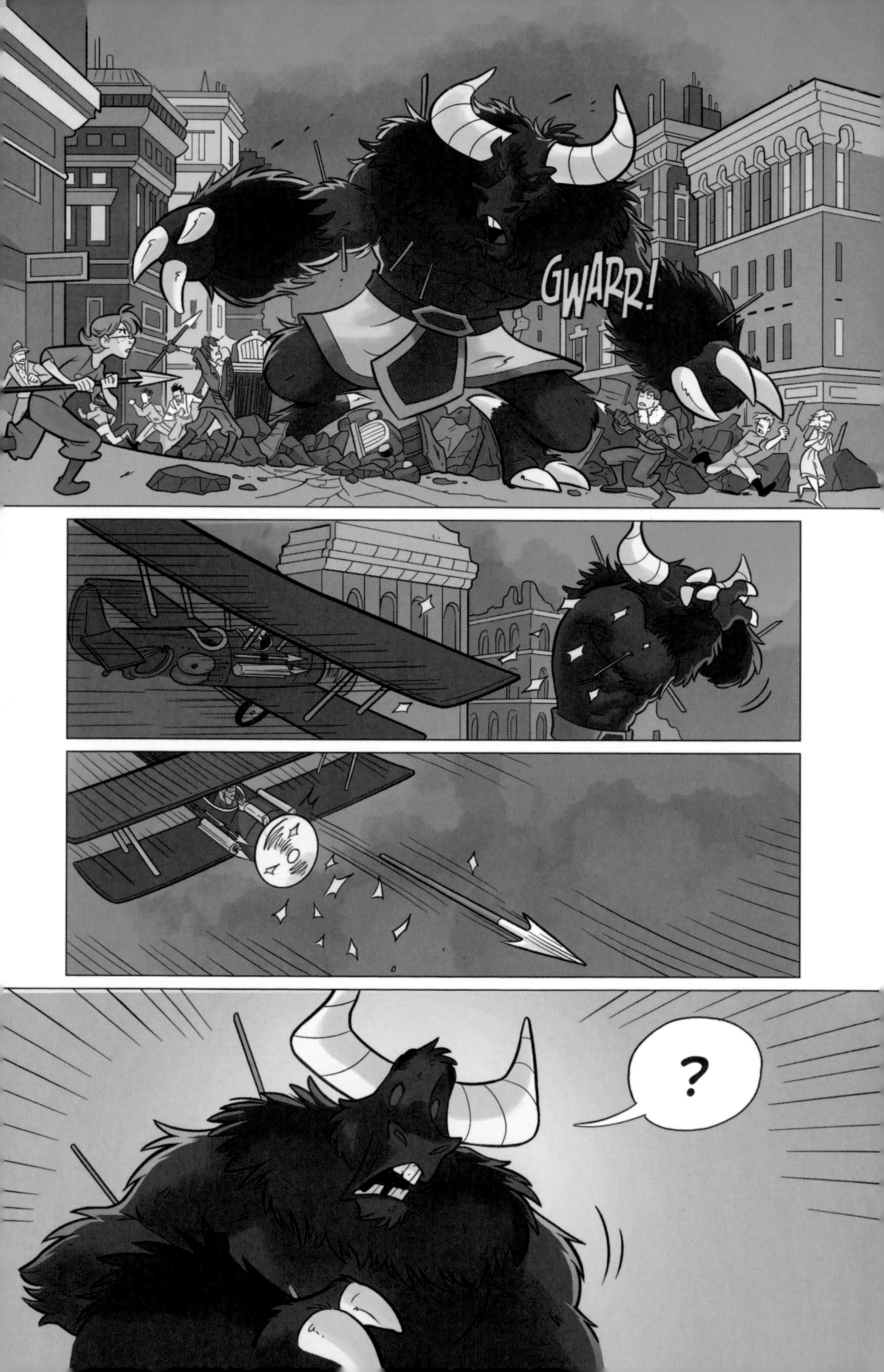
GWARR!
?

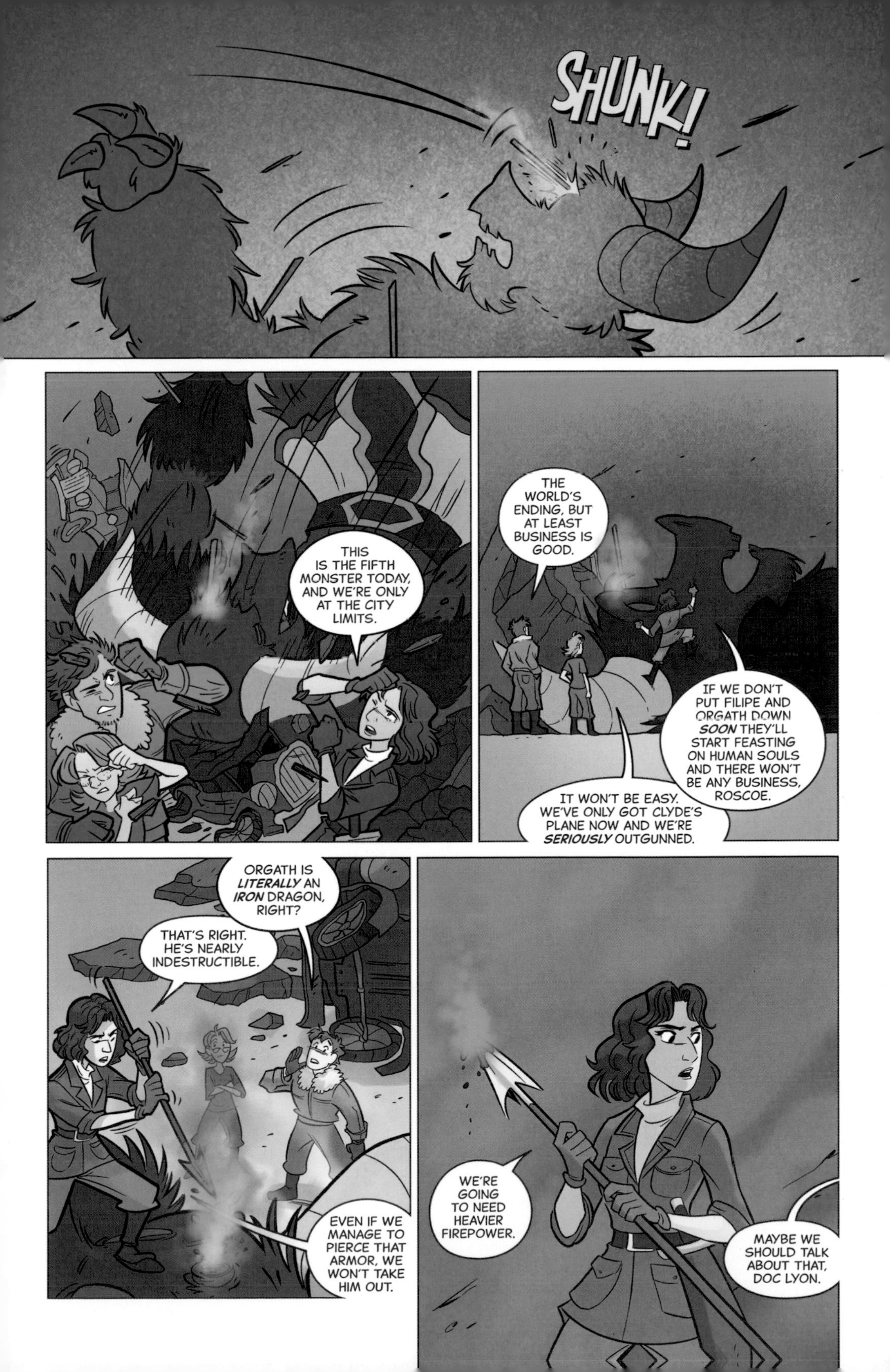
SHUNK!
THIS IS THE FIFTH MONSTER TODAY, AND WE'RE ONLY AT THE CITY LIMITS.
THE WORLD'S ENDING, BUT AT LEAST BUSINESS IS GOOD.
IF WE DON'T PUT FILIPE AND ORGATH DOWN *SOON* THEY'LL START FEASTING ON HUMAN SOULS AND THERE WON'T BE ANY BUSINESS, ROSCOE.
IT WON'T BE EASY. WE'VE ONLY GOT CLYDE'S PLANE NOW AND WE'RE *SERIOUSLY* OUTGUNNED.
ORGATH IS *LITERALLY* AN *IRON* DRAGON, RIGHT?
THAT'S RIGHT. HE'S NEARLY INDESTRUCTIBLE.
EVEN IF WE MANAGE TO PIERCE THAT ARMOR, WE WON'T TAKE HIM OUT.
WE'RE GOING TO NEED HEAVIER FIREPOWER.
MAYBE WE SHOULD TALK ABOUT THAT, DOC LYON.

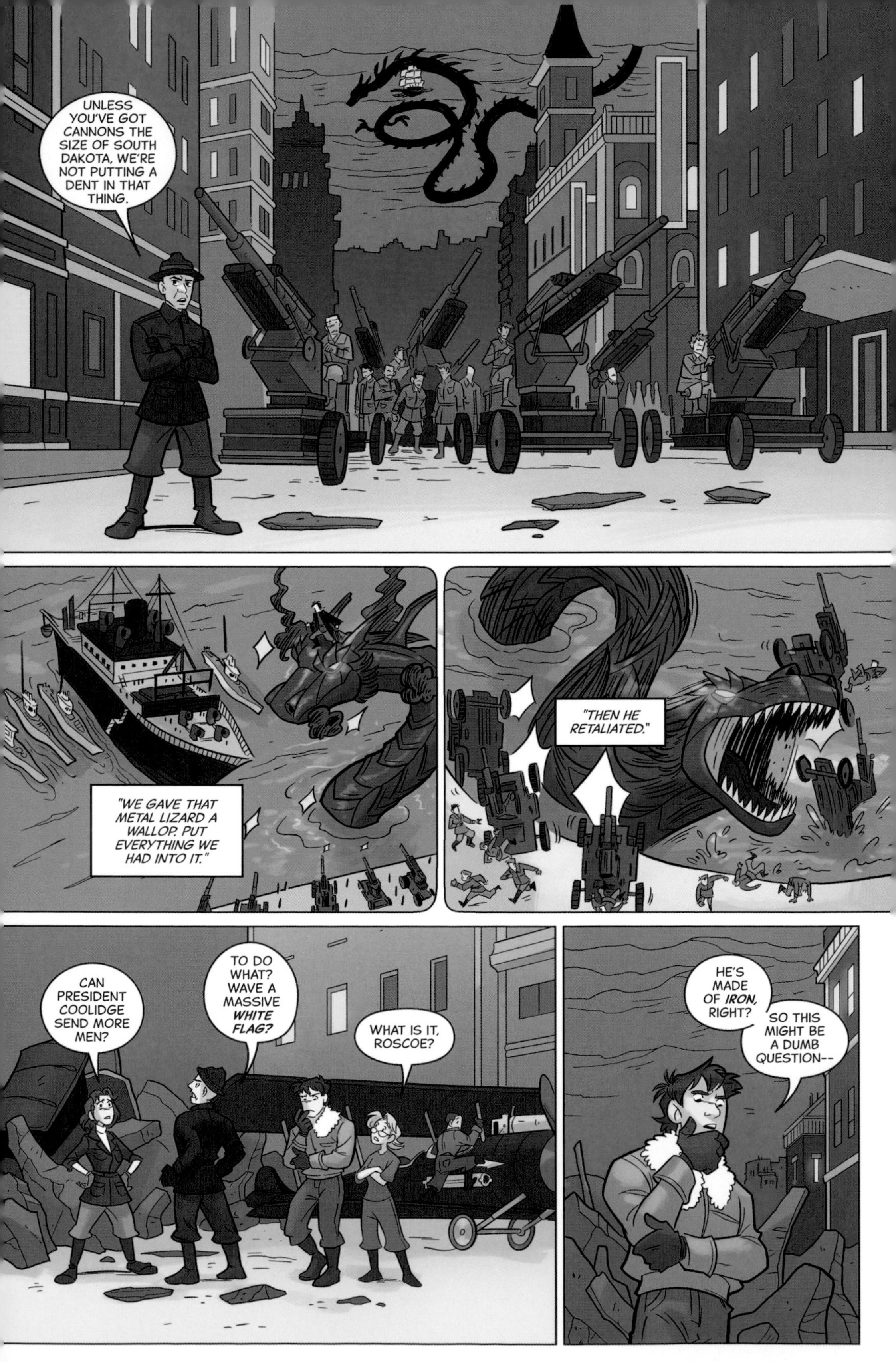
UNLESS YOU'VE GOT CANNONS THE SIZE OF SOUTH DAKOTA, WE'RE NOT PUTTING A DENT IN THAT THING.
"WE GAVE THAT METAL LIZARD A WALLOP. PUT EVERYTHING WE HAD INTO IT."
"THEN HE RETALIATED."
CAN PRESIDENT COOLIDGE SEND MORE MEN?
TO DO WHAT? WAVE A MASSIVE WHITE FLAG?
WHAT IS IT, ROSCOE?
HE'S MADE OF IRON, RIGHT?
SO THIS MIGHT BE A DUMB QUESTION--

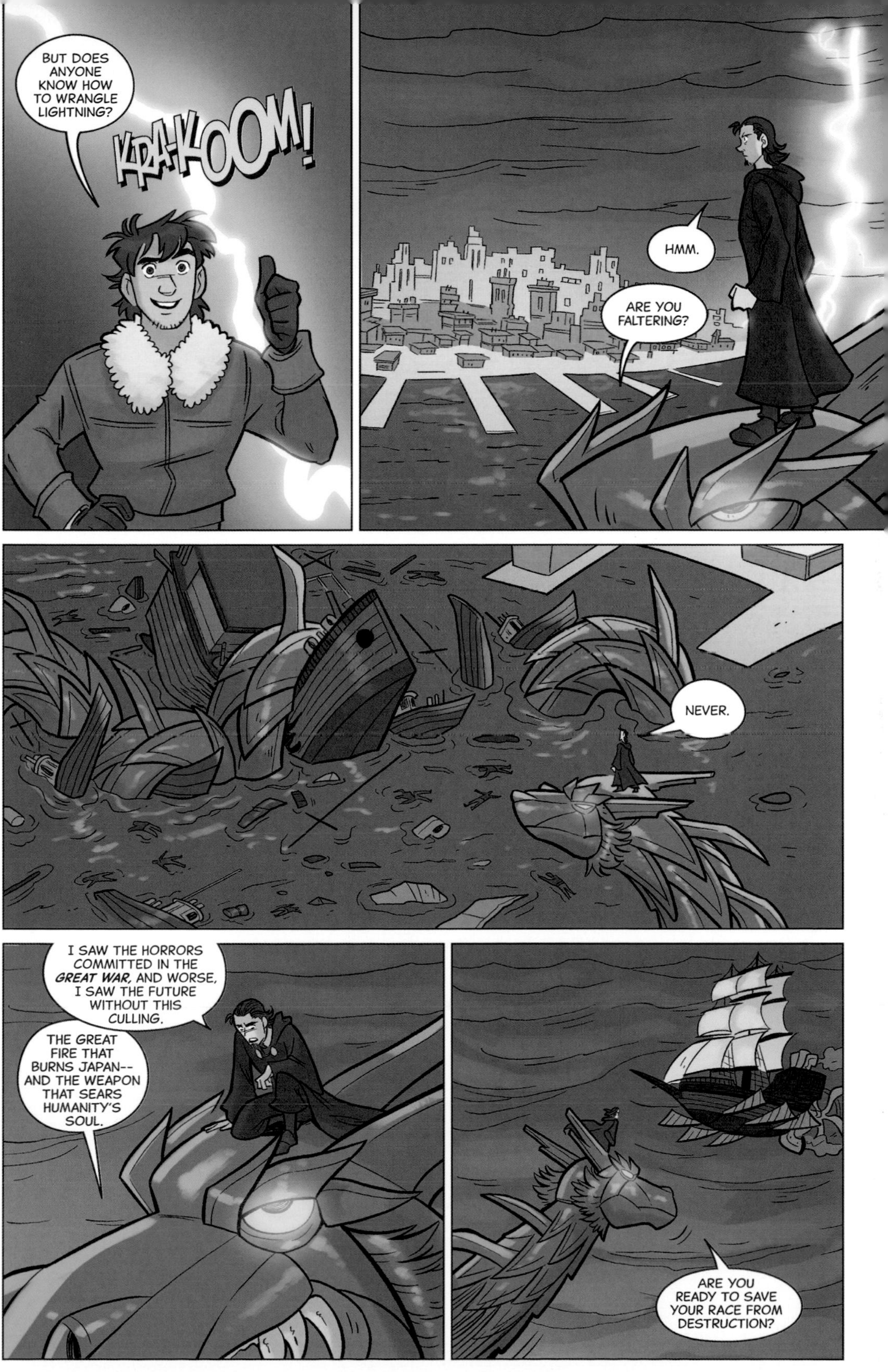
BUT DOES ANYONE KNOW HOW TO WRANGLE LIGHTNING?
KRA-KOOM!
HMM.
ARE YOU FALTERING?
NEVER.
I SAW THE HORRORS COMMITTED IN THE *GREAT WAR,* AND WORSE, I SAW THE FUTURE WITHOUT THIS CULLING.
THE GREAT FIRE THAT BURNS JAPAN-- AND THE WEAPON THAT SEARS HUMANITY'S SOUL.
ARE YOU READY TO SAVE YOUR RACE FROM DESTRUCTION?

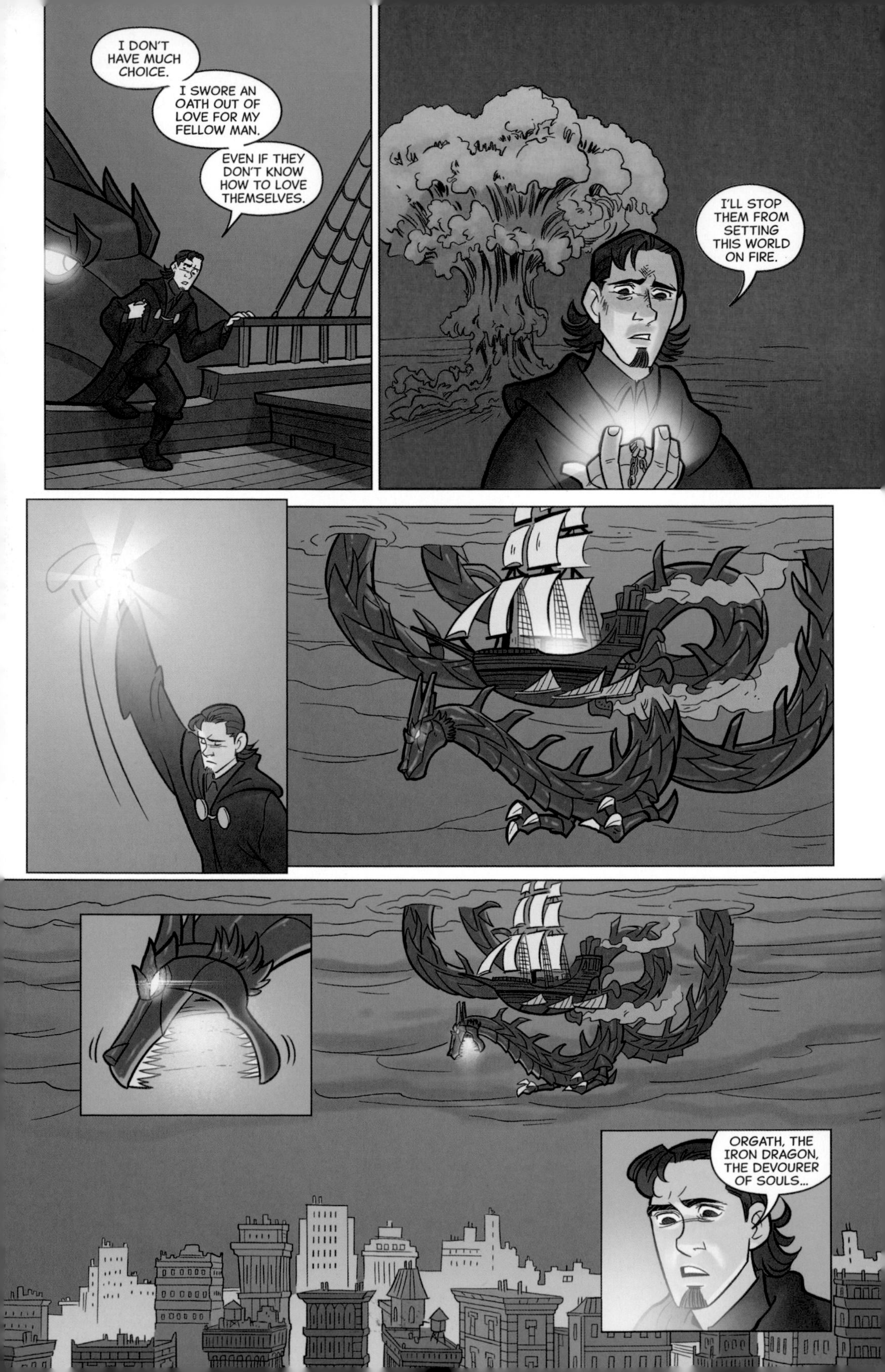
I DON'T HAVE MUCH CHOICE.
I SWORE AN OATH OUT OF LOVE FOR MY FELLOW MAN.
EVEN IF THEY DON'T KNOW HOW TO LOVE THEMSELVES.
I'LL STOP THEM FROM SETTING THIS WORLD ON FIRE.
ORGATH, THE IRON DRAGON, THE DEVOURER OF SOULS...

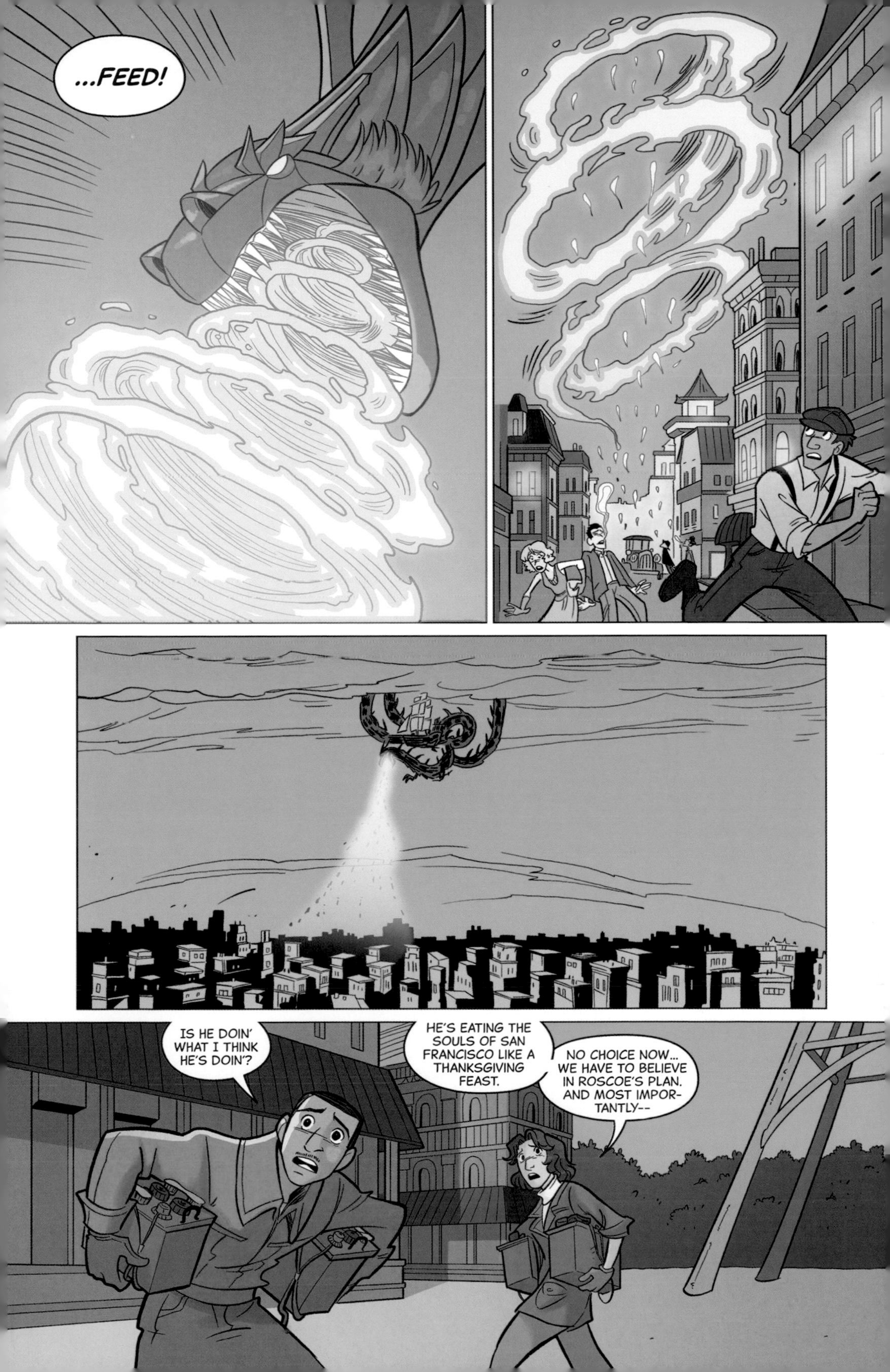
...FEED!
IS HE DOIN' WHAT I THINK HE'S DOIN'?
HE'S EATING THE SOULS OF SAN FRANCISCO LIKE A THANKSGIVING FEAST.
NO CHOICE NOW... WE HAVE TO BELIEVE IN ROSCOE'S PLAN. AND MOST IMPORTANTLY--

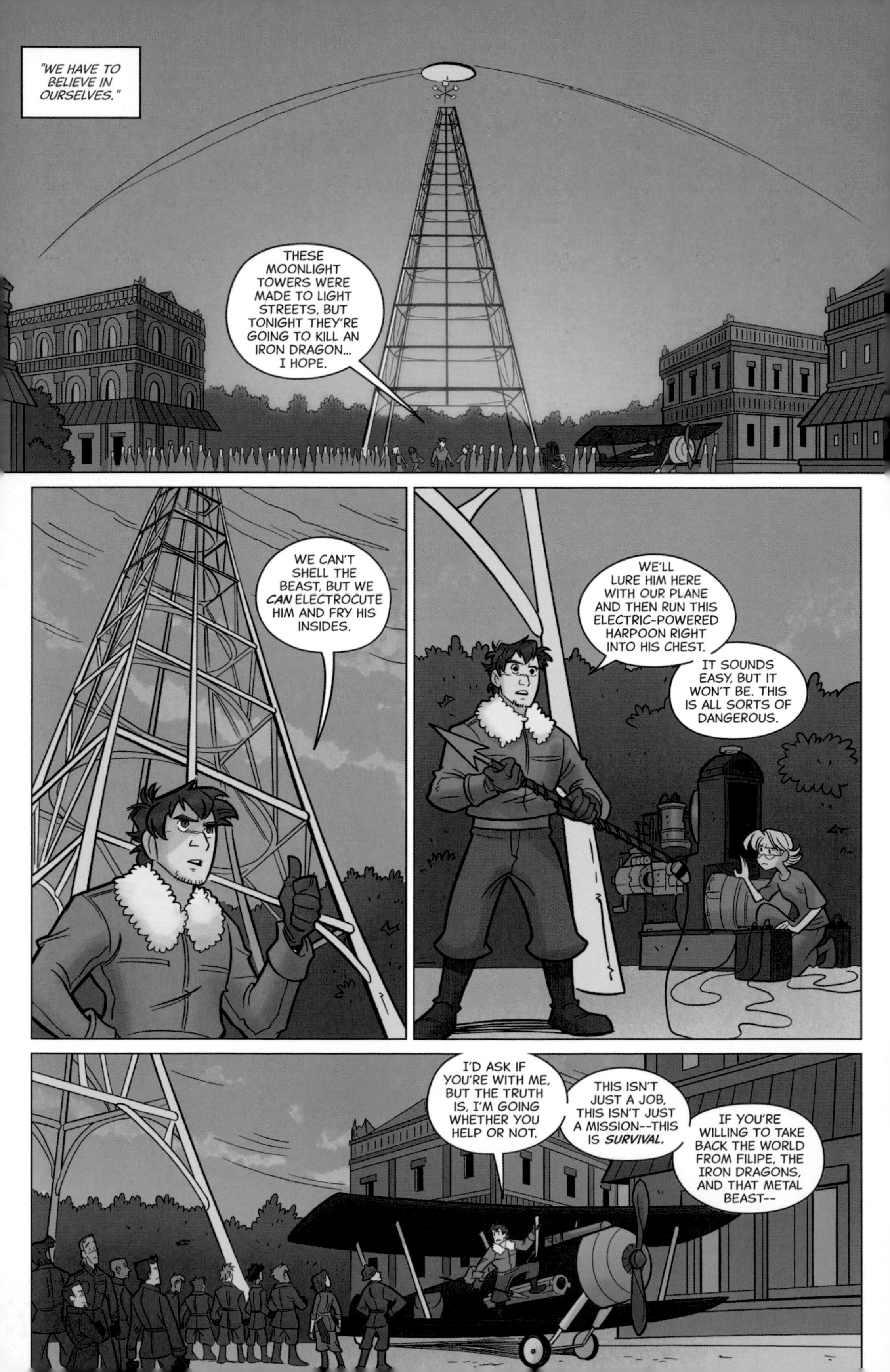
"WE HAVE TO BELIEVE IN OURSELVES."
THESE MOONLIGHT TOWERS WERE MADE TO LIGHT STREETS, BUT TONIGHT THEY'RE GOING TO KILL AN IRON DRAGON... I HOPE.
WE CAN'T SHELL THE BEAST, BUT WE *CAN* ELECTROCUTE HIM AND FRY HIS INSIDES.
WE'LL LURE HIM HERE WITH OUR PLANE AND THEN RUN THIS ELECTRIC-POWERED HARPOON RIGHT INTO HIS CHEST.
IT SOUNDS EASY, BUT IT WON'T BE. THIS IS ALL SORTS OF DANGEROUS.
I'D ASK IF YOU'RE WITH ME, BUT THE TRUTH IS, I'M GOING WHETHER YOU HELP OR NOT.
THIS ISN'T JUST A JOB, THIS ISN'T JUST A MISSION--THIS IS ***SURVIVAL.***
IF YOU'RE WILLING TO TAKE BACK THE WORLD FROM FILIPE, THE IRON DRAGONS, AND THAT METAL BEAST--

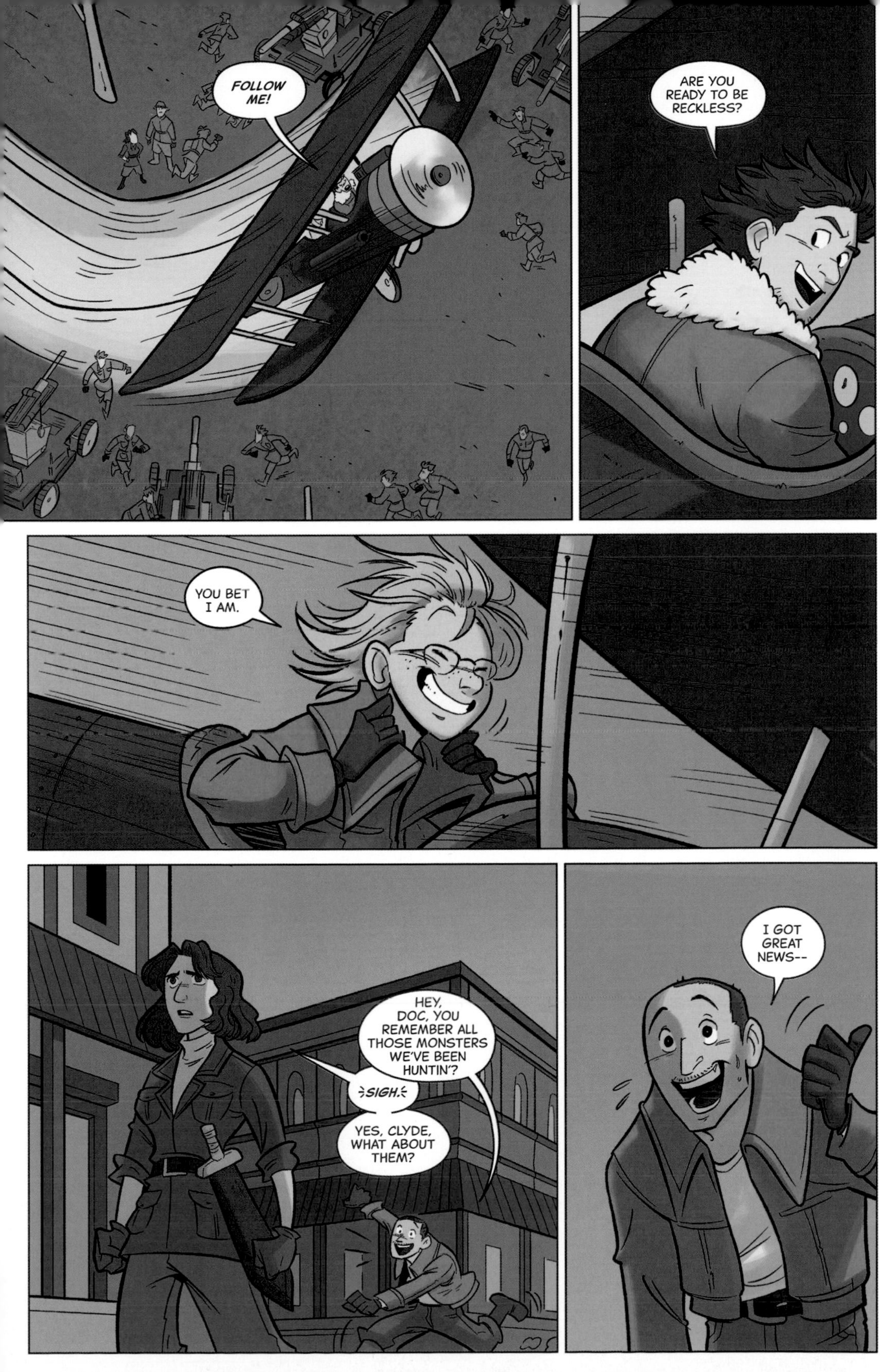
FOLLOW ME!
ARE YOU READY TO BE RECKLESS?
YOU BET I AM.
HEY, DOC, YOU REMEMBER ALL THOSE MONSTERS WE'VE BEEN HUNTIN'?
SIGH.
YES, CLYDE, WHAT ABOUT THEM?
I GOT GREAT NEWS--

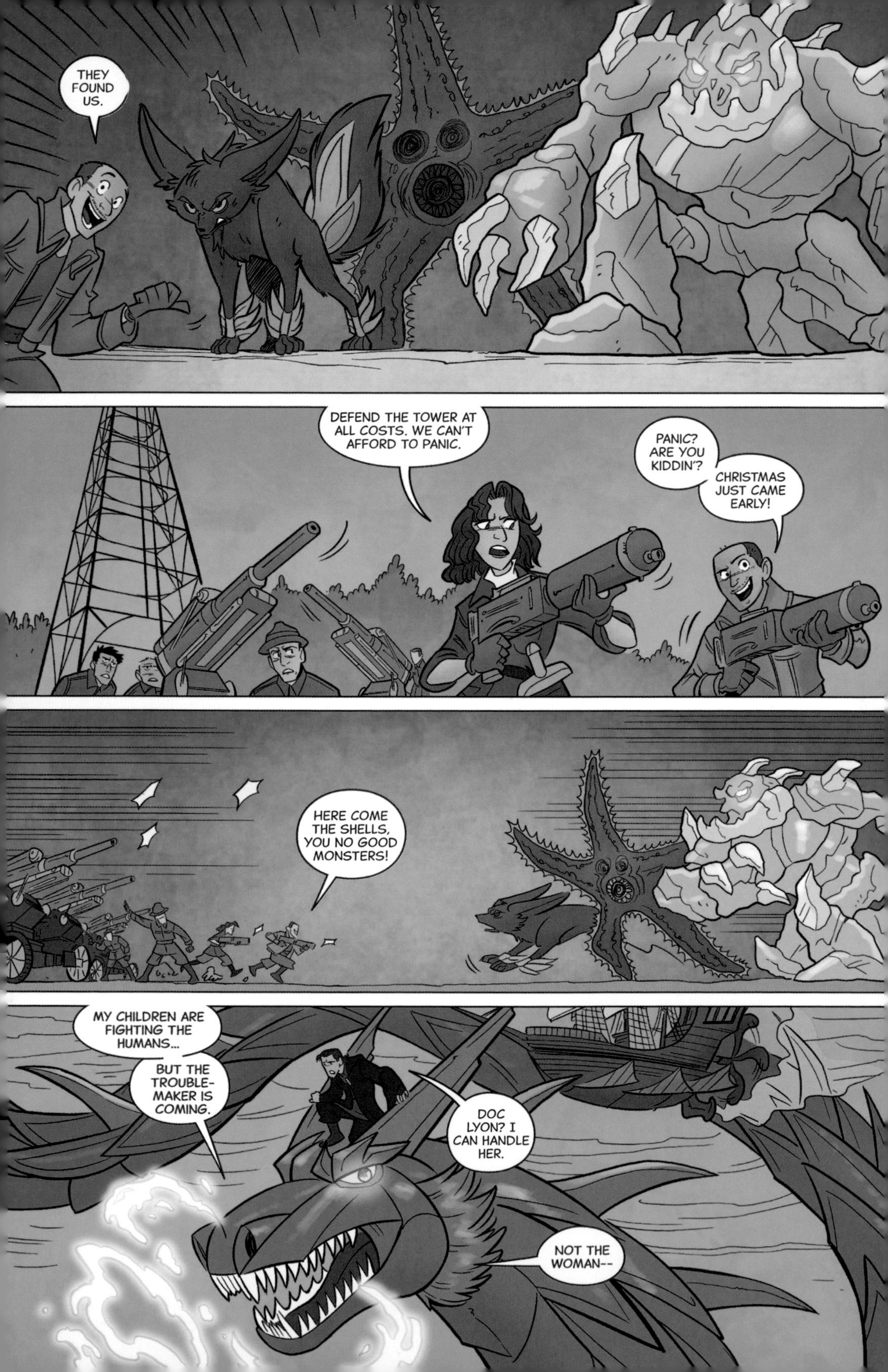
THEY FOUND US.
DEFEND THE TOWER AT ALL COSTS. WE CAN'T AFFORD TO PANIC.
PANIC? ARE YOU KIDDIN'?
CHRISTMAS JUST CAME EARLY!
HERE COME THE SHELLS, YOU NO GOOD MONSTERS!
MY CHILDREN ARE FIGHTING THE HUMANS...
BUT THE TROUBLE-MAKER IS COMING.
DOC LYON? I CAN HANDLE HER.
NOT THE WOMAN--

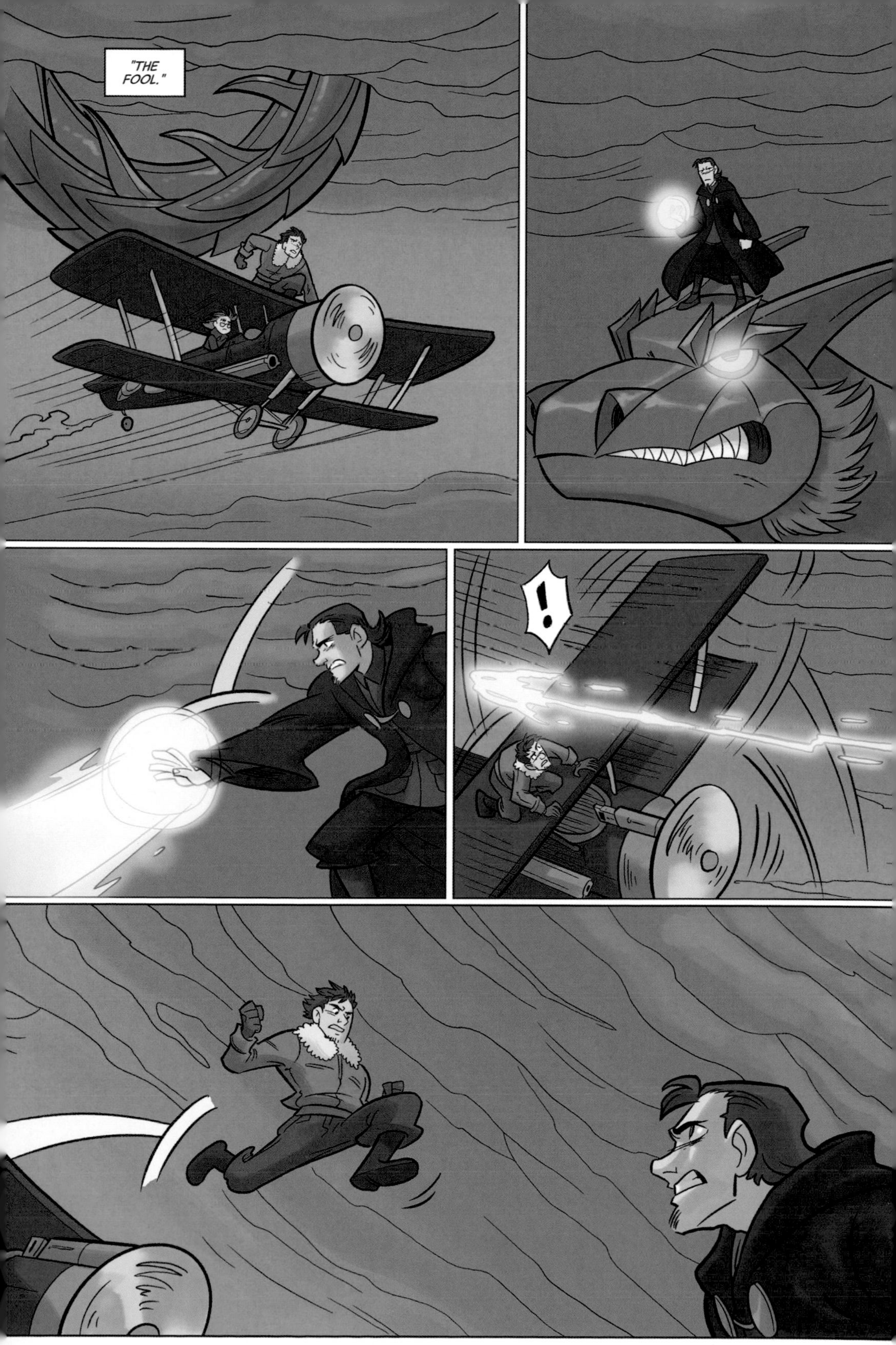
"THE FOOL."
!

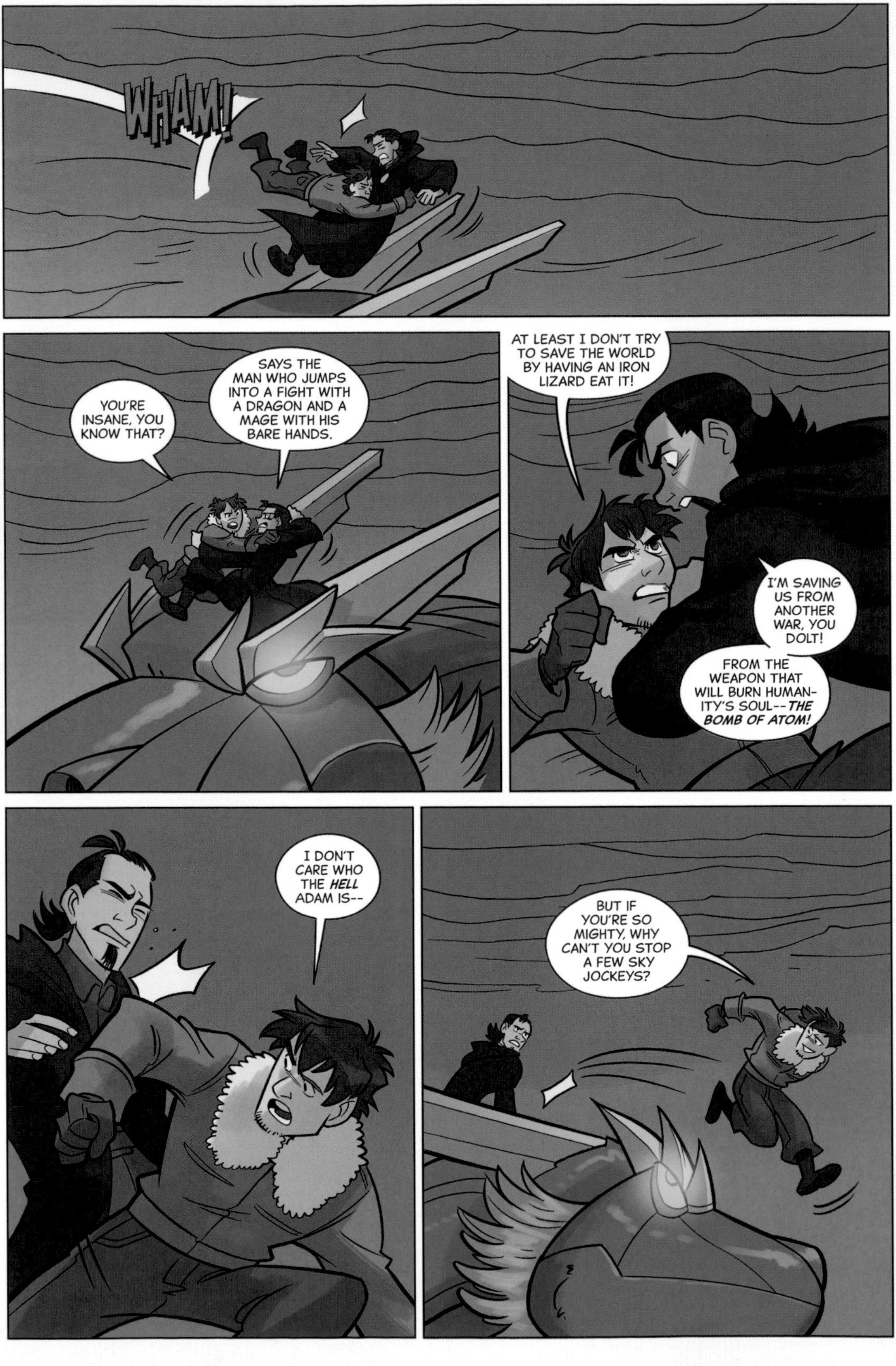
WHAM!
YOU'RE INSANE, YOU KNOW THAT?
SAYS THE MAN WHO JUMPS INTO A FIGHT WITH A DRAGON AND A MAGE WITH HIS BARE HANDS.
AT LEAST I DON'T TRY TO SAVE THE WORLD BY HAVING AN IRON LIZARD EAT IT!
I'M SAVING US FROM ANOTHER WAR, YOU DOLT!
FROM THE WEAPON THAT WILL BURN HUMAN-ITY'S SOUL--*THE BOMB OF ATOM!*
I DON'T CARE WHO THE *HELL* ADAM IS--
BUT IF YOU'RE SO MIGHTY, WHY CAN'T YOU STOP A FEW SKY JOCKEYS?

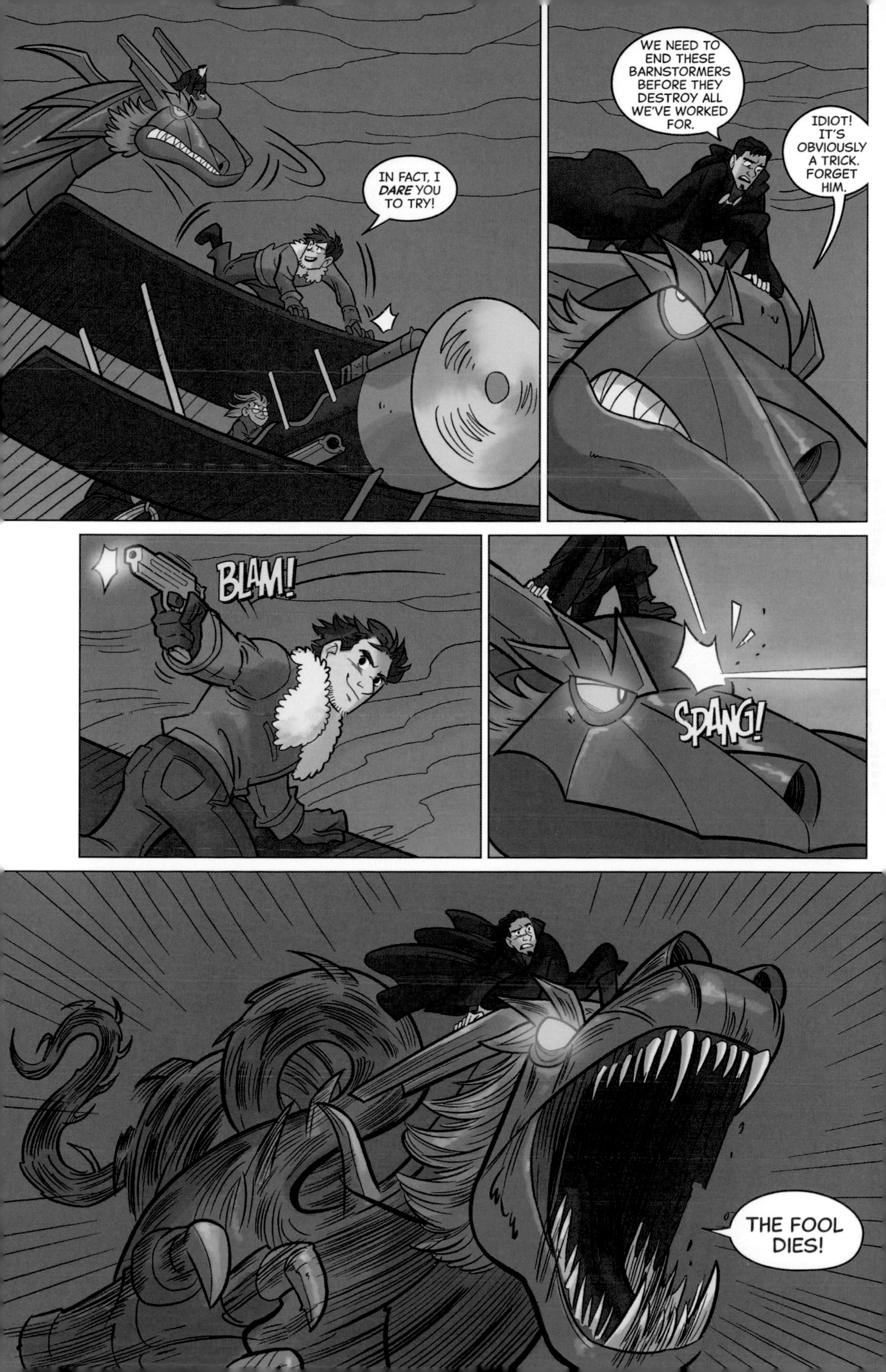
IN FACT, I *DARE* YOU TO TRY!
WE NEED TO END THESE BARNSTORMERS BEFORE THEY DESTROY ALL WE'VE WORKED FOR.
IDIOT! IT'S OBVIOUSLY A TRICK. FORGET HIM.
BLAM!
SPANG!
THE FOOL DIES!

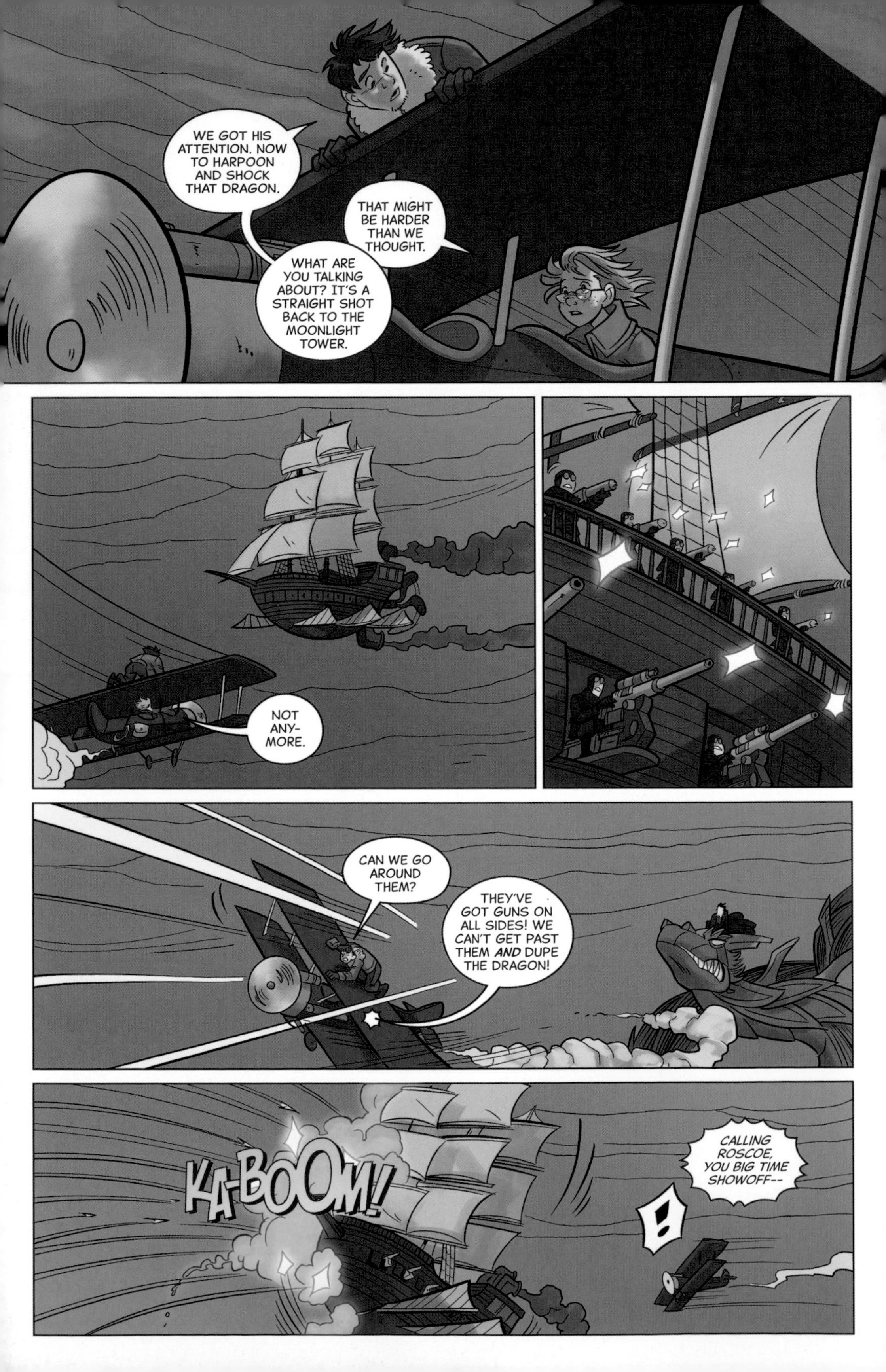
WE GOT HIS ATTENTION. NOW TO HARPOON AND SHOCK THAT DRAGON.
THAT MIGHT BE HARDER THAN WE THOUGHT.
WHAT ARE YOU TALKING ABOUT? IT'S A STRAIGHT SHOT BACK TO THE MOONLIGHT TOWER.
NOT ANY-MORE.
CAN WE GO AROUND THEM?
THEY'VE GOT GUNS ON ALL SIDES! WE CAN'T GET PAST THEM *AND* DUPE THE DRAGON!
KA-BOOM!!
CALLING ROSCOE, YOU BIG TIME SHOWOFF--
!

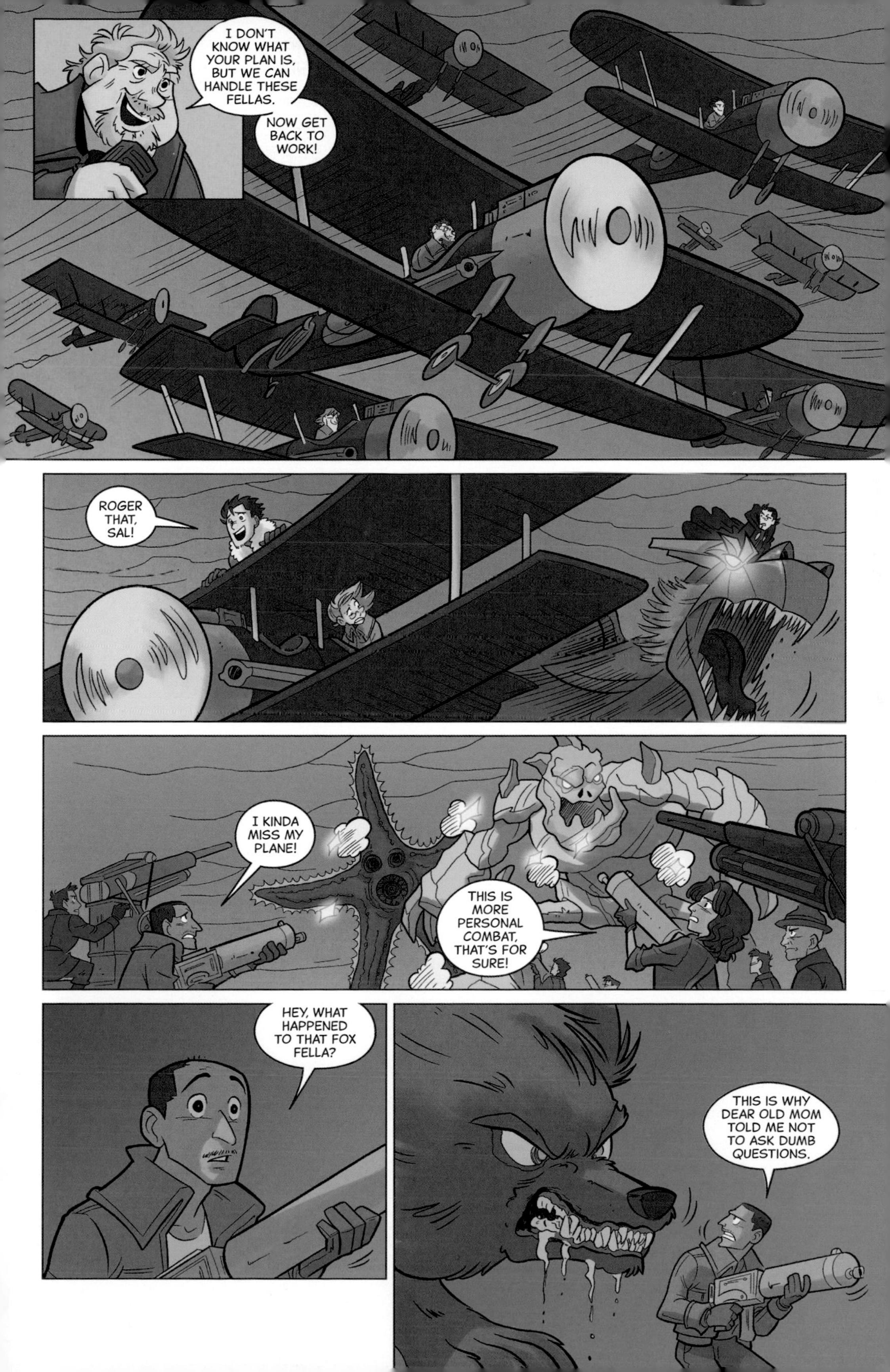
I DON'T KNOW WHAT YOUR PLAN IS, BUT WE CAN HANDLE THESE FELLAS.
NOW GET BACK TO WORK!
ROGER THAT, SAL!
I KINDA MISS MY PLANE!
THIS IS MORE PERSONAL COMBAT, THAT'S FOR SURE!
HEY, WHAT HAPPENED TO THAT FOX FELLA?
THIS IS WHY DEAR OLD MOM TOLD ME NOT TO ASK DUMB QUESTIONS.

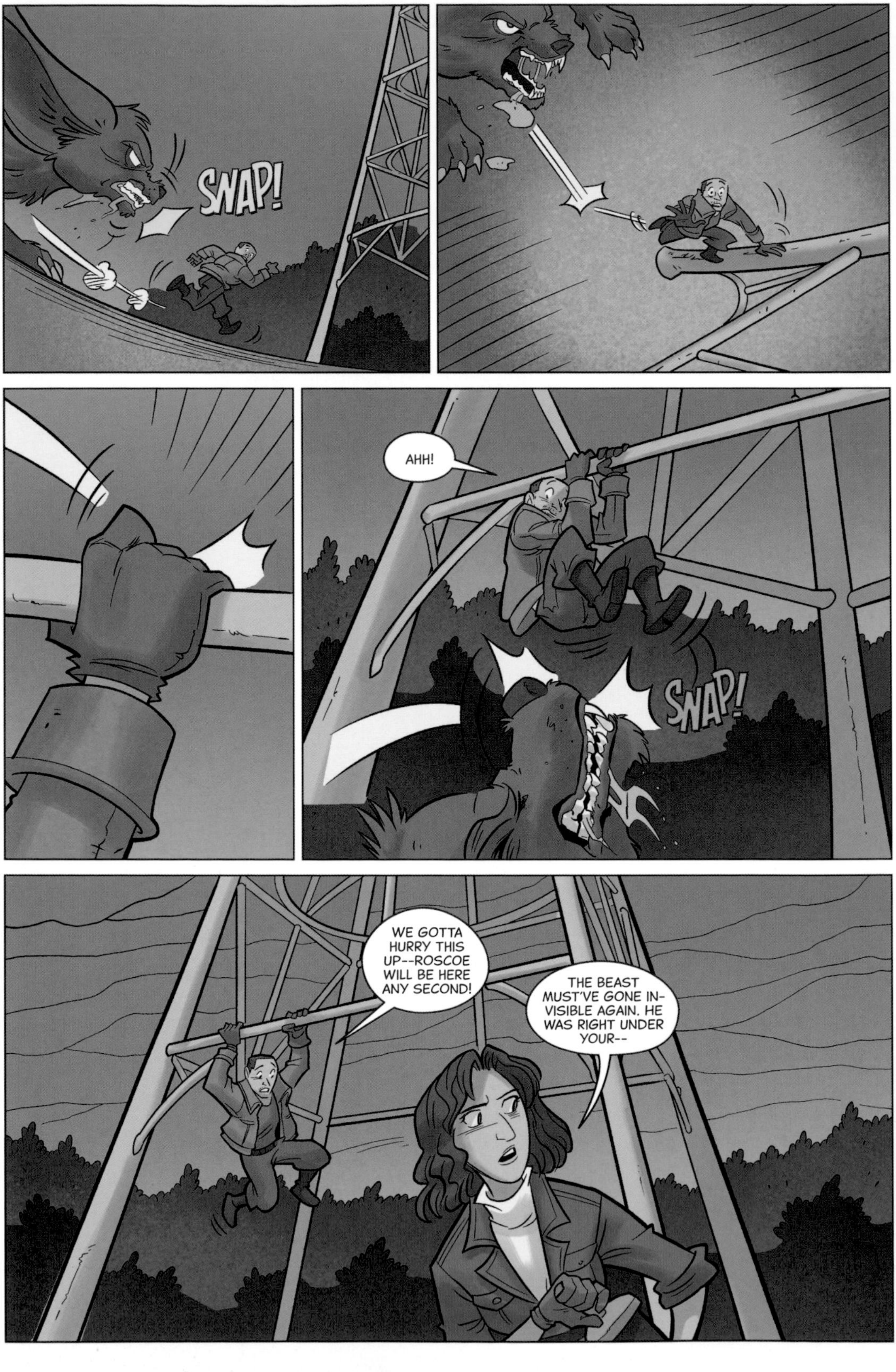
SNAP!
AHH!
SNAP!
WE GOTTA HURRY THIS UP--ROSCOE WILL BE HERE ANY SECOND!
THE BEAST MUST'VE GONE IN-VISIBLE AGAIN. HE WAS RIGHT UNDER YOUR--

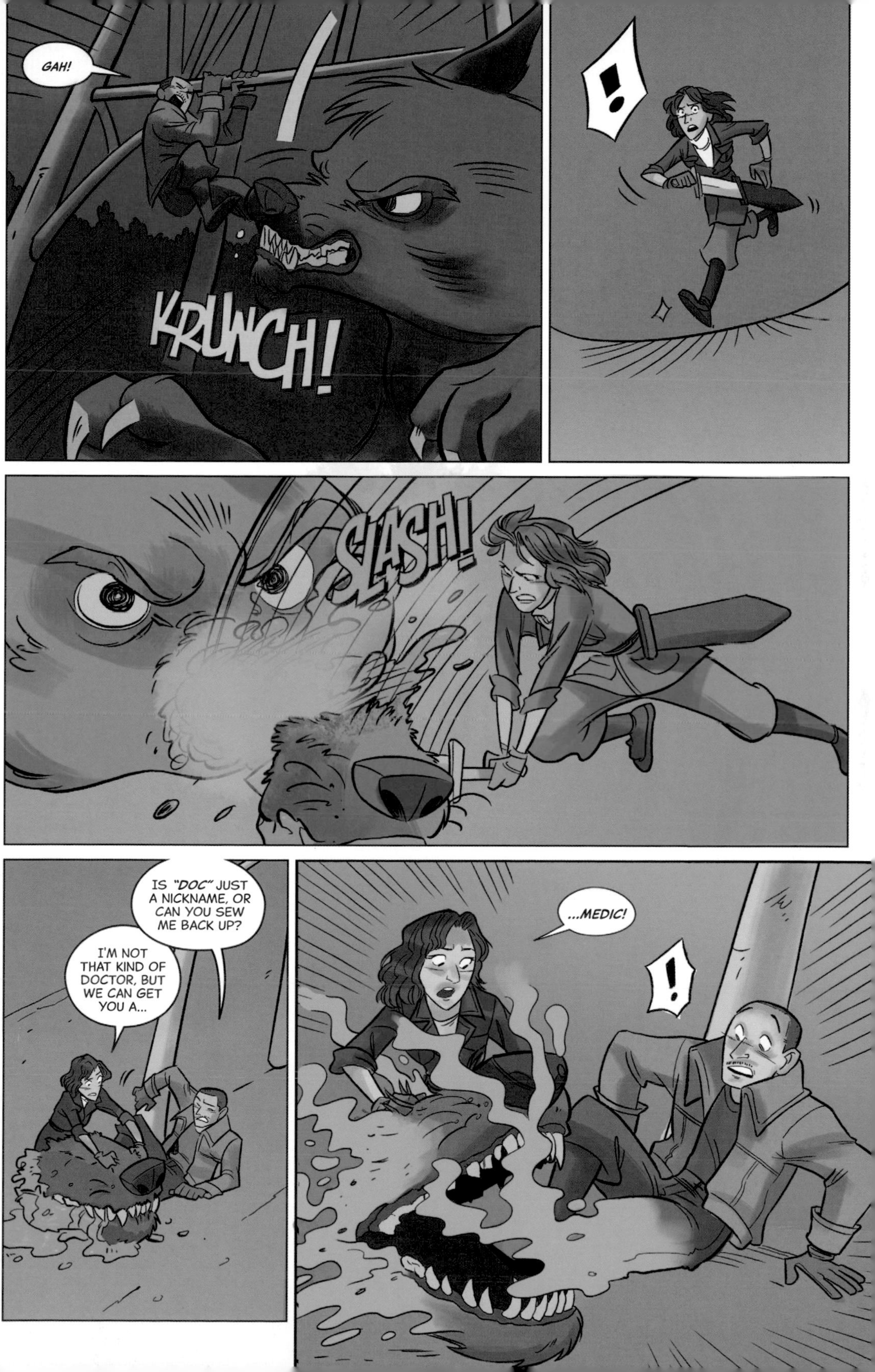
GAH!
KRUNCH!
!
SLASH!
IS "DOC" JUST A NICKNAME, OR CAN YOU SEW ME BACK UP?
I'M NOT THAT KIND OF DOCTOR, BUT WE CAN GET YOU A...
...MEDIC!
!

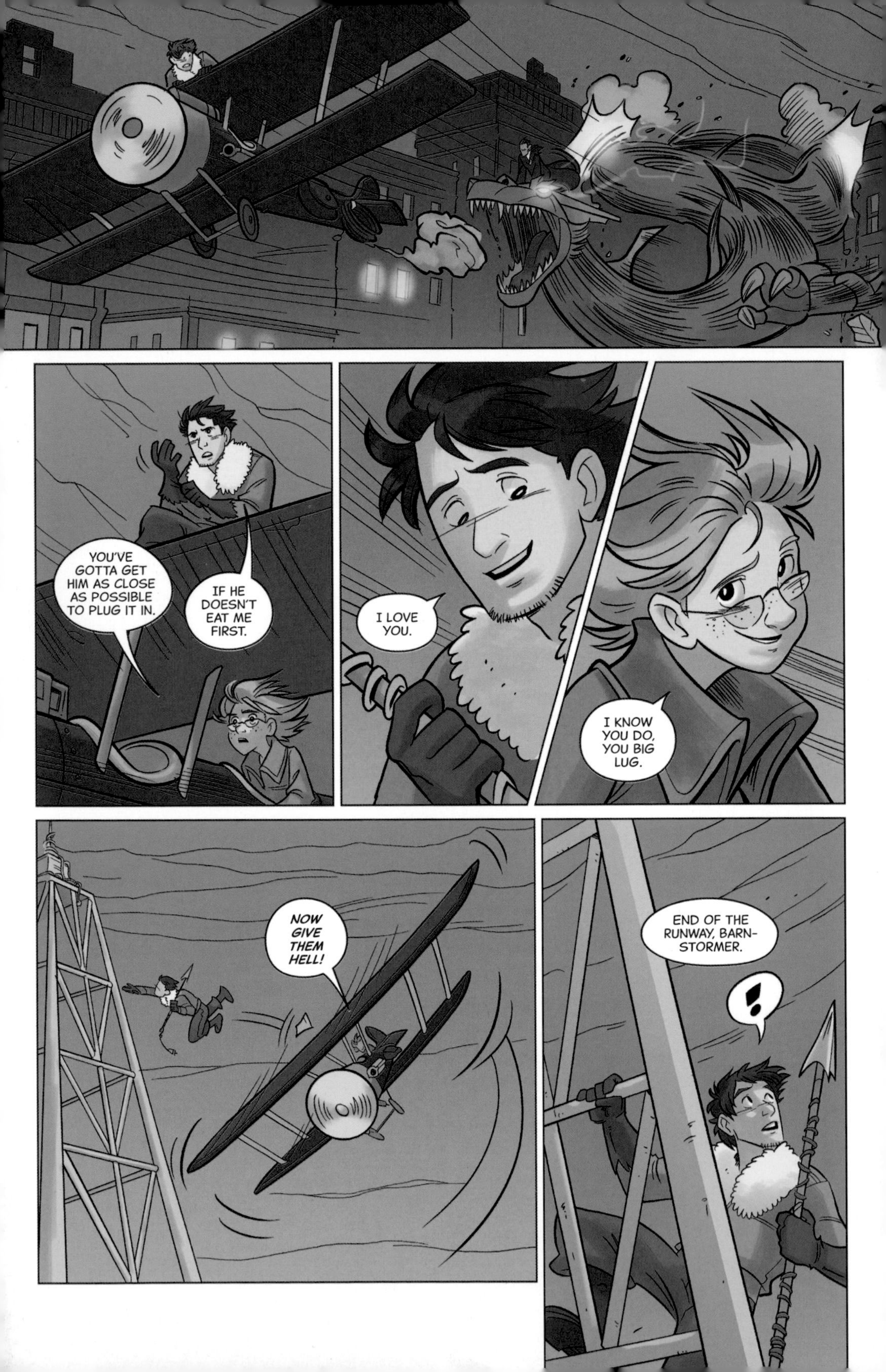
YOU'VE GOTTA GET HIM AS CLOSE AS POSSIBLE TO PLUG IT IN.
IF HE DOESN'T EAT ME FIRST.
I LOVE YOU.
I KNOW YOU DO, YOU BIG LUG.
NOW GIVE THEM HELL!
END OF THE RUNWAY, BARN-STORMER.
!

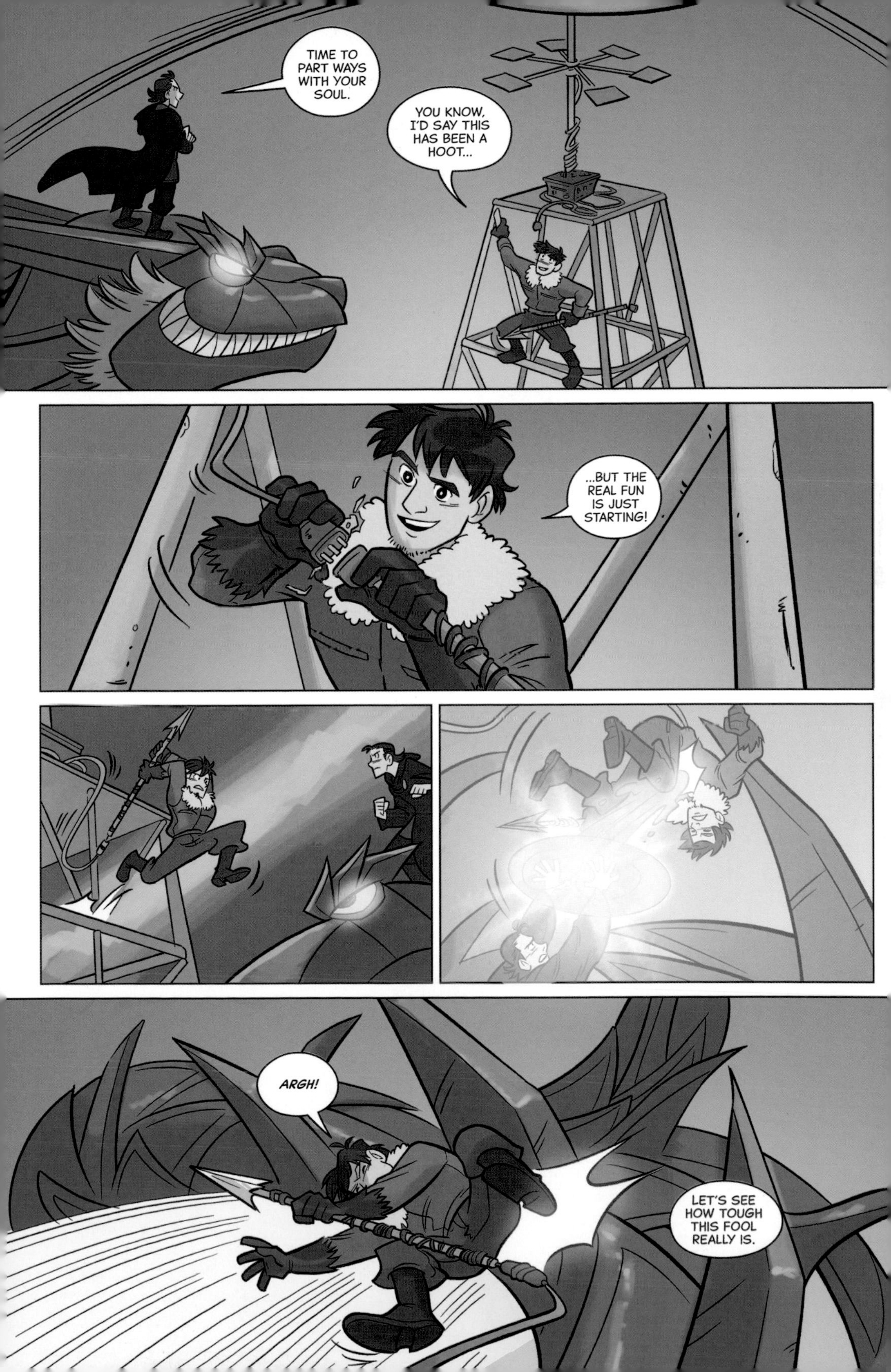
TIME TO PART WAYS WITH YOUR SOUL.
YOU KNOW, I'D SAY THIS HAS BEEN A HOOT...
...BUT THE REAL FUN IS JUST STARTING!
ARGH!
LET'S SEE HOW TOUGH THIS FOOL REALLY IS.

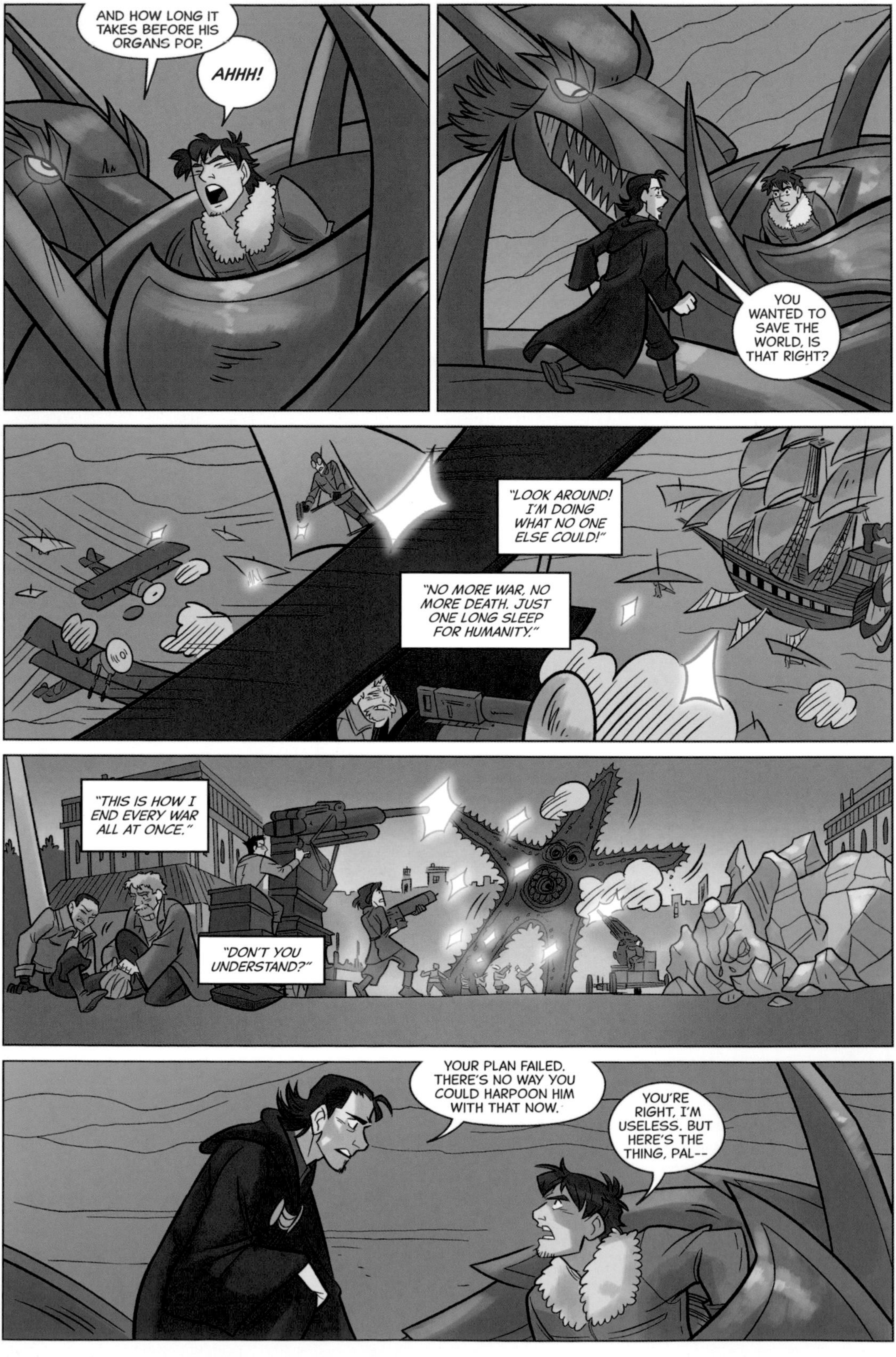
AND HOW LONG IT TAKES BEFORE HIS ORGANS POP.
AHHH!
YOU WANTED TO SAVE THE WORLD, IS THAT RIGHT?
"LOOK AROUND! I'M DOING WHAT NO ONE ELSE COULD!"
"NO MORE WAR, NO MORE DEATH. JUST ONE LONG SLEEP FOR HUMANITY."
"THIS IS HOW I END EVERY WAR ALL AT ONCE."
"DON'T YOU UNDERSTAND?"
YOUR PLAN FAILED. THERE'S NO WAY YOU COULD HARPOON HIM WITH THAT NOW.
YOU'RE RIGHT, I'M USELESS. BUT HERE'S THE THING, PAL--

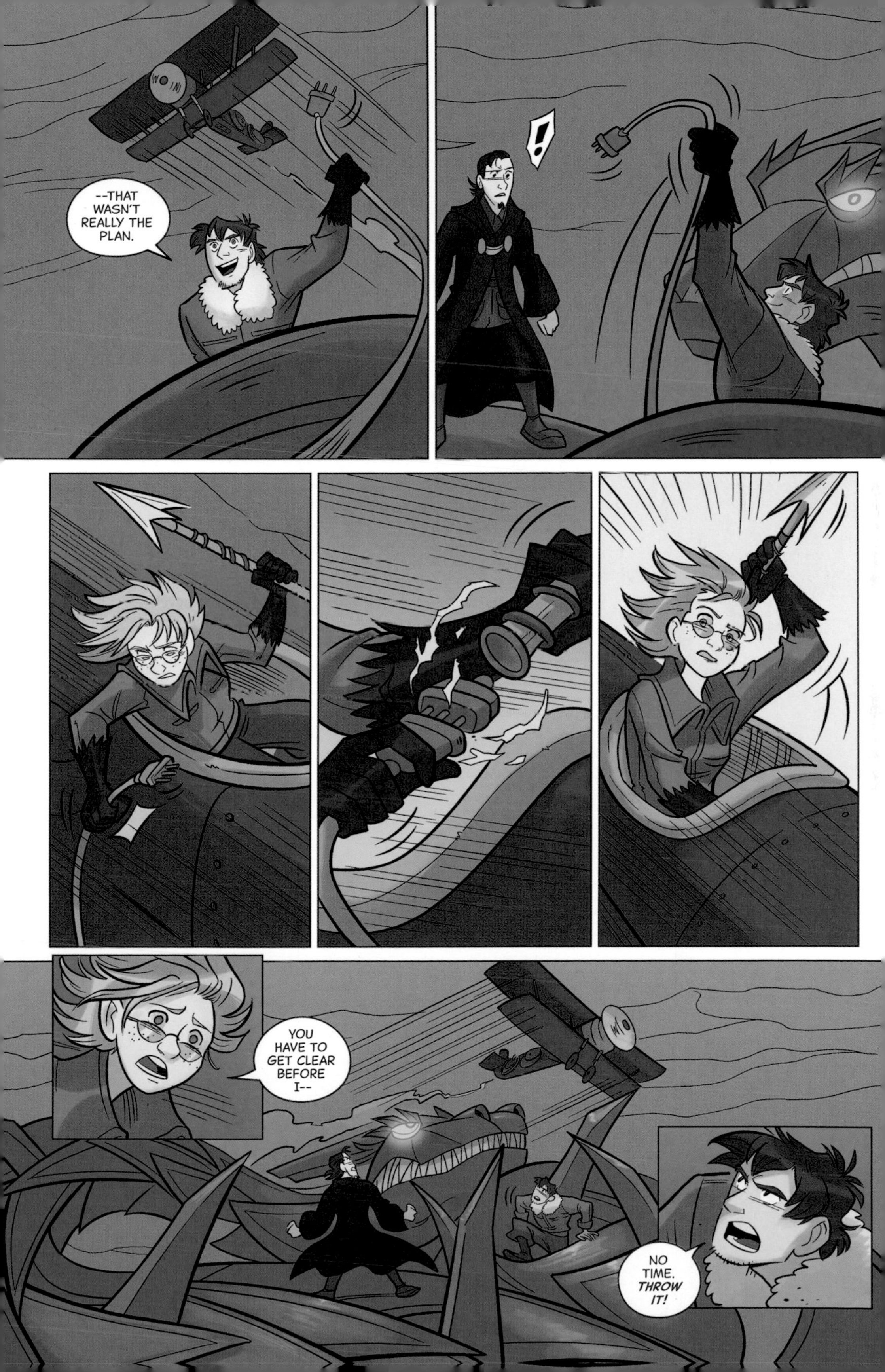
--THAT WASN'T REALLY THE PLAN.
!
YOU HAVE TO GET CLEAR BEFORE I--
NO TIME. *THROW IT!*

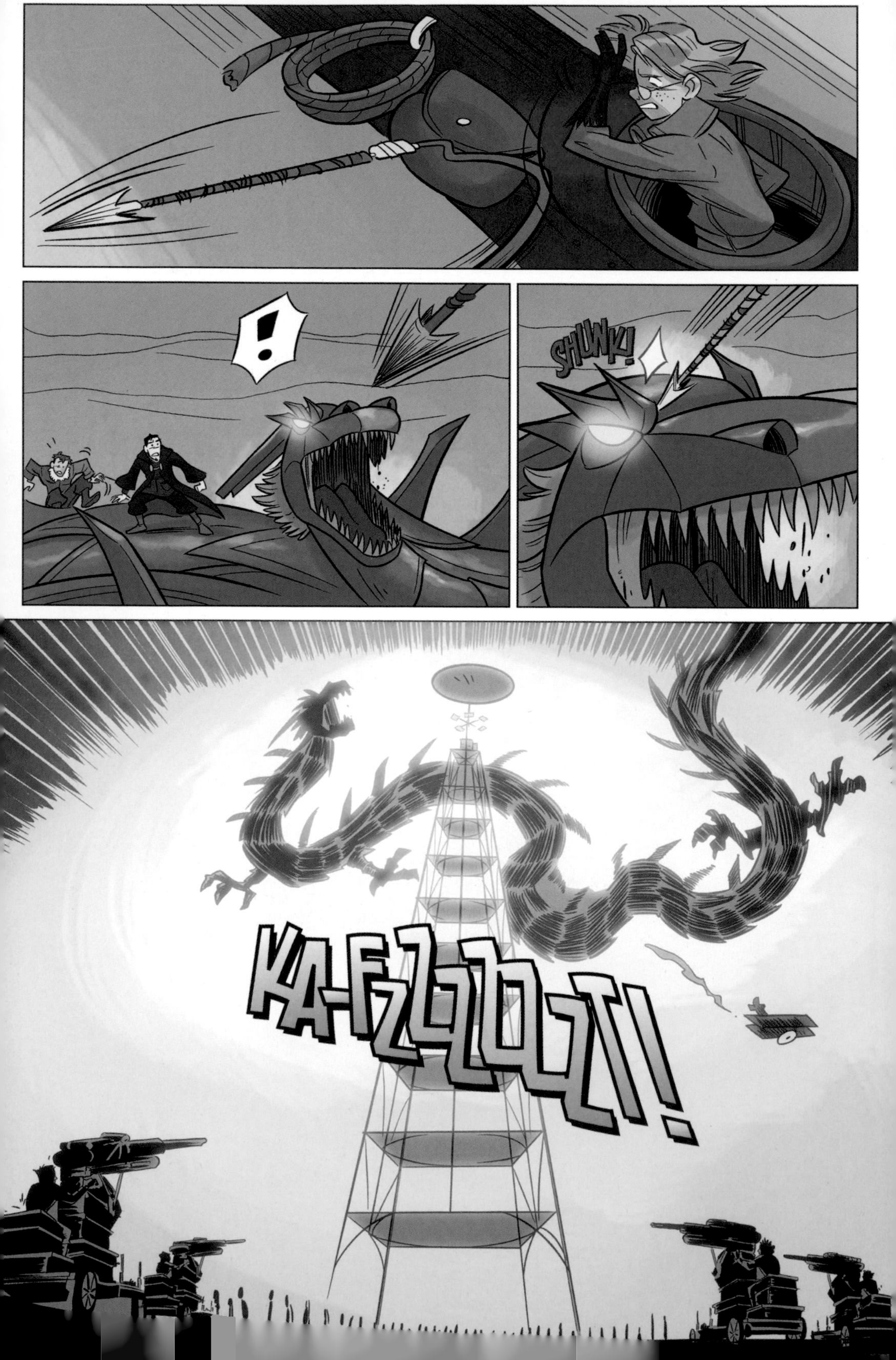
!
SHUNK!
KA-FZZZZZZT!!

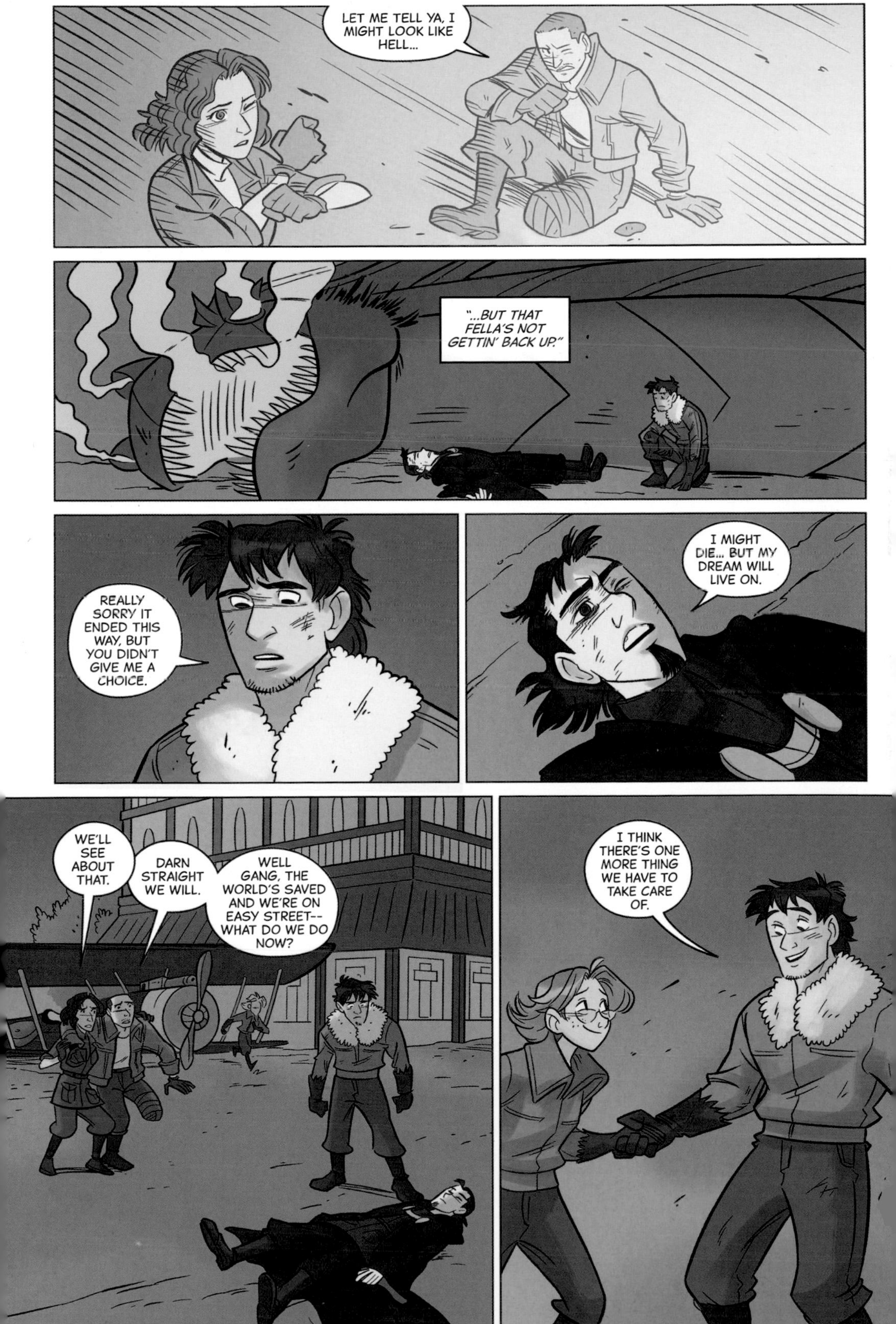
LET ME TELL YA, I MIGHT LOOK LIKE HELL...
"...BUT THAT FELLA'S NOT GETTIN' BACK UP."
REALLY SORRY IT ENDED THIS WAY, BUT YOU DIDN'T GIVE ME A CHOICE.
I MIGHT DIE... BUT MY DREAM WILL LIVE ON.
WE'LL SEE ABOUT THAT.
DARN STRAIGHT WE WILL.
WELL GANG, THE WORLD'S SAVED AND WE'RE ON EASY STREET-- WHAT DO WE DO NOW?
I THINK THERE'S ONE MORE THING WE HAVE TO TAKE CARE OF.

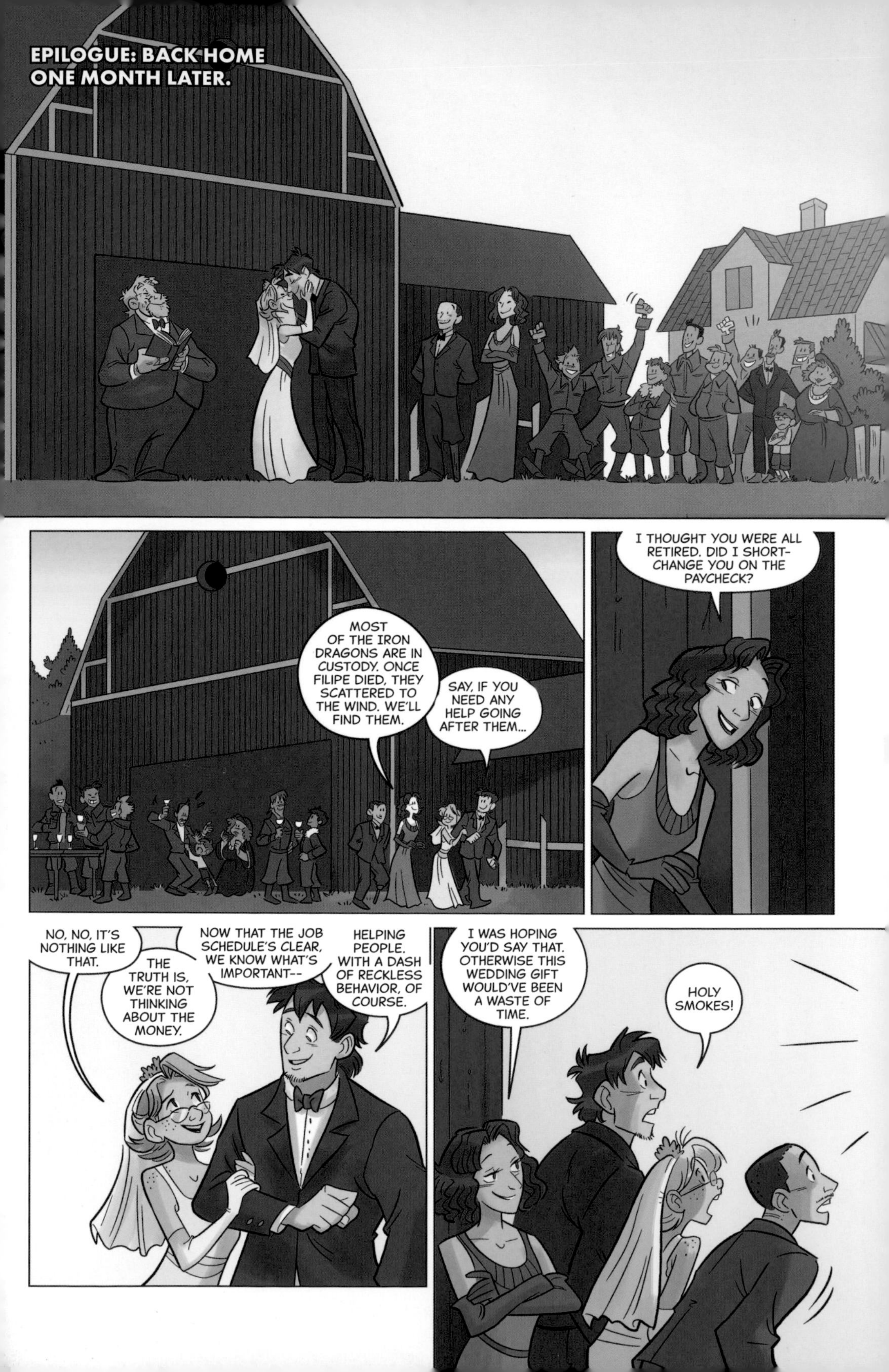
EPILOGUE: BACK HOME
ONE MONTH LATER.
MOST OF THE IRON DRAGONS ARE IN CUSTODY. ONCE FILIPE DIED, THEY SCATTERED TO THE WIND. WE'LL FIND THEM.
SAY, IF YOU NEED ANY HELP GOING AFTER THEM...
I THOUGHT YOU WERE ALL RETIRED. DID I SHORT-CHANGE YOU ON THE PAYCHECK?
NO, NO, IT'S NOTHING LIKE THAT.
THE TRUTH IS, WE'RE NOT THINKING ABOUT THE MONEY.
NOW THAT THE JOB SCHEDULE'S CLEAR, WE KNOW WHAT'S IMPORTANT--
HELPING PEOPLE. WITH A DASH OF RECKLESS BEHAVIOR, OF COURSE.
I WAS HOPING YOU'D SAY THAT. OTHERWISE THIS WEDDING GIFT WOULD'VE BEEN A WASTE OF TIME.
HOLY SMOKES!

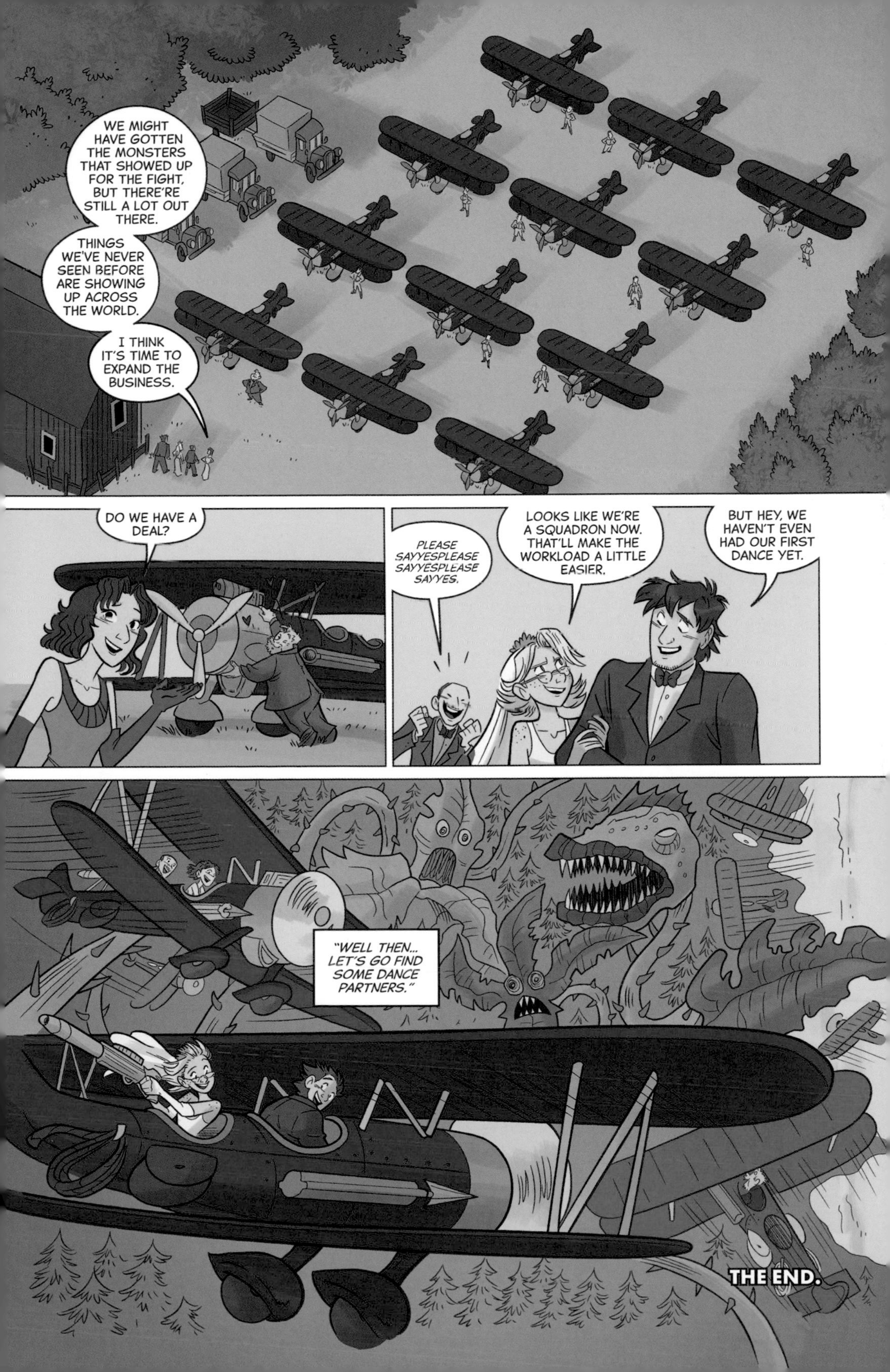
WE MIGHT HAVE GOTTEN THE MONSTERS THAT SHOWED UP FOR THE FIGHT, BUT THERE'RE STILL A LOT OUT THERE.
THINGS WE'VE NEVER SEEN BEFORE ARE SHOWING UP ACROSS THE WORLD.
I THINK IT'S TIME TO EXPAND THE BUSINESS.
DO WE HAVE A DEAL?
PLEASE SAYYESPLEASE SAYYESPLEASE SAYYES.
LOOKS LIKE WE'RE A SQUADRON NOW. THAT'LL MAKE THE WORKLOAD A LITTLE EASIER.
BUT HEY, WE HAVEN'T EVEN HAD OUR FIRST DANCE YET.
"WELL THEN... LET'S GO FIND SOME DANCE PARTNERS."
THE END.

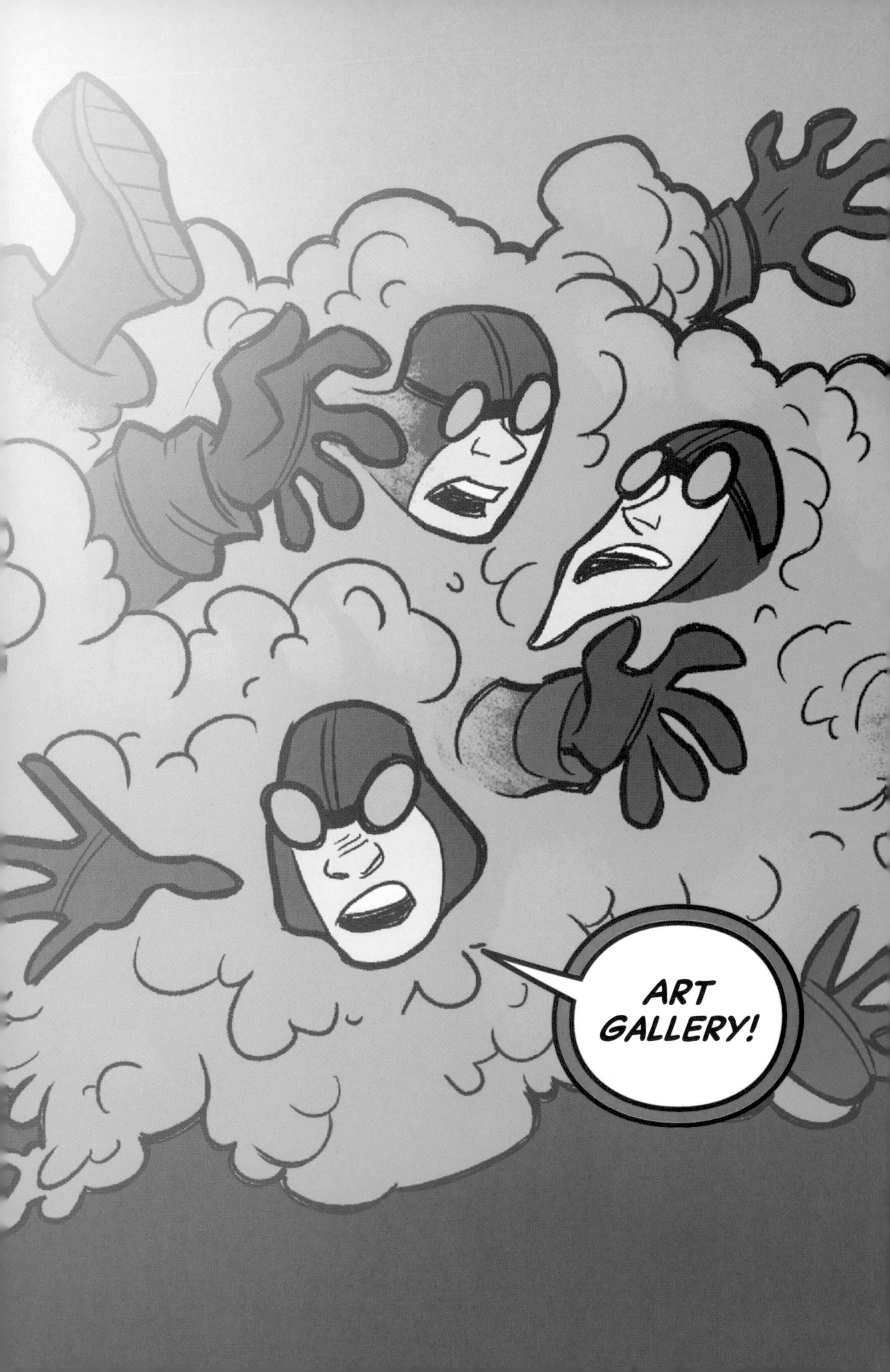
ART
GALLERY!

Pinup by **Ryan Lee**

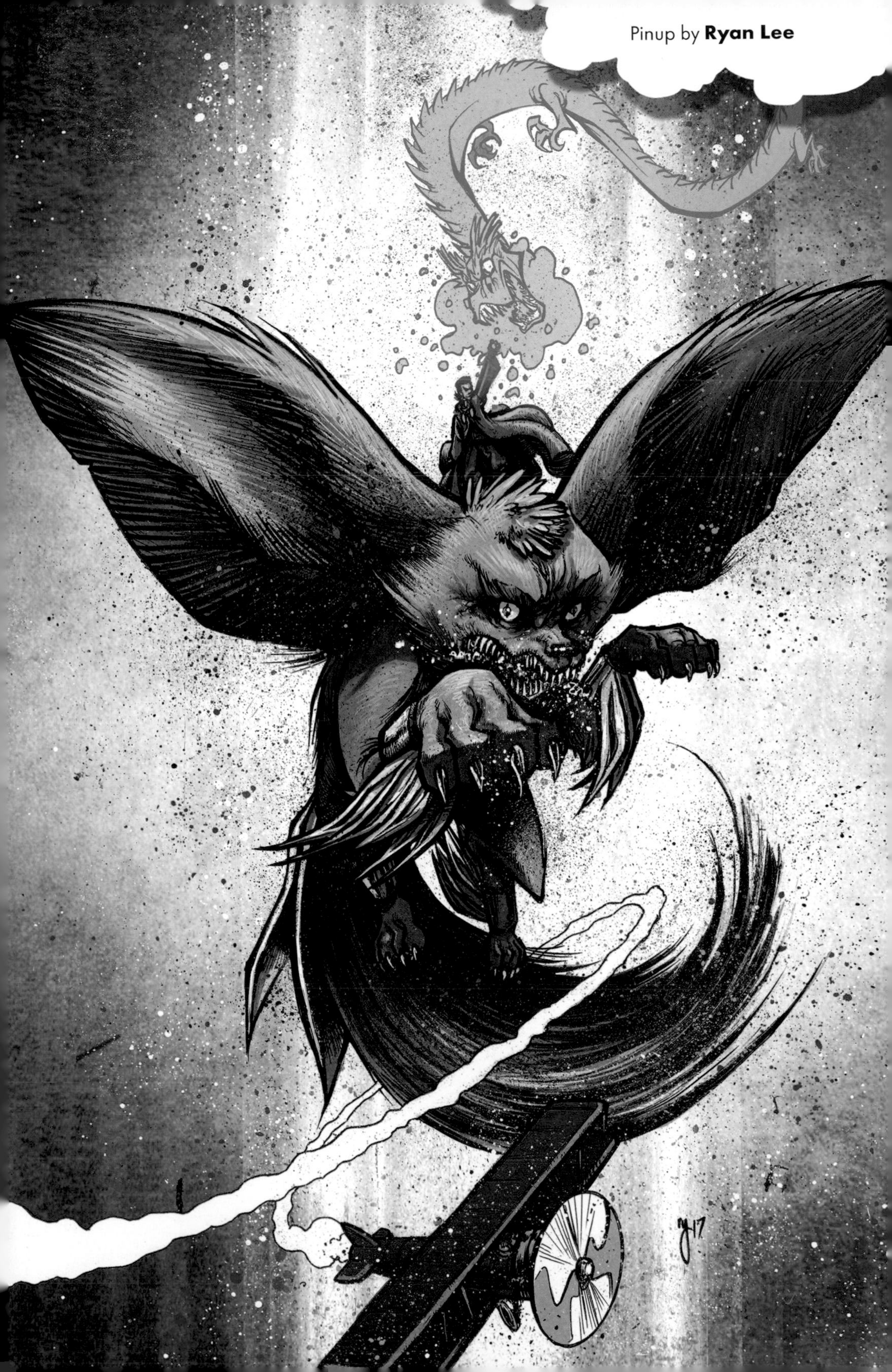

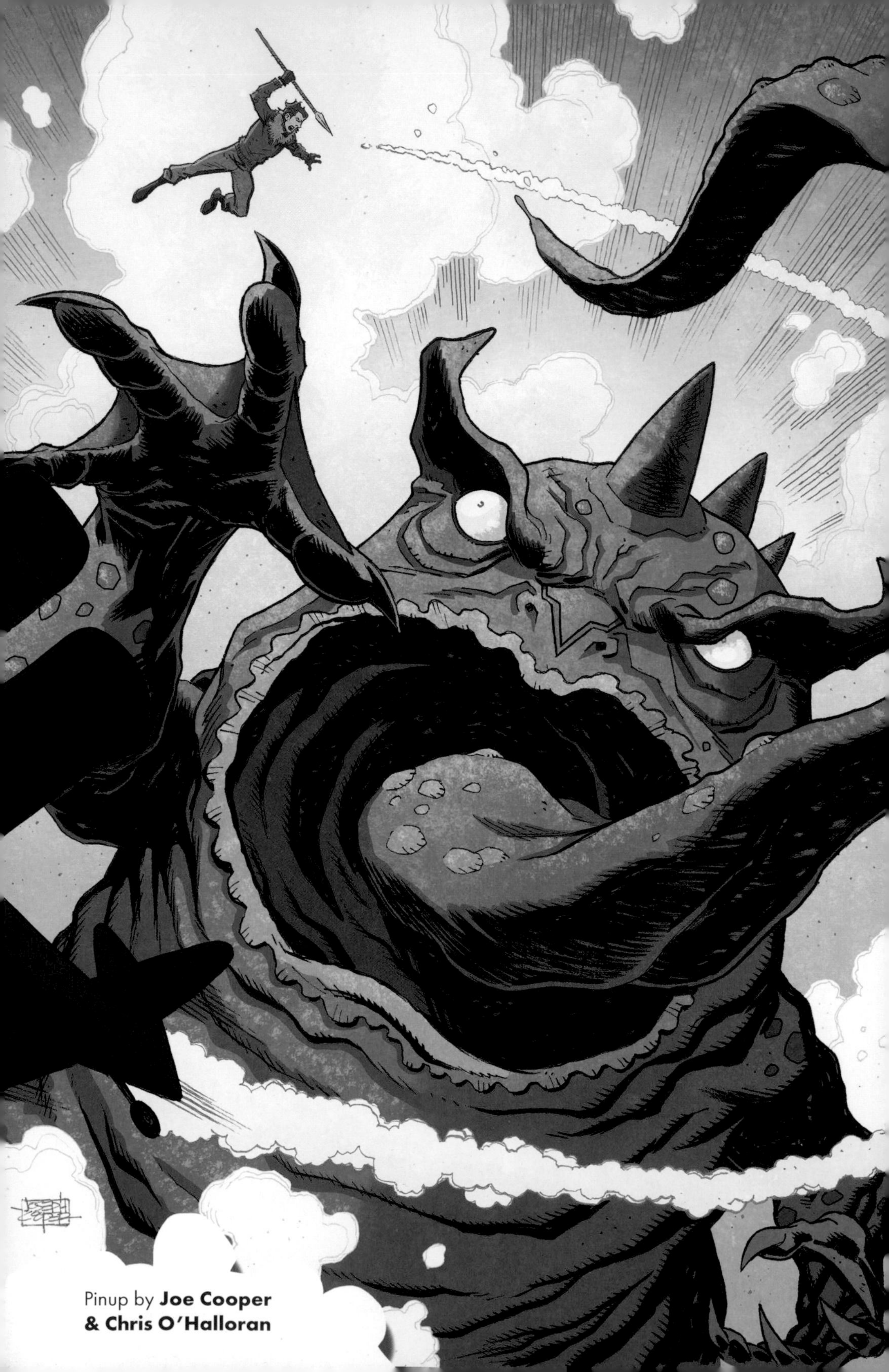

Pinup by **Joe Cooper**
& Chris O'Halloran

Pinup by **Renny Castellani**

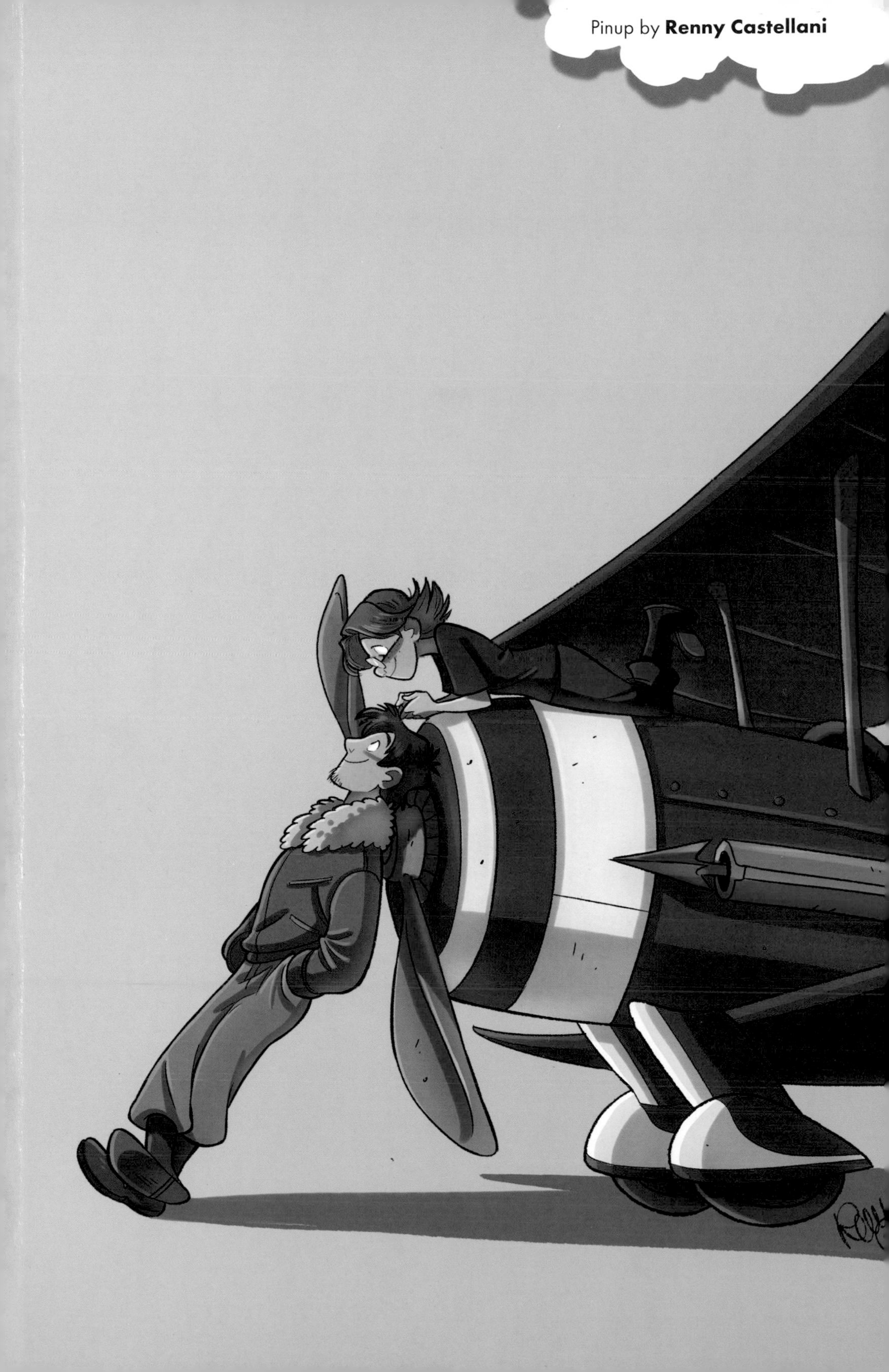

An Imprint of Insight Editions
PO Box 3088
San Rafael, CA 94912
www.insightcomics.com

Find us on Facebook:
www.facebook.com/InsightEditionsComics

Follow us on Twitter:
@InsightComics

Follow us on Instagram:
Insight_Comics

Library of Congress Cataloging-in-Publication Data available.

ISBN: 978-1-68383-663-6

Publisher: Raoul Goff
President: Kate Jerome
Associate Publisher: Vanessa Lopez
Creative Director: Chrissy Kwasnik
VP of Manufacturing: Alix Nicholaeff
Designer: Brooke McCullum
Executive Editor: Mark Irwin
Associate Editor: Holly Fisher
Senior Production Editor: Elaine Ou
Production Associate: Eden Orlesky

ROOTS of PEACE   REPLANTED PAPER

Insight Editions, in association with Roots of Peace, will plant two trees for each tree used in the manufacturing of this book. Roots of Peace is an internationally renowned humanitarian organization dedicated to eradicating land mines worldwide and converting war-torn lands into productive farms and wildlife habitats. Roots of Peace will plant two million fruit and nut trees in Afghanistan and provide farmers there with the skills and support necessary for sustainable land use.

Manufactured in China by Insight Editions

10 9 8 7 6 5 4 3 2 1